The Ship-Master

A Novel of Viking-Age Wirral

H. A. Douglas

Copyright Hrolf Douglasson (writing as H.A. Douglas) 2011 All rights reserved. Revised Edition Copyright Hrolf Douglasson 2017

The right of Hrolf Douglasson to be reconised as the author of this work has been asserted in accordance with the Copyright, Designs and Patents Act 1988. All rights reserved. No part of this publication may be reproduced, stored in or introduced into a retrieval system, or transmitted, in any form or by any means (electronic, mechanical, photocopying, recording or otherwise), without the prior written permission of the author. Any person who does any unauthorised act in relation to this publication may be liable to criminal prosecution and civil claims for damages.

This book is sold subject to the condition that it shall not, by way of trade or otherwise, be lent, resold, hired out or otherwise circulated without the author's prior consent in any form of binding or cover other than that in which it is published and without a similar condition including this condition being imposed on the subsequent purchaser.

This story is a work of fiction. Any similarity to persons or characters alive or dead, or to events or places current or historical, is purely coincidental.

DEDICATION

This book is dedicated firstly to my wonderful wife and family, and secondly to all my good friends in Regia Anglorum, who served as an inspiring force to write this tale in the first place.

INTRODUCTION

This story is set in and around the Wirral peninsular, between the Mersey and the Dee rivers, in the year 919 AD. The political situation is as follows:

Sihtric Caech is the new Viking king of Dublin, having beaten off an assault by Niall Glundub, the Irish king of the northern Ui Neill, to secure his position. His kinsman Ragnar, having assisted in the re-establishment of a strong Norse presence in Ireland, has returned to Northumbria to be proclaimed king.

In what will soon become a united, single kingdom of England, Edward the Elder is consolidating his position as the new king of Mercia, following the death of his sister Aethelflaed "The Lady of the Mercians". Since the death of her husband Aethelred, she and Edward, the children of Alfred the Great of Wessex, have been systematically reconquering those parts of England surrendered to the Danish invaders by their father.

English Mercia still follows the line of Offa's Dyke at this time, and so includes a large chunk of what is now North Wales. Beyond the Dyke is the Welsh kingdom of Powys, but this will be reduced in both size and influence by the emergence of Gwynedd.

The Wirral peninsula itself, although nominally Mercian, has since 902 been occupied by Norse-Irish refugees from a Dublin attacked and overrun by the Irish. Their numbers are such that within five years of arriving, they felt strong enough to claim Chester as well, and although this claim was comprehensively rebuffed by the Mercians - who refortified the city by way of answer - northern Wirral is effectively an independent Norse enclave, making its own laws and following its own, Norse, way of life. By the time of Aethelstan's accession to the Saxon throne in 925, however, Norse and Irish moneyers will be an integral part of Chester's economic miracle, making it the largest mint in the country. But that is still to occur; for now, there is an uneasy peace, while the Norsemen look to what Edward's plans are, and also watch the tangled skein of events across the Irish Sea.

CHAPTER ONE

Rain blew from the east, as fast as the clouds before the gale; trees swayed, their leafless branches bending to the storm god's will. Sheep bleated; men muttered, and drew hoods and
cloaks tighter as they squelched out of low, leaky houses, with walls of wattle and roofs of turf, to their day's work.

"Time to awaken, husband! Thurbrand has the cows back from their milking already, and you said you would look at the byre with him!"

At least, thought Hrolf, those words were accompanied by a full cup and the first of the day's baking - the main strategy for sleeping late, as far as he was concerned. His mind still
occasionally wandered over the problem of stale bread every morning when shipboard, but he had not as yet come up with a method of securing a hot oven - even a makeshift one - amid the timbers. The firebox he had was dangerous enough, and that was only ever lit on a calm sea, when his crew dropped the anchorstone and slept under the awning. Beer was not such a difficulty; it could only spill, and wash away. So why not do away with the bread

altogether? He could see advantages to this idea, but perhaps the disadvantages might outweigh them... more immediately, there were signs of a good mood in the house today: the ale in his cup had been put by the fire to warm.

Hrolf swung his legs out of the bed-closet, pausing to push a bit more of the bracken from under his mattress into the cold, damp gap between two of the wall-timbers. The house was
as low and dark as it ever was, with only the orange light from the newly raked-out fire giving any sort of light beyond that which filtered in from outside through the uncounted cracks in the walls - of good, upright wooden staves, as befitted a lord's residence - and roof. Inside, Hrolf found that he relied just as much on his ears and nose to guide him around as he did his
eyes. Now in his late twenties, he still had the dull browny – red colour of his hair, even into his beard - although that was beginning to grey in places - and so far, not too much of a
paunch. He rescued breeks, hose and his woollen overshirt from their own habitual sleeping-place (over his wife's feet) and pulled them on over his linen shirt, touching as he did so the

amber bead around his neck (he had not been struck by lightning yet, so it must work), tightening the drawstring around the square neckhole, and then stopping to count his fingers. Still only nine... which left Unfinished Business with Pawl the Welshman, across the Dee and beyond the narrow channel of the seaway to the south.

Yngvar the house- thrall looked over as his master rummaged for his shoes, and cleared his throat. "Sir? We will need more firewood soon, and the barley is getting low for the time of year..."

The lord's deep green eyes stared back at the slave's pale grey ones. "So go to Arnkel or Thurbrand and ask them for wood, they're the ones who own the wood-axes. As for the wheat...well, perhaps we will have to stop our thralls from making extra bread to eat when they think nobody is watching!"

He slapped Yngvar's stomach for emphasis; the slave had the decency to look suitably abashed. Hrolf was certain that besides eating, Yngvar had a talent for making things too, but he had yet to catch him at it, and thus have an excuse to get the greedy oaf out of his kitchen. They *couldn't* be low on bere this early into the spring… could they? He added this item to his memory-list of Things To Do, and hoped nothing equally important had dropped off the other end of it.

His wife and daughters looked up as he reached the fire.

"Good day, my husband," smiled Var, pausing from her examination of a pot. "Another one cracked, I'm afraid." She held the offending article out for his inspection with one hand, and tried to tuck a stray wisp of flaming auburn hair back inside her headscarf with the other. Three children had left their marks on her body, but Hrolf could never see it. To him, she still
looked as youthful and vibrant as she ever had, and the flowing cut of her dresses only served to accentuate this. He tore his eyes back to the pot and, taking it from her, carefully rapped it with his knuckles. The sound was dull, flat, which even in pottery was a bad sign. He wondered why they bothered with the stuff; he knew there were places that dealt in the soft pot-stone that his grandparents had used, without the need to go all the way round the North Way to where they cut it from the hillsides. Iron pots were perhaps a little

too much for him to afford, but he still reckoned them the best answer. Certainly better than the amount of silver he kept paying out for pots that lasted only a handful of times in the fire.

"Chester again?"

She nodded. "Next time that merchant comes through my door, I'll have his skull to stew the pork in."

"Ugh, short rations that way!" Elle laughed. She was teaching her little sister to spin, slowly adding yet another skein of wool to those already hung from the pegs in the wall- plates. Hrolf rubbed his beard and reflected that there could be a new shirt in all that lot, somewhere. Did they have any dyestuff in, currently? He rather fancied a red one, which might be more easily achievable than blue, if more expensive, considering how far the raw materials for it had to travel; he hadn't ever been that far south, and knew nobody else who had, either. But it would
be far more noticeable than his everyday green garb. Maybe he'd get it, if his luck held…but he knew a way to increase that luck.

"It must be nearly spring," he mused aloud.

"Long past midwinter," Var agreed, with the smile of one who knows what is coming next, "we've finished all the ale from that brew." Her soft face, with its delightfully shaped nose,
looked indulgently into his, waiting for him to speak the next line of a speech they went through every spring.

"...So it must be getting on for Ship Time!" Hrolf finished happily.

Var patted his arm. "Yes dear, nearly time to pack you off out from under my feet for a few months - but not before you mend the byre! If you want cheese for your homecoming, you
have to keep the cows dry."

Hrolf opened the door a crack and peered out. "Lovely day for mending roofs," he muttered, seeing nothing but rain beyond the eaves.

"You've got a cloak," his wife replied, and turned smartly back to the fire.

CHAPTER TWO

The problem with being a Man of Standing, Hrolf reflected, and thus one possessed of Wealth and Power, was that it didn't seem to have left him with very much of either on a day-to-day basis. Being the local Hauldr didn't remove the need to clamber up Thurbrand's rickety old ladder clutching a handful of nails, an axe and a hammer borrowed from Jon the smith's toolchest; indeed, it sometimes felt as if, whenever something needed doing, his farmhands and hangers-on looked to him to do it. On the other hand, he could be fairly certain that Yngvar *would* go and politely ask Arnkel to attend to the wood shortage, since power and status were always relative to those around you, and the thrall would be on his master's business; but it still removed the need for Hrolf to do so, and thus left him free to mend the roof on the cowshed instead.

Thurbrand passed up a new rafter on command; Hrolf didn't bother to ask where the timber had come from, as it clearly wasn't from the ship. At least, he reflected as rain cascaded off his huddled, cloaked form, he could reach the damaged area from the top of the ladder, and wouldn't have to spreadeagle himself across the sodden, spongy mass of the turf, and thus get even wetter. Easing up the corner of the turf roof took only moments; Hrolf called for the axe, firstly to knock out the remains of the old wood, then to scarf the new joint before he slid it in. Thurbrand steadfastly held the foot of the ladderpole, his grey eyebrows drawn deeply over his eyes, giving no opinion away about anything; if he spoke, it was lost in the tangled web of his beard, or in the wind that continued to blow.

Hrolf generally had a lot of good things to say about a lot of people, including Jon the dark- haired, pale-eyed resident blacksmith, who was also by turns companion-in-arms, explorer and fellow-drinker; now he added "makes a good nail" to the list as he hammered them in. The other timbers that made up the roof- frame seemed to be holding up alright, so he left them alone, and presumed that the prevailing winds had hit this section more than any other... or that the goats had got up here for a snack, and somehow weakened the structure.

Thumping the turf back into place, he pulled the brortches from his belt and hammered them home again before descending the ladder to rejoin

Thurbrand in the mud. They stooped under the eave as if on some unspoken signal, and went on into the byre, where the new work could be inspected underneath, and its soundness checked. At their feet, the usually dry earth floor had degenerated into a morass of slick, wet mud. No wonder the cows hadn't liked it.

Thurbrand picked up the remains of the old rafter from where it had dropped. "See what I mean, lord? Rotten through and through."

Hrolf grunted. "Put it on the fire, then, and get some use from it on a day like this." He shook the water from his cloak; it ran off in little streams towards the hen's dustbowl by the doorway, raising clucks of disapproval. Hrolf glowered towards the cock as if to forestall any answer, but to no avail. "Where did you get the new wood from, Thurbrand?"

"I had to get a piece from the fence around the pigsty this morning. Don't worry," he added, seeing the look of horror on his master's face, " I didn't leave a hole, I promise. I had a bit of driftwood all ready, nice and dry and just the right shape - but when I looked for it yesterday, it had gone."

Hrolf scratched his damp head. "Bits of wood don't just up and walk away, man! You must have moved it somewhere. It'll turn up, and no doubt we'll use it somewhere else."

"Maybe timber doesn't walk on other farms," muttered Thurbrand, "but it does around here, and other things besides. It comes of not having any ghosts, I reckon."

"Talk any more of that rubbish and I'll make you a ghost! You just make sure your tongue has consulted your brains - or better still, *my* brains - before you go sending me to the Thing with your accusations and lawsuits."

"I'm not accusing anyone of anything!" Thurbrand's weatherbeaten face wore a look of surprised outrage. He opened his mouth to say more, but the words never made it out.

Hrolf looked at his cowherd. "I've known you long enough to see that you're on the verge of beginning a case, Thurbrand. All I say is to be certain of your ground before you take it further than the fence of your own head, and risk us all being laughed out of court for the loss of a lump of wood. At any rate, your roof is fixed, and according to all the authorities around this farm, that's all that really matters. Go back to your – my - cows; I have more enjoyable matters in mind for the rest of the day."

CHAPTER THREE

Hrolf sneaked back into the warm, smoky gloom of the house for an early-morning horn and a spoonful of last night's pottage by the side of the fire before he headed out to the boatshed; thanks to Var's awakening him, it was still too early for anyone else to find him other jobs to do. The lady herself was occupied with sorting the day-meal in the little room that served as a larder, built onto the side of the main hall, and if she noticed her husband, he failed to make any impression. So he slipped out again, and nobody was any the wiser.

On the short journey from the hilltop to the shore, however, like the supernatural spirit Thurbrand claimed they didn't have, he still managed to gather companions around him,
despite that early hour. Jon the smith; Arnkel, who owned the other axe on the farm, Grim the tree-smith (who owned lots of axes and other things besides, but never advertised it), and Hrolf's own son Kendrick, usually asleep at this sort of time, but who, like the others, could smell ship-business a mile away, and who only ever had one question regarding the ship, and seemed determined to

repeat it over and over until he got the answer he wanted.

The noust itself was one of the most substantial buildings on the farm, as well it might be, containing as it did the main source of all their incomes - and thus Hrolf's ability to pay their collective taxes and rents to the sons of Ingimund, the nominal (and in Hrolf's view, very much so) owners and lords – maybe even Jarls - of these lands to the west of Chester. So, rather than wattle-and-daub walls under thatched or turf roofs, the boatshed had firm planks of solid timber, cut tightly together, and held upright by vertical posts rammed deep into the ground
along their length. The roof was high, although it still overhung the walls by a respectable amount, and was also of wood, albeit with turf over the top - a later addition to help keep the water out and any warmth in.

Now, as Hrolf and his followers entered the building at the open, river-end, pale shafts of light shone in and over the sail, draped across the hull in an attempt to keep the rain out over the winter. Eager hands pushed and wrestled the heavy, sodden, oily, fat-soaked wool over the rail of the vessel, and listened for the splash or thud of it's landing to gauge how successful they had been in their protection. Critical eyes and loving hands ran over the faded paint and the well- worn wood beneath.

"Well now, my beauty, my love," whispered Hrolf, more to himself than even to the boat, "and how have the rimethurses treated you this winter, hmm?"

"It don't seem too bad," croaked Grim into the heavy air of the shed, "Nowt broken, at any rate. Bit o' warping where it's dried, but it should tighten up alright once we get it back in the water. Give it a week or so once in, mind, before you go off anywhere."

"Smells a bit inside, but no worse than other years," added Jon.

"Well, remember the weather we put it away in," said Arnkel slowly, "didn't really have time to clean up, after all."

"It's been a wet winter, and no mistake," agreed Hrolf, helping Kendrick over the rail to clamber around inside. "Shall we ask for better this time?"

The ship, and indeed its shed, strictly speaking, were not Hrolf's. When its old crew had returned one autumn long ago, they had brought with them the news of his father's death, along with the proposal that he take over Dubhnjal's share in the vessel, in lieu of a wergild his ship-fellows could not afford to pay - unless he and his mother would accept their bruises and
spear-cuts. He had been around ten, then, and had demanded to see those wounds, as if judging the accuracy of their story before he took the deal. Year had followed year, and the faces at the oar-benches had changed, until now all but a few were of Hrolf's choosing - or of his generation - and they mostly looked to him as leader. But still, technically, it wasn't his ship, for all that under him the crew had done well, the gods had smiled, and he regularly "borrowed" it to support his position at home and with his neighbours. He still had to go and see each of his fellow-owners, and discuss, slowly, carefully, what they wanted to do this coming season, without seeming too eager for them to sell their share. It was a long, wearying process, involving much drinking, much long talking, many gifts given and got, and many
long nights away from the comforts of home.

In the meantime, however, there was a ship to prepare... it struck Hrolf as strange that this part of the business was always, somehow, left to him to achieve at his own expense,
whilst the profits were always divided. Kendrick, heading for his seventh year, was already aboard, having worked out the answer to his question for himself (or having remembered it from last year), and deciding to make the most of what access he could have before the vessel left him behind once again. Already he was at the prow, waving an imaginary spear at imaginary enemies, as imaginary waves carried him and his own (imaginary) crew to new exploits and mountains of plunder, sadly also imaginary. The grown men cheered him on, lost in similar dreams or memories of their own, whilst uncoiling ropes, fighting the sail into a roll in order to carry it outside for inspection and patching, sighting down the oars for warping, and generally inspecting the timbers. The fabric of the ship appeared sound enough; as they went about their tasks, Hrolf mentally made a list of people to visit, work to organise, and tasks to delegate.

*

"And how is the Second Wife, after her long confinement?" asked Var sweetly when he returned

to the house late that evening. "Is she as eager as ever to dance on the waves,
singing the whale's songs, and bringing me fine gifts for tolerating her presence this winter and next?"

Hrolf laughed. "You're in a fine mood today, oh First Wife...she is well enough, thankyou, but as usual she will need your help to mend her fine woollens before she is fit to go anywhere."

"This comes as no surprise... just as long as you don't expect us to lay the pitch or put that yuck on the sail." Hild and Ymma, Var's Ladies of the House, looked suitably shocked at
the thought, and hurriedly returned to studiously examining the state of their day's weaving.

Hrolf nearly choked on his ale. "You know the recipe better than any of us! No? Well, just some sewing in places, then, and I will find someone else to waterproof the wool again."

He chuckled, and looked towards the shadowy figure by the ale-vat. "Perhaps Yngvar would like the task? It would get him out into the fresh air for a while. I'm sure being cooped up with you and your ladies is doing him no good at all." He smiled savagely as the butt of his joke hastened out of sight.

"I will have to go and see Brynjolf," he continued, turning back to Var, "and ask to borrow his man Brand...the net-maker, remember? Some of the lines are a little frayed, and something tells me a few lengths of netting might come in handy this summer."

"And why might that be, hmm? And what of the walrus hide lines you paid so highly for? Are they a bad bargain already?" As if to emphasise the words - or perhaps to tease him - Var casually chinked the keys that hung from her clasp. Hrolf frowned at her through the fire-smoke, and looked again, this time more longingly, at the ale-cask in the corner. To return the
imagined emphasis, he tapped his empty cup on the table.

"The hide ropes are fine, as far as I could tell, but let's wait until we float again, in the daylight, before we decide." He mischievously added, "I'd lay money on them being in better condition than your pot."

"What will you do if they have suffered? We can't afford more."

Hrolf snorted. "If they don't last even a winter, I wouldn't buy any more! If - if, mind you - they are bad, we can shorten them, and find another use."

"Such as?"

"How about a noose for the pirate who sold me them?"

Var laughed, and signalled Hild to refill her husband's beaker. "Ah, husband, once again you remind me why we married all those years ago! Two people so alike in their view of the world."

"Indeed… one day and already we've killed a pot-merchant and a rope-maker. We're doing well; who shall we end the day with?"

"Don't you go looking at Yngvar like that! Fat and lazy he may be, but he's also useful. You'll be getting me a replacement before he hangs from the ash trees with our other victims, if you please."

CHAPTER FOUR

It was Hrolf's duty and custom, as ship-master, to report to his co-owners on the health of the *Felag's* biggest single investment as soon as he had opened up the boat-shed every spring. As the oldest of the fellowship, Snorri got the first visit, which was a matter of some irritation to Hrolf as he also lived the furthest away, beyond the bay at the mouth of the northern river. It meant a day's sailing - Hrolf flatly refused to even consider riding that far - and the usual practice was to get a minimal crew aboard, sail the ship to Snorri's farmstead in the lands of black earth, and let Snorri and his share of the full crew help them sail it back. But this year was different. There seemed to be fewer free hands available, and the ship was not even in the water yet. Where had the time gone? Hrolf realised glumly that he would have to make other arrangements, and he resented the intrusion of yet more hassle and annoyance into an already complicated process. Why couldn't the boat just get itself ready, and be done with all this messing around?

*

Arne and Kol were half-brothers, fishermen for the most part, although Hrolf did not doubt that their

little boat found other employment besides hauling in cod and salmon, when the
opportunity arose. They were free men, of a free family, not beholden to Hrolf in any way beyond the obligations that went with residing on his estates, and that freedom was in danger of becoming a problem. He could easily imagine that, with the right sort of luck, they could have the foundings of a Felag of their own, and a bigger ship to boot. Did he want rivals on his own doorstep? Hrolf wasn't particularly comfortable with the idea, and he doubted if his fellow ship- owners would look favourably towards potential competitors. Thinking along those lines gave him an idea, however, a further wedge to widen the cracks in their slowly crumbling unwillingness to ferry him up the coast on his visit to Snorri, and turn their wyrd into a more favourable direction besides.

"It's not as if you're going to lose by the deal, now is it?" asked Hrolf, exasperated by the unnecessary stubbornness, to his mind, of the men opposite him. He had approached them with the proposal to sail him north almost as soon as he had finished in the noust, and here it was nearly evening, with the matter still not settled. "It's only a day's sailing to Snorri's beaches, instead of three day's riding- and a river to cross even then! And besides," he leaned forward, "I *know* you fish in those waters anyway. Many a time you've come to me asking for money to put yet another patch in that tub of yours after you fell foul of the currents beyond the rivermouth." As his visitor's faces fell, Hrolf leaned back against his wall with a slight glow of triumph, and he allowed them a minute or two to consider a better reply than their original one. He decided now was not the time to remind them that, in theory, he could just take their boat from them, and leave them to starve. After all, he was the one who had the most men, and more weapons to hand; besides which, they looked as if they were well on the way to famine by themselves. Their faces were lean and drawn, with that dark and shiny quality to the skin around their eyes, along with lank, dull hair that just seemed to hang from their heads, that spoke of little food to spare - or anything else, if it came down to it. Kol and Arne had come to his house without even a spear between them.

"You must understand, sir," said Arne eventually (having been nudged in his prominent ribs by his elder sibling in way of encouragement), "it's not that we are unwilling to give you transport… but as I'm sure you realise, this would put us in something of a deficit ourselves, not being free to fish for that day - or the return day, either. We have to make our way in the world, as do we all."

Hrolf nodded wisely, a faint smile on his lips. "I do see your predicament, Arne; I am also aware that it will be rent-time again soon, too. And, had I a smaller vessel of my own, I would not need to trouble you, of course. Perhaps I should talk to Grim, see if he can be persuaded to build me one this next winter, hmm?

"Mind you," he went on suddenly, as if only then thinking of it, "perhaps there could be suitable compensation for your trouble. Perhaps - just perhaps - this journey would finally convince me of your seamanship; my partners in the Felag are getting on in years, and Brynjolf for one seemed uncertain whether to sail again this year when I spoke with him at the Thing. There might be a chance for enterprising young men like yourselves to... *persuade*... me of their own worth as Felagmen..."

He left the words hanging in the smoky air, like bait sent down to the world-serpent in his dark, briny deep... and like that snake in the old tale, finally, the brothers took it. Words were spoken, hands were clasped, and a silver ring passed across the table to clinch the deal. As they left, chuckling to each other like young boys who had seen their first glimpse of a girl's arms uncovered, Hrolf finished his ale and considered wider pictures.

He could leave his household bondsmen behind for this trip, for which he was glad, since Kol and Arne would hardly go home without attempting to impress Snorri of their worthiness, and so in them he had suitable companions for his journey without any need to disrupt the entire farmstead's working. If Jon was available, he might ask him along, if only to keep those two in
line somewhat, but he suspected the forge might be too busy for that. Solmund would surely want to stay behind with his new wife, which also suited Hrolf perfectly well. So; time to finish
lazing by the hearth like an old man, and get to work. He'd probably have to pack his own bags, from the looks the Ladies of the House were giving him. Or maybe he was just in the way
of the broom.

His sea-going satchel, a large and unwieldy bag of leather, spent its winters under his pillow, and now was the time to haul it out. Feeling the silent pressure of female eyes, he took it into the brewhouse before opening it. To his surprise, Yngvar and Thurbrand were already there.

"What's your business here?" he demanded of the kitchen thrall.

"I'm told I have many skills, sir," the slave replied, nothing but innocence on his shaven, slightly flaccid face. "I thought I'd see if brewing was one of them." He held up a sack of barley by way of illustration.

"I came in to check on the fire," muttered Thurbrand. Something in his tone bothered Hrolf, but as he couldn't immediately put a finger on what, exactly, he ignored the potential for problems. The pair of them looked - and sounded – for all the worlds like trespassers caught in the orchard.

He opened the bag (it had enough ties to hold down a wolf, but at least the insides kept dry), and

emptied the contents on the floor. Most of what it held was also leather: a hood, a
heavy over-shirt, and a set of hose. There was also a long coil of walrus-hide rope, for tying the owner to the ship if need be. This gear was awkward and heavy, but in a storm it was a lifesaver. It was also one of the few things his father had owned that had come back after his death, and it was too good to have wasted it.

"Yngvar, go find me some fat." His hands ran over the hide, noting the dry patches, testing the seams. The sack also held linen thread, a block of beeswax, and a little roll of cloth with an awl and a pair of long bone needles in it. Tucked right in the corner was a little bag of silver coins and scraps, and amber beads - his emergency funds.

Yngvar returned with a little bowl of lard, muttering about being told to make beer and casting dark looks across at Thurbrand. Hrolf creased his brow, enough of a warning to those
that knew him well, and abandoned his intention of getting the kitchen-thrall to grease his gear. The cowherd got the job instead, which gave Hrolf a reason to remove him from the

brewery, and thus away from Yngvar. Beer always struck Hrolf as far more important than firewood, and if Yngvar by some chance did have the brewer's skill, his master was not about to ignore it.

CHAPTER FIVE

"I smell a storm coming," murmured Hrolf to Var later that evening at the benches. The pillars of his high-seat, resplendent in their carved and painted figures as they flickered in the firelight, had been set far enough apart to allow two people to sit side by side, and their very presence conferred an impression of space and privacy. Around them, the farmhands
and house-bondar sat filling the wall-benches at the night-meal, eating, talking, but all at a discreet enough distance for their lord not to be overheard.

Var raised an eyebrow. "Really? And with the second wife so eager to be off? This is unlike you, my husband, and unlike our weather here. Will it delay you, do you think?"

He smiled "Delay? Not likely, I'll take ship on my mistress and leave it here on shore!"

Var nodded sagely. "Ah. One of *those* storms."

"Mmm. Thurbrand is on a vengeance-quest, I suspect it's over a piece of wood of all things, and

Yngvar is right in the path of the storm - without the wit to move."

"Oh, well, that'll be fun then, won't it? Good to know I won't have a dull summer without you." She smiled. "I can deal with Thurbrand well enough, and as for Yngvar..." she
shrugged.

"As ever, you understand completely, my love. Just don't let them kill each other before I get back, eh?"

"Why should I have to wait for that?"

"Aren't I allowed any entertainment, then? Besides, if I'm here, I can set out the hazel rods, and make 'em do it properly." He took a spoonful of his fish stew, and continued. "If that doesn't scare them into their senses, I don't know what will. Think Yngvar could persuade anyone to second for him?"

"Doubtful. He's never been one for making friends, after all. But Thurbrand keeps pretty much to himself as well. It could be a very short holmgang."

"Yngvar was in the brewhouse earlier, wondering if he could make ale." As if reminded, Hrolf took a sip from his cup, and looked around him at familiar faces shining in the heat of his hearth. "Could be an expensive way of removing him from the kitchen…"

Var patted his arm and reached for the jug. "Never you mind, husband dear; leave such matters to She Who Holds The Keys. Besides," she added, leaning and whispering in his ear, "I
think I saw him cutting leather."

"Ahh!" Hrolf whispered back. "Anyone else catch him at it?"

"Not yet; but again, leave it to those who can best manage such matters. We'll have nailed him by the time you return in the autumn."

Hrolf nodded. "All well and good, then." He looked through the haze over the fire to the doorway, feeling a breeze, and waved Kol and Arne into the room. "I've done a deal to take
their boat - and them - up to Snorri," he said by way of explanation. "We should at least feed them before we go."

The half- brothers presented themselves to their host, awkwardly, stiffly, uncertain of how to do such

things, it seemed. Hrolf welcomed them in, Var poured them ale, handed them the washing- bowl for their hands, and found them seats further down the bench, along with someone to talk to who wouldn't frighten them too much. "They don't keep much
company, do they?" she observed of them on her return to the high seat. "They seem rather impressed by it all."

"I never thought I'd hear you say that in a worried sort of tone," grinned her husband. "I thought the whole idea was to frighten people into subservience by all this."

"I heard you with them earlier," answered Var. "I thought they'd been frightened and bullied enough for one day, surely?"

"I was polite…"

"You tied them up good and proper, you beast! I told you, I was listening, and I was most impressed. Is this what you do to all those poor merchants you meet while you're away with

Second Wife? No wonder we're so rich from it." She took his arm and nestled in close to him. "The Felag is lucky to have you, and I'm sure they know it."

Hrolf kissed her. "Hmm. Well, tomorrow it all begins again, my love."

"Everything is ready: Hild even helped me start sorting through the larder. We have sausage for you to take, and ham, and the fish has dried out really well; and I think we might just
spare you all a cheese, too. And if we put extra bread to bake from now on, you ought to have plenty, at least to begin with, until you can get more. How does that sound?"

"As always, my wife, it sounds wonderful. I'm sure you will cope as well as ever while I'm gone."

Var shrugged. "I met you when you were voyaging; I can hardly claim not to have known the sort of life I'd have with you. Remember my father was the same, and Mothir taught me well. I miss you, especially at night, but I'd miss the silver and the thralls if you didn't go out every summer. So I'm content. It's not as if I'm ever short of company, either."

"No indeed; we have a houseful, and no mistake. And you could always go visiting…"

"Now there's a thought! I haven't seen Gytha in years, and it was lovely when Asa came with Brynjolf last year. Do you know, I think I might do that. Who could I take with me?"

"Solmund has a new wife, she might like the trip, and her husband would be suitable escort, too. Any of the men here would ride with you, I'm sure. Lambing will be over soon, the wheat and barley are growing…it's a good time for going out on journeys, especially with so many here to share what work there is."

"I could leave the children with Hild and Ymma. Neither of them care for travelling." She looked thoughtful. "I suppose Elle is old enough to come with me, really. Definitely a good reason to go visiting, it's time to start looking for possible husbands!"

"There's a happy thought…anyone in mind? While you're at it, Kendrick will be wanting a foster- father soon, too. It's time to widen the family ties again."

Var leaned back into the cushions behind her. "My brothers on Mann would be happy to have him, maybe in a year or two more. They have ships, and good contacts all over the place. They'd do him a lot of good, and Ragnar has always said he would foster him."

"I'd like that," said a little voice by the side of them. "I suppose I don't get to sail with *you* this year?"

"No you don't, my boy, but only because I still have to lift you over the rail! You want to go and live with your uncle Ragnar on Mann? Well, if the wind takes us that way, I'll go see him for you, and ask." Hrolf regarded his son for a long moment. "You're nearly a man; it's time we started thinking about your future, and your reputation. Ragnar has friends in the North Way still, and among the Western Isles." He nodded to himself. "Yes; I'll ask him. Maybe next summer, eh?"

"Thankyou," said Kendrick. "I'm tired; Rowan is asleep already. I think I'll go to bed too."

"A wise choice," agreed Hrolf. "It's an early waking for me as well, so I won't be far behind you."

"Will you be here when I wake up?"

Hrolf smiled. "Surely that depends on *when* you wake, son of mine?"

"I suppose so..."

"I tell you what, lad. You just sleep, as late as you like, providing you get your work done afterwards. If you are awake when I go, you can walk to the river with us - but you'll have to walk back on your own."

Kendrick nodded. "I'll probably see you when you get back, then."

Hrolf ruffled his son's thick, tousled hair. "More than likely, son of mine. More than likely."

CHAPTER SIX

As predicted, and to nobody's real surprise, Kendrick was not awake to see his father depart with Kol and Arne the following morning. It was no great hardship for Hrolf to be up at such an hour, used as he was to shipboard life and the demands of his homestead; and so, even before the brothers had sorted their gear aboard the boat, he was swiftly descending the slopes down to the river. Passing the noust, he turned towards the sea, only a mile or so away across the marshes beyond the end of the little river, where Kol and Arne habitually kept their boat on the shore. Hrolf was also used to travelling with very few belongings, and so he had his small stock of spare clothing, a little extra food and a few useful gifts for Snorri all bundled into the one bag, which in turn was carried inside his big, shaggy, grey cloak, worn pinned at the hip in the style of the Irish and the Dalriadans, where it made a useful satchel by itself. It took him very little time to cover the distance; the morning was clear and dry, with only a hint of wind, and the only moisture being that of the sea. Soft and boggy though the land around here was, Hrolf knew the paths, where drier, firmer ground snaked its unpredictable way through the marshlands and pools. Long grasses grew, along with short, scrubby bushes; the soil was just too poor for trees, and so when he needed timber, Hrolf had to go upland, to the long ridge on which his own hall sat (although that had lost all its woods long before his time), or further into Wirhalh, around the parts where Ingimund's Irish followers had chosen to settle, where timber was more easy to get.

Although the fishermen around his lands ought to know him by sight, he didn't see the point in taking chances, and so warned them of his arrival with a blast on his horn. The brothers looked up and waved; Hrolf quickened his pace slightly to eat up the remaining furlong. Their boat slid into the surf as he approached, leaving only the lightest of traces in the shingle and sand.

"Need anything doing?" he asked by way of greeting, as Arne stepped aside to let him aboard. The elder brother shook his head.

"All is ready, lord. We'll even beat the tide, I think."

Hrolf followed his gaze. "Hmm, maybe. Could be close, but of course, you've less depth than I'm used

to." He settled amidships, where the other two could get past him at need, and
pulled a leather bottle from his bag. "Ah, we're floating already. I'd forgotten what a small vessel can do. Want a drink before we go?"

Kol, who was overboard pulling up the anchor-stone at the time, looked up. "If that's the ale you were serving last night, sir, then yes indeed!"

"You should come and eat with us more often. You look half- starved as it is, and far too sober." He passed the bottle round. "To a good journey," and tipped a little over the side, just
to help stack the odds in their favour. "Are we ready, then?"

The brothers took the oars and, with Hrolf at the steerboard, they made their way out towards open water. At some unspoken signal, the oars came inboard and Arne ran the
sail up, whilst Kol moved aft and took over the steering from their passenger. Hrolf soon realised that the little boat was very responsive to even the smallest changes in its loading, and took care not to move around more than he had to. He had not been sure how well the brothers would cope with his

minimal weight aboard, used as they were to day after day in their own company, hauling in fish, setting lines, and so forth; but they handled it well, shifting their own positions within the hull to compensate for the presence of a bulk far smaller than any decent load of fish. As soon as they were able, Kol pushed the steerboard over, and sent them northward, following the coastline towards the mouth of the big river that separated their home from the lands of the black earth. The sail bellied out in the breeze, the mast creaked, and the lines drew taut as the boat surged onwards.

For reasons known only to himself, Snorri had settled in a largely deserted area that had lain unclaimed by either Ingimund, the Mercians, or the Westmorlanders. Yet he had not been the first there, as a number of mounds could testify, so exactly what the attraction of the place was, Hrolf could not really say. He knew that the soil was good, perhaps even remarkably so; but would that be enough of a lure to such an otherwise bleak and uninviting place? Snorri was not a native of the area; much like Grim the treesmith, his past was shrouded in mystery. Some had said that Gytha, his wife, was not only his second wife, but also an Anglian by birth, from the lands of the

Northumbrians. Snorri himself had been described as everything from a failed merchant, to a once-famous warrior, to a dangerous outlaw from overseas, convicted of numerous killings and driven from his homeland in consequence. Hrolf's problem was that he could see traces of all these in the man he had known all his life. He sometimes suspected that it had been Snorri who had persuaded the other Felag-men to give him his father's share all those years ago. But then, he could also easily believe that it might have been Snorri who had got them into the mess in which his father had died in the first place. It was idle to guess, and dwelling on the past served no purpose; especially when in a small open boat, accompanied by two men whose seacraft he had never before experienced first-hand.

Hrolf was well aware that Kol and Arne repeatedly had problems trying to navigate the currents that swirled around the mouth of the northern river, and so as they approached, he
shuffled closer to the stern, so that Kol could hear the suggestions he shouted. Their little boat behaved far differently than the twenty- bencher of the Felag did in these waters: every

little eddy and cross- current seemed to take hold of the vessel and turn it around in ways Hrolf could never have imagined from his own fore-deck. Suddenly, the problems these two fishermen had told him of began to seem more real than he had given them credit for; the boat moved so swiftly at each tug of the water that predicting anything was out of the question. Nevertheless, he watched the waves around them, and felt the movements of the strakes under his feet (for there was no space for any decking in a vessel this small). Slowly, between the three of them, they fought the boat across the rivermouth, and into the calmer waters to the north. Once clear of the worst of the tides, Hrolf considered that a victory celebration was in order, and after a brief session with the baling- bucket, he passed the bottle round again.

By late afternoon, as the sun was beginning to visibly dip into the open ocean, the coastline opposite began to look familiar. A long, wide beach, capable of stretching over a mile at the lowest of tides, began to appear along the shore, and Hrolf paid less attention to the sailing, and more to the finding of further landmarks. As it was, their landing- place was easily chosen, for a thin plume of

smoke rose from slightly inland, behind a point at which a small group of men stood on the sand, watching their approach. Hrolf knew at least three of them from
previous years, and hailed them as soon as he judged the distance sufficient for his voice to carry. Kol and Arne ran out the oars, and rowed the boat high up onto the beach; the waiting
men grabbed the bow- line and helped pull it further, above the high-water mark.

"Welcome back, lord!" smiled Olaf from beneath his tight-fitting helm. Hrolf grasped his outstretched hand warmly.

"Good to see you too, Olaf; how is the old man, then?"

Olaf looked cagey. "Ah, not so fast, and no clues, either. Come back to the hall, and I'm sure you'll find out all you want to know."

CHAPTER SEVEN

Even as they walked into his hall, before their eyes had even adjusted to the darkness of the interior - with its fire banked lower than his own, Hrolf noted absently, and not blazing so
Brightly - Snorri was rubbing his hands with joy. "Spring already! Who would have thought the winter could pass so quickly, eh? This is the day I wait for through the rain and the sleet! And where do you propose we go hunting this year?" His grey eyes twinkled amid a nest of wrinkles and equally grey hair, and his few remaining teeth showed in a perpetual grin.

"It's alright for you," muttered Gytha to Hrolf, as she filled his horn," you've only just got here. I've had to live with him ever since you got back last year!"

"Ah," replied the old man, "but you look forward to my trips too, do you not? Hmm? You've worn the proceeds of last year's ventures across your breast all winter after all," he flicked
a finger to point at the silver chains that hung from his wife's brooches, and the ingots, coins and bits of

precious stone that dangled from them, "and a safer place for them I cannot
imagine. We mended the byre, I bought the timber for that myself; we laid in food and the makings of ale - what do you think of it, Hrolf? - and got some of the cloth we didn't sell, too. I'm happy to sail again; you're happy with the profit and prestige our ventures bring home. I don't see why you keep on trying to stop me from going."

Gytha frowned at him. "It's because, husband dear, you're not getting any younger, and your days in this world are not endless, and it would be nice to spend some of the warmer ones with you! We are rich enough to afford for you not to go, and every year you come back aching more, and less able to move around the farm. One year, not so far away, you'll either
not get your limbs back, or not come back at all - as Dubhnjal didn't. You're the oldest of the Felag who still go, and I've told you often enough that I think it's time you sold your share and
paid more attention to what happens here at home."

Snorri rubbed his beard, but the smile never left his lips or his eyes. "Well, I reckon that tells me where we stand! I'll listen to you, wife, but I'll not act on your advice. I've always travelled; it's a part of me, and if I die while we're away, well, talking of Dubhnjal, his son here hasn't exactly done badly from our fellowship, so I think you can be certain of getting my share, should it come to that. But something in my bones tells me it won't; not this year, at any rate."

"There's no point in asking you to talk sense into him either, is there?" said Gytha, switching her attention to Hrolf.

Their guest shrugged, whilst his companions tried hard to melt
into the shadows around them. "He's a useful man aboard the ship; I'd be sorry if he didn't come, and, to be honest, to stay at home just for the worry of getting hurt would be less than I'd expect of him. Now, if he were old and decrepit, it would be different; I'd side with you
against him, and as shipmaster, I have the final say in who goes and who stays. But at the moment, I have to say that I came here expecting him to come with us, and wanting him to. I cannot argue your case in this matter, my Lady."

"Oh, I thought as much." Gytha seemed to sag perceptibly as she sat down. "Ah well, another summer of trying to keep things running here while you go off and risk life and limb again; I should be used to it by now, but somehow it never gets any easier. And we're short on help this year, what with Sigmund going away and Gunnar injured after his fall from the roof."

"Has he not recovered from that?" asked Hrolf. "I can send a man or two, if it eases things."

"Yes, it would help," answered Gytha, cutting off Snorri's protest to the contrary. "I'm as old as he is, after all, and my joints ache more than his appear to. Some of the younger bondar seem to think they can run around me and get out of their share of the work, and I find myself more tired more quickly by it."

Hrolf thought for a moment. "I'll ask Solmund to come for a few months; he'll appreciate the chance, I think, and he'll bring his new wife with him. Var is thinking about paying a visit, too, so she could bring them over and go home without them. He doesn't sail, you see, so he's an ideal choice for this. Who knows, he may like it enough to want to move over here with you, and then you'll have all the help you could wish for."

Snorri chuckled. "You say that as if there might be a sting in the tail."

Hrolf raised an eyebrow. "Really? Well, he can be a bit of a pain sometimes, and if he decides he knows best, there's often no dealing with him. But he'll whip your farmhands into shape for you, and then there's only him for you to keep in line. I still say it's better than trying to run it all yourself, Gytha, and his wife's a kind woman, a good companion and houseworker.
Makes a seriously fine cheese..."

Gytha raised her hands in submission. "All right, let him come, and whatever help he gives us will be gratefully received; we can sort out any problems afterwards, I 'm sure." She turned
her gaze back to her husband "And as for you, just be careful, and mindful of your creaky joints and such. I expect you back here for the autumn harvesting, and you'd better be fit for it, or I'll be dealing out bad fates to the lot of you!"

"Don't worry," smiled Snorri to Kol and Arne, who were hanging back and looking worried, "I'm sure she doesn't include you - yet. So;" he continued, waving them closer to the fire,
"Hrolf says you are men of character and worth, and yet I've never met you." He sat down, and motioned for them to do likewise. "So tell me about yourselves…"

"We - my half- brother and I - are fishers and sailors," began Arne. "We have our own boat; that is why we are here, in part. Lord Hrolf says he might think of us should a share in the
Felag ever come up for sale."

"We are happy to work, and to share in the adventure," added Kol. "We want to do well in the world, and be more than just fishermen."

Snorri's smile had warmth in it. "You sound like me, forty years ago! I remember my first venture - I was around nine when I had my first trip, but I was too small to do much, so it
doesn't really count. Gytha, my lady, could we have more ale, please? Where was I - ah, yes. Ever been on a proper ship, as crew?"

Kol and Arne both confessed they had not. "We only have our little four-oared skiff," explained Arne, "although it does have a sail. We built it ourselves."

"I'm impressed; ship-making isn't easy. But you've rowed, and you can handle a small sail, so you know the basics probably better than I do, I shouldn't wonder." Gytha returned
with the ale-jug, and Snorri poured for all of them, an unspoken honour in itself. "The trick to doing well on a bigger ship," he continued, "is to just do as you're told, which, in your own boat, you may not be so used to. We all follow the word of the shipmaster, no more and no less. Very often, the rule is not to think for yourself, or you'll be in someone's way!" He grinned over the edge of his cup. "Still keen?"

"Even more so, if anything, sir." Replied Kol.

Snorri nodded. "There's a guest-house through the door over there; I suggest you sort out your beds before we eat tonight." As the brothers bowed and went out, Snorri looked over at Hrolf.

"They'll do. Quite a find, I'd say: sailors and shipwrights all in one."

"They're untested…"

Snorri snorted. "So were we, once upon a time. Don't hold that against them, or we're all done for!" He leaned closer. "Not a word to Gytha, or I'll have your hide; but what she says about my aches and pains is all true. But I'm damned if I'll sit at home waiting to die! I couldn't; to go from the ship would be too much for me. I was very glad to hear you say I was welcome still."

"You always will be. I don't expect you'll miss a trip until the year you die, and likely as not you'll do that while we're away."

Snorri laughed. "Still, these two of yours could be useful, for all that I get the impression you don't care for them all that much, hmm?" He stretched. "Their day may yet come, friend, and when it does, we may all want them with us and not against us. Let them come; my vote is with them. It's about time we all started looking to who is to follow us."

CHAPTER EIGHT

Hrolf and his companions stayed the customary three nights with Snorri, during which time the old man put a lot of effort into Kol and Arne, teaching them what he thought they ought to know about life on a larger vessel, and indeed about the wider world in general. They went hunting, although the exercise largely consisted of fruitless chases across open, wild heaths; Olaf and the others of Snorri's hearth-troop gave them a brief, but thorough, introduction to spear, shield and axe. This last exercise was one where Hrolf felt he could benefit as well, and so took the chance to polish his own war-skills. One of the biggest differences between Snorri and he was that the older man chose to maintain a warband at his own expense, something Hrolf had sometimes toyed with, but never actually done. Most of his encounters with professional fighting men had convinced him that they were, in the main, lazy, greedy, boorish, and potentially dangerous even to their patron, and with an extended farmstead and children to look after, Hrolf had never felt the investment in soldiers to be worthwhile, or indeed wise. Yet Olaf, Ragnar and their mates were old friends now, so perhaps it was the feeling that any others he found would be inferior that stopped Hrolf from wanting a band of his own.

Snorri - and Gytha, once she was reconciled to the fact of her husband sailing again - saw all three of them off with fine gifts, chosen for their ease of transport and usefulness: spare
shirts, new cloaks, and bronze finger-rings. Hrolf considered it to the brothers' credit that they quietly asked him if such gifts had to be matched, for they were not wealthy men, and they
might have to rely on his assistance to repay the gesture. Their lord smiled, and assured them that gifts such as these would not have to be reciprocated - this time. Snorri was investing in his own future, and Hrolf recognised that this future held great things for his lowly fishermen. But he advised them to keep something back from any share in the profits of the coming
summer, and use that to return Snorri's gesture.

The winds were with them on the return to Walea, speeding them southwards with far less effort than had been required to reach Snorri's coast. Their spirits were high; Kol and Arne had conducted themselves impeccably in high company, and so,

Hrolf considered, it was probably time he put himself to elevating them somewhat as well. He made a mental note to make regular space for them in his own hall, and to be a little more generous towards them from now on. Strange, he reflected, how it sometimes took somebody else to point out what should
have been clear without such help. That was a dangerous failing in a ship-master, and one he would have to be aware of in himself.

Once again, it took the three of them working together to get across the mouth of the big river, and Arne was heard to wonder at one stage whether it would be worth buying in an
extra pair of hands on trips to the north, simply for the time and effort it would save. Hrolf could easily imagine that such a comment, long ago, could have started his own Felag on its long career, and he was suddenly glad that he was bringing these two half-brothers into it, helping it grow and stay strong, instead of sending them away and potentially watching them begin on their own.
"Come and feast again tonight," he suggested, as the hillside and low marshes of home began to show around them, "in fact, come more often. We should be better friends, I think,

especially with Snorri taking such an interest in you." He grinned at their faces. "You are rising in the world, as you asked - it happens, don't worry about it." He leaned back against the rail. "Once the initial journeys like this one are done with, and the Thing has come and gone, I usually put the word out to fill my share of the crew. Your names are already marked for the
trip, if you still want it. Providing we do well, there should be enough in your share of the proceeds to keep this fine ship afloat for another winter - or longer."

Kol, who usually left the talking to his brother, beamed. "We'll be there, sir; we won't let you down."

Hrolf put a hand out to seal the deal. "Friends, you've already shown me that."

CHAPTER NINE

Brynjolf possessed what, in Hrolf's opinion, was probably the fiercest beard in all of Mercia. Blacker even than the winter nights, it jutted belligerently from his chin, whilst his cheeks were carefully shaven; coupled with his thick, dark eyebrows and receding hairline, it gave this most pleasant of men a look of towering anger and outrage at everyone and everything around him, no matter what his actual mood. He had his dwelling at a point where the more northerly river, that which formed the boundary between Ingimund's lands, Mercia and those of the Westmorlanders, naturally widened into a shiphaven, and the tide lessened. On the basis of having put a fence atop a bank, piled up as the ditch was dug, Brynjolf called it his Burgh, after the English fashion. It showed fine humour and imagination, Hrolf thought, but he also considered that his own people would never furnish even a half-decent poet, as they showed little if any sign of either quality. Hrolf's house was The Hall On The Rock, which was exactly what it was, no more and no less. And Hrolf did feel the want of a skald, especially over the winters.

Good manners dictated that Hrolf take not only gifts when visiting (he had already taken a good silver armring with him on the trip to see Snorri, but found an axehead in his chest that he thought Brynjolf might like, and so had it hafted by Grim), but also companions; since Brynjolf was often noted for being open- handed towards guests, on this trip there was no shortage of volunteers. One in particular was desperate for the journey.

"It's been a long winter, sir. I've not seen her since last Harvest, when you sent us over there with Lord Brynjolf's overseer to help with his fields. I didn't disgrace you, or her, or the lord Brynjolf then, sir, and I won't now; but I do so ache for even a sight of her."

Hrolf sighed, and surveyed the man over the rim of his cup (he never planned even the shortest of journeys on an empty stomach). He was tall, well-built, with an angular face and an air about him that spoke of better days in the past; under close-cropped hair, in the accepted fashion for thralls, dark eyes burned, full of mystery and unfathomed depths. He sat now, quietly awaiting his master's answer, where a moment before he had been leaning over the table, intent in his passion and blind to all else.

"Erlend, I don't even know if we'll be staying a night – although perhaps, given your feelings, it might be better for us all if we didn't. If we do come straight home again, how will that help, except to make this longing worse? My business is with Brynjolf, and it involves ship matters, not the lovesickness of his - or my - thralls. You have no right to start trying to make it otherwise, and you know it."

"Yes, I know that, sir, but all the same, you will have need of attendants, companions…"

"What! You'd have me ride out with a thrall as my shield-man? Put yourself above your place in this world, and expect me to pay the price of it? What of my standing here? I earned mine, remember, while you lost all your reputation the day you laid your spear at my feet in surrender! Remind me never to let you be free in these parts, Erlend, or you'll be the
death of us all with that sort of pride! No doubt once at Brynjolf's, you'd be wanting me to put in an offer for the girl, and bring her back for you?"

Erlend's face showed Hrolf he had hit close to the mark.

"You must be mad: mad to think you, a thrall, one of many, could sway me so far; mad to think I wouldn't see it, and maddest of all to think you'd get away with it!" In a sudden lunge forward, Hrolf sent his cup flying, grabbed Erlend's shirt at the neckline across the table, and pulled him over the board; from the corner of his eye he saw Hild trying to keep the children out, but they pushed around her to watch, and, he hoped, to learn, for one day such problems might be theirs. All this was peripheral, however; his rage towered over the cropped hair of his slave as he pulled him to eye level.

"I remember how I got you by my own force of arms, Erlend, just as I remember that this is not your birth name. You seem to have forgotten… you are not in bond to me, working your way back to free status, you are in thralldom to me forever…" he hissed the last word into the man's face, "…and I could kill you now for your plots and schemes, and nobody – nobody - would think anything of it, much less lift a finger against me for it. You are without the law here, Welshman: there are none to speak for you, none to protect you, none to further your interests or ambitions. You lost all this on the day when you chose to live as my slave instead of dying with your friends and your lord. You are *nothing* here! And you would do well to remember this a bit more, or it will be the end of you. I can always get another thrall, Erlend, but if I ever lose Brynjolf's good will, I may never get it back, and believe me, his friendship is worth far more than you could ever be." To drive the lesson home, he promptly sank his fist into Erlend's face, and sent him sprawling over the floor, dangerously close to the fire. Clutching his nose and trailing blood, the thrall headed for the door, and this time the children *did* get out of the way.

Thralls he had plenty of, but they counted for little when playing games of status and influence with the neighbours. How busy was Jon, he wondered; he did not doubt for a minute that the smith would travel with him if commanded, even though he was a freeman. Grim was a stay-at-home, destined for a strawdeath, but Hrolf had never got the story of his earlier years out of the man. All he knew for sure was that he wasn't a local lad; having grown up in Walea since around his eighth or ninth year, Hrolf had known everyone who had been born here since

his childhood. Who else? Even if he did decide to take Erlend along, and he had to admit the man was useful with a spear – the only reason Hrolf had even considered his surrender last summer - at least one other of good family and free birth was almost a necessity. Solmund, perhaps? He had useful qualities, and he had travelled, but he could be insufferable at times, and affected riches he could hardly afford: a free man who thought this made him an earl. Hrolf went to the vat and got another cup of beer, racking his brains to remember who he had gone with last year... ah, no, wait... last year, Brynjolf had come to *his* hall, and his wife, Asa, had brought that thrall-girl, the one Erlend was so smitten by, with her as an attendant. So *that* was where it had all started! But by any sensible reckoning, it was a long time ago; there had been a summer of trade and *Strandhogg* since
then, and a winter of wind, rain and no skalds. Why in all the worlds did Erlend, of all his thralls, have to be the one with a memory? He knew the answer, of course; the man had not
always been a thrall. He had placed himself in Hrolf's service on the day his new master had lost his finger to the sword of Erlend's old lord: Pawl the Welsh prince. Hrolf had thought at

the time that it was odd for him to have done so, but had been in no fit state to worry too much. Ever since then, however, Erlend had been a growing source of unease. Hrolf got the feeling that he was just biding his time before doing something terrible to all of them, and then going on his way, free at last from any obligations to anyone. But until the Welshman made his move, there was little that could be done against him; to simply kill him for no obvious cause was not something his master cared to contemplate. It went against all sense, reason, and decency.

Hrolf finished his drink and declined the offer of another from Ymma; he had made up his mind. Jon and Solmund would go with him to Brynjolf, and much as he might wish to punish Yngvar by taking him along, he threw caution to the winds, as Asa had last year - or was that being unfair to the lady? – and settled on Erlend as a horse-guard for the three of them. Yngvar could be pushed out of the kitchen- house to cook up the weatherproofing for the sail while he was gone. Perhaps not an entirely satisfactory solution, but he could live with it. His plans thus made, Hrolf gathered up his cloak against the prevailing wind and wet, and went out to gather his companions.

He did not doubt that Erlend would be insufferably smug about it.

CHAPTER TEN

The journey to Brynjolf's Burgh was not particularly long, or arduous - Hrolf had heard from Icelanders passing through how it could take days to get from one farm to another where they hailed from - but it could be somehow lengthened or lessened by the company one travelled with. Jon knew him well enough to speak when required, and of suitable subjects, whilst
Solmund either said nothing, wrapped in thought, or made lofty-sounding pronouncements that somehow never even made it into his lord's head. Hrolf's mind tended to centre on the business at hand, whatever it happened to be, and there was not much to be said until they knew how Brynjolf and the other co-owners of the ship viewed the coming summer's work. Erlend followed just a pace or two behind, silently leading the spare pony, his eyes clear of trouble, but his face still showing the bruises.

They followed the shore of the northern river, albeit a little inland, where the ground was higher and the footing more certain. Of the three who rode, only Hrolf had a saddle: its high

pommel and seat kept him firmly seated, while his legs stretched out in front, a comfortable enough position one the rider got used to it. He would have preferred to take a boat upriver, but the currents were strong and in the wrong direction, and he knew of at least two vessels that now lay on the riverbed after falling foul of them. Jon and Solmund had only their cloaks,
folded and laid over their mount's backs, and the spare bridles from the store-house, but this did not seem to cause them any difficulties. They kept the pace slow, in order for Erlend to keep with them, but even then, Hrolf reckoned they could be with Brynjolf by nightfall.

The track wound along, going through patches of scrubland but around the stands of birch along the shoreline that gave the place at least one of its names; nobody had ever thought
to organise what part was called what, and so place-names tumbled over each other like leaves in the wind around these parts. Hrolf's own holdings did not stretch so far, but these parts were, to his knowledge, not owned outright by anyone else, either, with the result that plenty of little steadings had grown up, all within sight of each other but all completely independent, and all with a voice at the

Thing. It could cost a lot of silver to get their support at times, too. None of the travellers knew more than a few of the settlers here, and so they blew their horn at regular intervals, as the law demanded, and rode on through the flat, muddy landscape, through the grass and the trees, until the ground began to rise still further: the first sign that they were approaching Brynjolf's lands.

As politeness dictated, Hrolf had sent a runner ahead on a fast horse to warn of their approach; he considered it plain foolish to be waylaid and killed as an unknown traveller on his own doorstep. As a result of this forethought, Brynjolf himself met them at his gate, and accompanied the party into the hall. Once seated (in suitable places, as also dictated by good
manners and ancient traditions), Asa came forward with her eldest daughter, bringing beer (not as good as his own, Hrolf thought) and fresh stew. The fire was prodded back into life, and after suitable courtesies, Asa and the girl, whose name escaped him, withdrew out of earshot. Brynjolf took a swig of his beer and regarded his visitors warmly.

"Been a long winter, Hrolf; doesn't take much to guess what brings you here as spring comes around."

Hrolf smiled. "No indeed; Snorri knew my purpose, as always, and I daresay Eyvind will say much the same when his turn comes for a visit! I have the pleasure to tell you that our ship is well, having been sheltered from the worst of the storms over winter, and that even now, Var and her ladies of the household are preparing to mend what needs to be mended – though they stop short of weatherproofing the sail this year. I will have to attend to that when I get home; I doubt if that shirker of a house-thrall can be trusted to do it well enough."

Seated behind him, Solmund coughed to disguise his laugh.

"Ah, well that's good news indeed. We've done well since you took your father's share, and no mistake; I think it safe to say we are all the richer for it." Brynjolf looked around at the carved and painted pillars holding his roof up. "So tell me, what do you plan for this next voyage?"

"I thought we might head over to my kinsman in the south of Erin, and take some captives aboard, if he has them; perhaps stop in Mann, either on the way over or the way back, and do some business with Var's family. They are wanting cloth, I heard last year, and the ladies have been busy at the loom in my hall - doubtless also in yours. I want to sound out my brother-in-law Ragnar about fostering Kendrick, too. We could sell the Irish cargo there, perhaps, or down in Wessex, or up in Hrossey – though that's not such a good market for such things, and the Hrossey-men aren't above getting in their ships and seeking their own thralls and timber. So, if we go to Wessex to sell, we can buy cloth, or take silver, and head back up the Welsh coasts, buying, selling, or taking as the mood pleases. Probably a better proposition than Mann, in that respect. Either way, we could be back in time to do the last of the year's business at Meols, or in Chester, before the weather closes in."

Brynjolf peered more closely at him. "What of that place where we had the trouble last time? How are your fingers, shipmaster?"

"My fingers are well enough..."

"Still less one than you were, though, eh?" Hrolf shrugged; Brynjolf seemed to relax, and eased his burly frame back into his seat. "Well, it all sounds very fine; I may come
along this summer and get some exercise."

Hrolf smiled. "I won't deceive you, Brynjolf; I had thought of going back to Pawl the Welshman and recovering this debt." He held up his damaged hand. "But, if you and the others prefer not to, I won't argue the point - this year."

"Oh, I'm not saying that you aren't owed vengeance, and if the tides push us that way, well, this year is as good as any other for settling the matter." Brynjolf put his empty cup down and sighed. "Snorri, myself, and the others in our *felag*, well, we are getting older, and faster than you are, it seems. If I'm being as honest with you as you are with me, I'll say that I don't know how much good we'd be in another fight. We got lucky last time, we only came away with a few scratches and a finger lost. Pawl very nearly trapped us all, and I at least can see it."

"Think Snorri will? He sounds as keen as ever this year. And you're not that much older than I."

Brynjolf snorted. "Snorri won't even notice he's in his mound until he tries to get out of it for the day-meal! But I sit here over the winter, and I get... comfortable with it. Good food, good beer, a warm hall... they are harder to give up for months aboard a cold boat, for all that the weather is warmer and it's the ship that lets me live so well in the first place."

Hrolf accepted another cup from Asa, who had glided silently into the firelight again. "If you want to sell your share, Brynjolf, you need not leave your fireside. Your fame and reputation would be secure enough, and we can talk about a price at the end of the trip. You have settled well here, it's a good farm; there would be no shame in retiring from the ship life."

"Ah, but there would be the fear," replied Brynjolf in a low voice. "The fear of dying in my bed, alone, and being put in my grave with nothing to show for my life."

"That would never happen," said Asa. "I've promised you before, but as usual you've been too busy talking to listen. If I'm not dead by then, I'll bury you properly, and if I am dead, then our daughters will do it for both of us."

"And you'll not be without friends to see it done right, either," added Hrolf.

"I'll come this season," said Brynjolf, "and then we'll see."

*

"He's not as eager as he used to be," murmured Hrolf into the darkness of the guest- house that night. "If he lives through this voyage, I'm expecting him to sell up when we get home."

"Age finds us all eventually, sir," replied Solmund. "And he does have a few years on you. If his bones creak and ache as mine do, I'm not surprised he's reluctant."

"I thought you'd never sailed, Solmund."

"Oh, I've done my share of travelling, my lord, but most of it was before I came to your part of the world. I went up the Frankish rivers one trip; I'm still living on the proceeds, in a way."

"I knew you had dealings with a lot of people, but I never saw reason to ask too closely. What made you settle on my lands?"

"We had bad luck with the Irish; when they took Dubhlynn, I got out with your father on one of Ingimund's ships. Found a wife; built a house; found a trade to follow. No children to look after me in my old age, so I'm gathering the silver for as long as I can."

Hrolf was silent for a while. "Yes, that sounds like the path Brynjolf is looking for," he admitted finally. "But I could do with him not taking it just yet."

"You want him on the ship," stated Jon.

"I *need* him on the ship; I can't afford to buy him out yet! And for all that I held out the chance of fellowship to Kol and Arne, it may be too soon to expect them to rise that far. They've got less free cash than I, after all."

"Maybe you could extend them - or others - some credit? And if it's a good trip again this time, who knows that you won't be able to buy him out."

"You looking for a loan as well then, Jon?" Hrolf scratched his head in the darkness. "I don't know; the Felag hasn't changed since I bought my father's share, for all that some of the faces who come along have changed over the years. I'd never really thought about what happens when Snorri or Brynjolf retire - Eyvind isn't likely to, and he's got cousins, nephews, people to pass it on to. Snorri and Brynjolf haven't; what did they plan to do with their bench when the time came? I haven't a clue."

"You might try asking them," came Solmund's laconic reply.

"Go to sleep, Solmund. Right now, that's not what I wanted to hear."

CHAPTER ELEVEN

Although custom dictated that visits should last three days, neither Brynjolf nor Hrolf cared so much about the social niceties as Snorri, or more precisely Gytha, did. So, whilst Brynjolf and Asa would have quite happily entertained them for much longer, Hrolf decided to head on towards Eyvind's steading at the southern edge of the lands Ingimund had won from the Mercians in the aftermath of his attempt on Chester.

Solmund was less happy about travelling on, having only recently married, but a little silver smoothed the waves of his brow. Jon seemed not to care at all, and was enjoyably even-tempered over it. Erlend was more of a problem.

"I can carry your message, sir, and as easily after another day as right away…"

"You will head for home *now*!" Hrolf stood face-to-face with his thrall in the guest house, where, thankfully, he knew Brynjolf would not enter or overhear. "There is no way in all the worlds that I would leave you alone near that girl – and under her master's roof! What are you thinking, Erlend?

Are you thinking at all? No; you go back to your lady Var now, and you tell her that we are going straight on to Eyvind. You do not dally, you do not stop… and you most certainly do not turn around once I am gone from here and come back like some thief in the night to see your little slave- girl!" He paused and drew breath. "Do I have your pledge on this, or do I have to ask Brynjolf for a guard to go with you, hmm?"

With no way out, Erlend grudgingly gave his word. Hrolf saw him out to the horses, watched him saddle one, and watched as the Welshman rode out of Brynjolf's gates, heading for the Hall on the Rock. Once Erlend was gone from sight, Solmund and Jon came out to join him.

"You'll be cutting his throat by the end of the year," predicted Solmund, his thick white hair blowing around his face in the gusty breeze. Hrolf turned to look at him.

"Be careful, Solmund; a loose tongue gathers few friends. All the same, I'd not be surprised if you turn out to be right." He sighed. "Erlend has not proved to be the investment I thought he was, and he's not the only one around my house I could say that of.

Still, we're rid of him for a day or two. Come on, friends, let's get ready and be on our own way."

CHAPTER TWELVE

Eyvind's farm had an air of neglect, dereliction almost, as Hrolf and his companions approached. There was nothing to see out of the ordinary: men still worked, and the fields held the same ploughlands of barley, wheat and flax as they always did at this time of the year; the animals appeared in good health, and the ground not ploughed and sown was certainly as muddy as ever… but something was unwell in the place. Not right somehow, Hrolf thought, as if the farm were out-of-sorts with the world around it.

Just behind him, Solmund sniffed the air, then spat it out. "Smells like someone's died," he drawled quietly, his eyes slitted and his nostrils pinched. Hrolf felt a chill around his own heart at the words. His had not been the only wound of last season's trip, although by far the worst, and whilst Eyvind had seemed hearty enough at the winter Thing, Hrolf had not had any further word from him since their meeting then. From their failure to mention anything, he assumed that Brynjolf and Snorri had not either. Again, that was nothing unusual, but…

At Jon's third blow of the horn, they were hailed by a man Hrolf did not recognise. Yet there *was* something familiar to him; not his hair, which was neatly trimmed and combed low over his forehead, and of a vibrant blonde, which continued down into his moustache and full, bushy beard, but more of the set in his features, and the shape of his body. Politely, yet with a growing apprehension, they stopped, and let the stranger approach them. Hrolf's hand casually strayed to the hilt of his sword, still hanging at his hip even when riding.

"You are coming to see Eyvind Asleifarsson?" the man enquired. Hrolf nodded, and introduced himself and his fellows. He noticed that this man kept his hands in clear sight, and although carrying a spear, seemed more inclined to use it as a walking-stick than as anything more ferocious. He wasn't exactly young, but nor was Eyvind, after all. Perhaps a brother? Hrolf couldn't remember much about Eyvind's family.

"I am his cousin: his brother's son, to be precise. I am Einar Ivarsson, that Ivarr who made his wealth from the British of Strathclyde, and the islands, before Men of Dubhllyn took over in those parts.

Eyvind said it was around the time you usually came to see him, sir, so I will take you to him directly."

"Is he not up to coming out himself, then?" Hrolf had to ask. If Eyvind had been dead, it would have been the first death of a Felag-man since his father's.

Einar looked grim. "He is not, sir. I suppose you would not have heard, but he fell from a horse over the winter, after the Thing-days, and has not recovered since. He can't even stand now, the leg is so badly smashed. It has taken this long to get my house-mates and I down here to attend to matters, and that is why we've not sent word out. But he still lives."

Einar led them through the fields towards the house; as they went, Hrolf reckoned he had never seen so many men working at this farm, and he guessed that Einar had moved his entire household, or perhaps even his father's, into Eyvind's home. It was a shrewd move, and a sensible one, but come the next winter, there would be a hard time feeding so many. Hrolf made a mental note to arrange for added security around his own house.

Eyvind's household had always been large, and given to displays of wealth, and what Einar had said of his own father went some of the way to explaining where that wealth had come from. Hrolf also knew that Eyvind had been a good man aboard their ship: even in his advancing years he had been keen and bold, with an eye for economy of action and maximised profits
that Snorri and Brynjolf had never quite matched. Yet here he sat, a prisoner in his own chair, his skin pale and his hair unkempt, with a suppressed fury in his eyes that was plain for all
to see.

"I never married," he began, once his guests were settled, "and so I have nobody to hand this place on to. I have kept myself alive while Einar and his kinsmen got to know the place, and I have extracted oaths from his men and mine that they will honour him as their master once I have died, for I have no intention of going on like this." He lifted the blanket that covered his legs: Hrolf dutifully peered underneath, and wished he hadn't.

"That is one mess of a leg, Eyvind…"

Eyvind nodded. "Not going to mend, is it? I doubt there's more than a few inches of solid bone anywhere within it. I knew as soon as it happened that it would be the death of me, so I've no bad feelings having lasted until spring."

Hrolf leaned closer. "Your cousin, Einar; does he treat you well enough? And how does he plan to feed all these mouths I saw working?"

Eyvind laughed. "Hrolf, you show more concern than you should! It was I who sent for him, and suggested he move in. As I said, I have nobody of my own to leave it to, and were I to die and leave it empty, what sort of squabble would break out among my neighbours over it, eh? So I've sorted out all my debts and legacies; had time to think while I've been sitting here." He waved to a woman passing them. "Thordis, another jug, if you would? This is Thordis, Hakon's daughter, Einar's wife. Thordis, this man is Hrolf, the ship-master I've talked about. As soon as your husband comes back, we can finish that bit of business."

Thordis smiled broadly. "Oh, I'll go find him, then!"

Hrolf stroked his beard. "You've passed him your share in our Felag, then?"

"I can't use it myself, can I? And not passed: sold. Which brings me to another favour I have to ask, and this involves all my ship-mates."

"Ask it of me then, and I'll ask them in your name, when we gather."

"Fair enough. I've sold my bench, but not for cash – what use have I for it now? No, I sold it for a good burial, on my own lands. Laid in a boat - only a small one - with my weapons and tools, and a mound heaped up over me. The favour I ask you is to see it done, and to take Einar as my successor once that's finished."

"That may take a while, unless you are planning on dying fairly soon. If you're alive when we head out, you'll have to hold on until we get back, or else trust Thordis and the farm-hands to bury you in our absence."

Eyvind smiled again. "Well, Hrolf, when did you ever know me to be reasonable? It may not be that long,

anyway; the pain gets harder to bear with every day that passes. I have a good
knife handy for when I know the time has come."

"Hmm." Hrolf regarded him for a long, silent moment. "Want me to send runners to Snorri and Brynjolf? Tell Var I'll be away a few more days? I have a tree-smith, Grim, who I know can make boats. I'll ask him to start on one."

Eyvind nodded vaguely. "Talk to Einar. I'm sure he'll spare a few men for you."

"You've had a good life, Eyvind."

"Oh yes; no complaints about that - or anything, really. There's a bench in a hall beyond this life, with my name carved on it, and it looks more inviting by the day." He sighed, but the smile never left his face. "My affairs here are settled, the deals are all done. What is there to keep me?"

"Beyond friends and the comforts of your own hall, not a lot - and with that leg you're even robbed of those, I suppose. Am I going to wake up tomorrow and find you cold and stiff?"

"Ach, you know me too well. Anything is better than a straw-death; my family have always said this, and I've seen nothing to make me think otherwise."

Hrolf grinned suddenly. "Come on," he whispered, "one last trip, and we'll throw you at some Welshmen…"

"Oh, but now I'm tempted, damn you!" Eyvind sat back, laughing. "Ah, if only we could, eh? If only we could." He put out his hand; Hrolf grasped it. "Fine shipmates I've had, Hrolf, and a full life. Time to be going, before I slide into decrepitude. This mess of a leg is already getting an unpleasant smell around it, and I'm sure it's turning black. Want me to say hello to your
father when I see him?"

He released Hrolf's hand, and stared long into his eyes. Hrolf nodded in understanding.

"As you say, then: time to be going." He stood up, and motioned for Jon and Solmund to leave, before he noticed Einar coming in. "Wait: we need witnesses for this business. Sit down
again; we'll sort everything else out afterwards."

CHAPTER THIRTEEN

True to his word, Eyvind was colder than last night's leftovers when Thordis went to feed him the following day. Tears were shed, and many of the old master's farmhands went out to their tasks quiet and morose, wondering where their futures lay now. Einar put men and horses at Hrolf's disposal, to carry the news to those who needed it, and then asked the ship-master to stay with him whilst he put the farm's affairs in proper order. Among the men sent out as messengers was one going to Oslac the Lawman, over at Thorstienn's *tun.* It would be his task to oversee the disposal of Eyvind's legacies.

"Where do you think he'd want his mound?" Einar asked during a break from going through the contents of the house. They sat by the hearth, scattered boxes and bags all around them, trying to make sense of all the contents. Eyvind, it turned out, had been something of a hoarder, and Hrolf was baffled as to where he'd found to put it all. Or, indeed, why he had bothered.

He sipped his ale. "Difficult to say; and do we put it where he would want it, or where it's most convenient? Digging up the home-field is hardly helpful, after all..."

"I had in mind that slope where it overlooks the river."

"That seems fair; if he ever wants to come out, he can watch for ships, and if he starts walking, he's as likely to fall in!" Hrolf considered the other man. "All in all, a good choice, I'd say."

Einar met his gaze. "Sufficiently respectful? You are a better judge of such matters than I, and I have no wish to insult either you or him."

"I have no quarrel with you, Einar, nor do I wish to start one. I knew Eyvind, yes, but I never met his brother, your father, so I do not know how the family got on with one another. Eyvind ran his farm well, kept a generous house, lots of thralls, both men and women... good man in a ship, too. Lots of wisdom; he was ship-master when my father was killed, and he got them out of whatever hole they'd found themselves in, then brought them home. As I came to be master in my turn, when I was old enough to do it decently, it was Eyvind I looked to for guidance and advice when I needed it." He sighed. "I'll miss him, but I don't doubt that you will fill his shoes well."

"What makes you that sure? I'm curious."

Hrolf laughed. "That's easy, no real riddle to it. Eyvind sold you his place at the oars. He would never have done that if he'd thought you weren't up to it; nor the farm. He must also have held you high enough in his regard to invite you in. He could have sold either ship-place or land to any of his neighbours - but he chose you, and that's more than enough for me to rate you on." He reached out and held the other man's shoulder. "You're not your father's son now, Einar: you're the master here. Better get used to it quickly, or the wolves around
you will be at the door sooner than you'd like." Einar chewed at his bread thoughtfully, watching dust as it danced in the light from an open door near the far end of the hall. "Hardly the best time to go off a-viking, then. Had it all turned out otherwise, I might have put off a trip for this first summer, and learned more about how this place works. But I'm assuming that's not really a choice, is it?"

Hrolf smiled. "Ah, it could be, if you really wished it; but you have good, loyal men here who know what needs doing, and can do it whether you're here or not. If there's anything you want to learn, there's always next year... although many would say, and your father and uncle along with them I suspect, that as master, your proper place is out getting the wealth to live on over the winter, and not grubbing about in the soil and the cowdung. You have a position to maintain now, and if your lady is anything like mine, she'll value the silver far above your
company! And as for the neighbours, don't worry: you forget the company you'll be keeping by coming along. We take all our local wolves in the boat with us!"

CHAPTER FOURTEEN

Oslac was an outwardly serious, dour man of nondescript colouring and a definite lack of ostentation, who used his general air of bleakness and gloom to disguise a wickedly sharp sense of humour with which he would bait the unwary. Coupled to an undoubtedly bright mind that revelled in the complexities of Mercian, Dubhllyn and Vestfold law codes - all of which he appeared to know pretty much by heart - Oslac had been for many years a natural choice for the position of Lawman in Ingimund's lands, with a responsibility and influence that none could rival, or would wish to. Rumours said that he had once attended the court of one of the kings of the Oslofjord, which, if true, put him into social circles far above any of his neighbours. Yet he lived quietly on the land owned by Thorstienn, on the high ground where the bones of the world pushed out of the soil, and looked out over the river towards the Welsh hills. Or, rather, he lived there on the rare occasions when he was not being called upon to discharge his duties somewhere else; when Einar's messenger arrived in his homefield he was less than welcoming at first. Nonetheless, he had a horse saddled, and rode back to Eyvind's farm the following day.

"Ah," he began, on seeing Hrolf and Einar at the doorway, "I might have suspected the hand of the shipmaster in this somewhere. Getting tired of sharing out the booty, Hrolf?"

"I started in the wrong place if I'd wanted an easy time of it!"

"Indeed, you should have come and seen me first. Never mind; I don't object to errors, providing they're in my favour."

"This one was, you're still breathing!"

"Mmm. So; Eyvind Asliefarsson has died. Where is he, by the way?"

Einar coughed. "We put him in the guest-house."

Oslac raised his eyebrows. "Really? Do none of your guests complain? He must have stopped snoring at least. I remember the time I got a tent next to his at the Thing; didn't sleep a wink." He sniffed and looked around. "This weather won't stay cold for long; better get him in his howe pretty soon, I'd say."

Einar led the Lawman into the hall. "I've got men digging already, and Hrolf has sent word to his ship-wright to start on a boat."

"I'd have said a stone-setting might be quicker…"

"You haven't met Grim!" countered Hrolf. "Besides, I sent word that if he doesn't have one to spare, to get the skiff from the big ship, and we'll use that. It would be very fitting, after all. And there's always the matter of finding enough stones of a suitable size, or getting them cut from the ground; it's liable to take just as long as carting a skiff over from the noust, after
all."

"Welcome news, then." He took the seat offered by the hearth - Einar was shrewd enough not to occupy Eyvind's high seat in front of a man who could still, in theory, take it away from him - and looked around, before settling his gaze on the farm's new owner.

"I take it you requested me to come and untangle the old man's legacy for you?"

"Yes. I am Einar Ivarsson, Eyvind's brother's son."

"Ah; yes, of course, Eyvind himself had no children, did he? Or none that he ever admitted to; I remember now. Well, the first thing to do is establish your right to be here. It would be too much to expect the old man to have written anything down, wouldn't it? Not to worry; he won't have said anything without witnesses, and if he did, what was said between just you and he counts for nothing if nobody else was there to hear it."

Einar scratched his head. "Well now; let me see. My wife Thordis was here to hear everything that was said, on every occasion…"

"A good start, but we need more."

"Alright; my head man Anlaf Osricsson witnessed his giving me the farm, as did his own bondsmen Kari and Sighvat. He also had Eirik, the farmer on the mere that borders the Mercian *tun*, as a witness." Einar got up and went to a chest in the corner. "I have a token here for it."

Oslac took the piece of wood, as long as his arm and covered in markings on one side, and examined it. "Hmm. I recognise Eyvind's sign, and Eirik's. Which is yours?" Einar pointed. "Ah. So this will be Thordis, then, and these others the bondar you mentioned."

He turned the token over in his hands. "This is certainly the token for this land-holding; if you look further along it, this group of marks is where Eyvind got it from Hadding the Mercian, as part of Ingimund's settlement after the business at Chester. There is my own mark on the deal, and so, having seen these marks, and heard your story, I am content that all is well with this inheritance, and so I add my mark to it, thus. Hrolf, you are to witness this."

The two men duly made their signs on Einar's token. "It is important that you declare this at the next Thing," went on Oslac, "and that all these who witnessed it also attend with you, to swear to the accuracy of it. So if I were you, I'd start buying their loyalty and good memory straight away."

"Fair enough," said Einar, "I'll take your advice, and thank you for it." He matched deed to word, and a

small bag of silver passed between them. "Eyvind also sold me his place in
the Felag; do I need to declare this also?"

Oslac stroked his beard. "Well, that depends, again, on how it was done. The business of the ship is a private matter between those involved, it has no bearing on my business beyond ensuring that the sale was legal."

"I came to see Eyvind as usual, and he was still alive to do the sale in my presence," put in Hrolf. "You know Jon Dagfinsson, my blacksmith, and Solmund Hrafnsson: they are my witnesses, along with Thordis and Anlaf for Einar's side."

"Fine; do your other Felag- men know this yet?"

"Probably; we sent riders to them when we sent yours. We expect them in a day or so, then we can put Eyvind in his mound."

"We are making preparations for the feasting now," said Einar. "We would consider it an honour if you would stay."

Oslac inclined his head gravely. "I would be happy to, and equally honoured." He looked hard at Einar for a moment, and joked: "Just as long as I'm not sleeping in the guest- house!"

CHAPTER FIFTEEN

Whilst Hrolf, Einar and Oslac continued to sort through Eyvind's tangle of belongings and bequests, the farm-hands dug the hole into which his boat would go, and Thordis gathered her companions around her to make a feast worthy of their benefactor. Brynjolf and Snorri arrived a day or two later, looking sombre and serious: none of them had expected this death, so suddenly had wyrd turned against Eyvind, their friend of so many years, and the whole of Hrolf's life. Despite the knowledge that he was free of pain, and enjoying the hospitality of higher beings than themselves, all those gathered felt the eternal sense of loss and bewilderment that seems to accompany such events. Grim arrived the next day, with the Felag's skiff tied precariously on the top of one of his wagons. Closer inspection of the load showed that Var had sent other things along with him: carefully sealed pots of food for Eyvind's voyage (she had no idea of how good a cook Thordis might or might not be, having never even heard her name), and shoes for his feet, to stop him walking. Shrewd gifts, to lend help where it might most be needed in a household still adjusting, but not enough to be overpowering should they not be required.

Once unloaded, the skiff was put directly in its new resting-place, the soil put back under it to hold it in place, and anchor-stones tied to both ends. Eyvind's longest-serving bondsmen claimed the right to carry their master into his ship, and Einar felt no need to deny them. So, as the Felag- men and the Lawman stood at the edges of the hole, Eyvind was brought out from his hall for the last time, carried shoulder-high on a wicker bier through his fields to the slope that overlooked the wide, fast river to the north. There, dressed in his best shirt and
breeks, his cloak laid over him as a blanket, he was laid in the boat, and the corpse-bearers stood back.

Through the gap in the piled earth around the boat came Thordis and her ladies, slowly and solemnly, bearing bread, stewed beef, beer and mead, which all went into the vessel around the old man. Once done, Hrolf stepped forward to tie the shoes on his old friend's feet. Brynjolf put in a spear, Eyvind's favourite, a long, sharp blade with a silver-inlaid socket. His
shield went over his face and chest; a knife was placed across his belt. Finally, Einar laid his uncle's sword by his side.

Two woven willow panels had been taken from one of the farm's fences, and these were erected as a sort of tent over the body and its accompaniments. Then the men took up their
wooden spades once more, and the soil was heaped up over the body of Eyvind Asleifarsson. That work went on long into evening, but when it was finished, Einar threw the doors of the hall open to everyone who had their living on Eyvind's farm, and feasted them all until morning.

CHAPTER SIXTEEN

The end of winter was always a busy time of year, and Hrolf often felt that if, somehow, he could stretch out all that had to be fitted into these few months, say to the rest of the year, he would be a lot happier about it all. As it was, he was occupied virtually every day, and the time he got to spend in his own highseat between visits to colleagues, organising the farm duties and then riding to the Thing and exercising his domestic and legal powers and obligations there, was, to be frank, minimal. And he *did* resent such a powerful and sustained assault upon his freedom of action (as he saw it; those beholden to him viewed it more as the time when he either won or lost their continued support), but then the memory of older men, in other places, would come and remind him of how life could be, as a bondsman to some other lord, should he shirk or stint his duties. Much as he might not want the petty problems of all his tenants, bondsmen and neighbours thrust upon him, he relied on those same tenants, bondsmen and neighbours to maintain him in his privileged position as Hauldr of Walea and Lisceardr; having inherited his estates, and built them up further by his own efforts, he could not be voted out - but he could be abandoned, or ignored. Then life would get much, much harder, with fewer hands to do the work of the farmstead and fewer houses to collect rents from. So, this year as every other year, he kept his grumbles to himself, safe in the knowledge that there was no sympathy to be had from his spouse, since she enjoyed their fine lifestyle just as much as he did, and was more than happy for him to strive constantly to maintain it. It was certainly better than working for a living, he thought, as he stood at his doorway one morning (one of the few he was there, but it was more of a flying visit) and watched Kol and Arne in their little boat, putting out into the bay.

Eyvind's death and burial had eaten into the time he usually had before the Thing-days, when he heard complaints, grievances, or other matters from his retinues that might require further action in the presence of Oslac the Lawman. Normally it was only little matters, such as grazing disputes, debt recovery, and the like, but it all took time, since many of the people who came to speak with him were poor, and not very well versed at good speaking in the presence of The Authorities. It was Hrolf's job to untangle their often rambling version of matters, find out what was at the heart of them,

and then put it into a form of words that he could take to the Wapentak Court. Very often, it turned out that the issue could be resolved without expensive and time-consuming legal actions being brought, and when this could be done, Hrolf would do so, the effect of as few as two armed men and a lord turning up at any bondar's door being out of all proportion to what they could actually do against even a
handful of obstinate peasants.

He had only got back from Eyvinds' - no, Einars' - steading the previous day, and even then he had arrived ahead of Grim and his wagon. The Thing would surely be called to order in only a few more days - although the obligatory messenger from Oslac had not arrived yet, of course - and so Hrolf would have to try and hurry a lot of business along. He was therefore somewhat displeased when he noticed Thurbrand coming up the path towards him.

"Fine day for standing outside, lord," began the herdsman.
"I was watching the ship in the bay; Arne and Kol have their lines out already. So, Thurbrand, are you here to exchange pleasantries, or is there business

behind your visit? Come inside and have a drink, whichever it is."

Hrolf led the man back into the smoky, warm darkness of the hall, noting that he had already caught his guest off-guard by so doing. There were stools set out around the firepit in readiness for a stream of visitors; Hrolf took his proper seat between his carved and painted roof-pillars, where the wall-hangings met behind him and spread out to either side along the
whole length of the hall, and poured ale from the jug standing ready.

"So," he went on, "What can I do for you this day? Is the byre roof still dry?"

"Dry as any other roof hereabouts, my lord, and my thanks again for it." Thurbrand took a drink, as if winding up his courage. "It's the matter of the wood that I came to see you over."

"Wood? What wood? A lot has happened since you and I shared a ladder, my friend; you'll have to remind me."

"The matter of a piece of wood set aside for mending that roof, that wasn't there on the day we came to need it."

"Ah, now I remember. What of it? Had any more go missing?"

Thurbrand frowned, and shifted awkwardly on his stool. "Not exactly, sir, but we do seem to be continually short of timber all of a sudden."

"Any ideas why this might be so? I'm not aware that we've any need to be using more than normal; or perhaps it's that we've not had so much washing ashore this year."

"It's my belief, sir, that the kitchen fires are being kept going for longer than is normal, and being kept brighter, too. Sometimes I can see the glow from them in the evenings, even
from my house. And then there's the brewhouse, too; that seems to be used more than in past years."

"What exactly are you saying here, Thurbrand?"

The herder leaned forward, his weathered face flickering in the firelight. "What I'm saying, sir, is that some people around here are using more wood than usual, and they don't care much where they get it from."

Hrolf leaned back against the wall. "If the lady Var has said we need more fire in the kitchen, or the brewhouse, then she says it for a reason, and I'm not going to argue with her,
Thurbrand. And nor should you; you must know that, surely!"

"Ah," countered Thurbrand, "but what if she didn't know? What if she hadn't said? What if some dim thrall was just piling up the fires to keep warm of a night? What then?"

Hrolf sighed in exasperation. "I take it you have someone in mind, having said all this?"

"I can't prove anything against anyone - yet. So I'll not mention any names at this time. I just warn you that your hall is burning more timber than it has before, and that if the woodsmen have to go further and further afield to collect more firewood, maybe - just maybe - they'll look to other means of supply, closer to home. The fences; Grim's shed of good, working timber. The walls of the buildings; who knows?"

"Thurbrand, unless you can say something definite against someone definite, unless you can point to an occasion when this can be seen to have happened - and not just by you – then you have just wasted my time, and a cup of better beer than you deserve. All you have are unfounded suspicions, and dubious coincidences, which I don't wish to hear. I don't have time to hear them, not this year. A great deal has happened already, and I'm having to be careful what I do with the few days I have left before the Thing and the ship-business. So unless you can bring me something more certain than what you have just said, I'm not interested."

Thurbrand stood up. "I'll keep an eye out just the same, sir, although I hear what you say." And with that, he nodded the briefest of bows before his lord, and strode out.

Hrolf rubbed his eyes, looking for the bright side. He supposed that if all the other people who came to see him had equally intangible matters to discuss, it might be a very short, and possibly even enjoyable, Thing this summer.

The day went on. Knowing it was a Business Day, Var kept her husband supplied with ale and food at the proper intervals, without him having to leave his seat except to use the midden ouside the porch wall. It was a support he was grateful for. His suspicions about the probable workload appeared to be holding good, since by the time the shadows began to lengthen he had only received a handful of other visitors. Ulfketil from the birch-wooded shore on the road to Brynjolf's Burgh claimed he was owed ferry fares from someone called Halfdan, who lived on the other bank of the river, but the name was not familiar to Hrolf (who, by the nature of his position, knew most of the settlers round about), and he had to wonder why, if he had not recognised the man, Ulfketil had ferried him anywhere without making him pay up front. But he promised to ask if anyone had somebody of that name either staying or working with them, and he assured his boatman that, if the man could be traced, exacting payment should not be difficult. In the meantime, Hrolf paid what was owed from his own chest; it was hardly right that the man and his family go hungry over such a matter, and the amount was small enough for Hrolf not to miss it too much.

Vigdis, a woman long widowed, sent a runner (as she did every spring) to enquire if Hrolf could ascertain the exact boundary of her home field, as there was the chance of a dispute with her neighbour Hrafn, and she wished to be sure of her rights before she started sending thralls over to his farm in order to kill him... Hrolf had something of a soft spot for Vigdis, on the quiet. It was the marsh on the edge of his own lands, and he sincerely wished her up beyond her withered, wrinkled neck in it. Gods forbid she should ever get friendly with Thurbrand! He occasionally worried about her sons, too, who showed every sign of inheriting their mother's charming and cheerful disposition, and would in time, he was sure, turn into most excellent Vikings and troublemakers. One day, not so far away, he could see a need to nip that branch of trouble in the bud - before it blossomed. He was not at all sure that those two would take to ship-life as he hoped Kol and Arne would, and so any action against them was likely to turn messy and violent - which was probably why he had done nothing about it as yet.

The most pressing, urgent and, in a way, unsettling, business only came with the night-meal. Var had put up a good, thick broth, with more than the usual amount of meat in it. Hrolf had barely had time to appreciate it, when she leaned over and put his favourite cup (the big one) in his hand.

"Husband: we must make plans."

"We must? And what about, exactly?" He frowned in thought, trying to work out what she could be on about. He gave up very quickly, and settled back to listen. It was easier, and made for fewer misunderstandings.

"Has it totally escaped your notice, my dear, sweet man, that our eldest daughter is of an age for us to be seeking her a husband? Or is it just that, in all your journeys and business, you had forgotten our earlier discussion?" She placed her hand over his. "I was thinking that this summer's Thing might be a good place to start the search. Plenty of eligible young men, of good families, and a good place to spread the word beyond the boundaries of the Thing-stead, too. You know how people gossip so…"

"Indeed, and your own companions often in the thick of it!" he chuckled. "Yes, I had not forgotten that she has some eleven or twelve summers behind her now, and I fully agree that the time is high to start looking around." He rubbed his beard in thought. "It's a fine idea; I wonder if we could get Kendrick fostered out, too?"

"I'm not so sure about that. He's getting boisterous, though."

"Yes he is, and he knows what ships are for, too! And spears, I might add. We need to get him in a house where they can help him along. Have we not discussed this already, since midwinter? I'm tired; it's been a busy year, what with Eyvind and everything else. We haven't even got the ship out of its shed yet, and the Thing is nearly upon us." He sighed, and drank, and looked his wife in the face. "Are you thinking of coming to the Thing, then, as well as travelling this summer?"

"Mmm, I think I will. It will be a good place to fish for invitations, too, I should say. And we did discuss you asking my brother Ragnar if he'd take the boy, as he's said he would so often."

"That was it, I do remember now. Oslac isn't likely to have got home before I did, but I doubt he'll delay over sending word out. I would guess we'll have a visitor from him tomorrow; I'll go and get the tent ready in the morning. We'll take the children, Ymma, Hild, and Yngvar. Maybe a few others." He stretched. "If we wait another few days for folk to come and find me, and then go. I'm not expecting it to take very long this year."

CHAPTER SEVENTEEN

"In the name of Ingimund, first Jarl over these lands and the people who dwell in it; by the right given to me by him and his successors, and by your consent, in my capacity as Lawman within these lands, in witness of all you gathered here, and in the presence of all Gods, both of our ancient lands and of the Church, I, Oslac, call this Thing to order, and do hallow the ground on which our business is conducted. Now is come the Law of the Thing upon this place: that all men shall conduct themselves peaceably and with due respect and regard to the Law. If any man here should argue with another, let it be dealt with as if he had struck that other. Should any man here strike another, it shall be seen as if he had wounded that other. Should any man here wound another, it shall be dealt with as if he had slain that other, with all the relevant penalties and rights of the slain man's family." He paused, probably, Hrolf thought, mostly

for effect. "Should any man here kill another, a full wer-geld will be paid for the slain man by the killer's family, and the killer shall forfeit his own life. Such is the Law of the Thing, as it has been since earliest times; if any have issue with this, let them speak now or forever after be subject to this Law without redress."

The initial business concluded, Hrolf and the other people in the crowd went about setting up their homes for the duration of the Thing. The ship-tent was a bit too large for dragging overland, and given this fact together with the marshy nature of the lands surrounding the higher mound of the Thingfield as they fell gently towards the welsh river at the south, Hrolf had long ago dismissed any thoughts of ever bringing it. Instead, he had set his household the task of constructing something more suitable, more easily portable. His idea had been to do something similar to tents he had seen on trips into Mercia, where the poles to hold it up looked like half his roof support at home, a long timber placed lengthways at the top with
two supports beneath, with the wool stretched down to the ground and keeping them up by that tension. It had worked well for many years now; the hard part seemed to be keeping the
fabric in good order between its annual outings.

Erlend, Arnkel and Grim soon had the structure up, and then they erected a little lean-to at the side,

just big enough for Hrolf to receive visitors in. This was a concession to Var more
than anything else, as they all slept in the tent together, and the interior rapidly degenerated into a messy tumble of bags, blankets and stools that no housewife worthy of the name would
ever want seen by guests. Solmund dug a little pit on the other side of the tent, into which he built a cooking-fire. The children were sent off to collect wood and anything edible they could find in the surrounding trees.

By early evening, their camp was set up. The pot was on to boil (the ship's only iron one, partly out of utility on the rough journey, but also as a subtle expression of wealth), and the ale-cask had been unloaded safely. Hrolf was sitting in his shelter, awaiting food and a drink, when Oslac approached.

"I've been speaking to Einar, and to the other men who live round about him," began the Lawman, taking a cup from Hild as he sat. "We'll make it the first bit of business tomorrow,
I think, because some of them aren't happy about not getting a chance to take a bit of land from Eyvind when he died."

"I can't see as they've got any right to be unhappy about anything, surely," answered Hrolf. "It's not as if Einar came in and took vacant land, or indeed their land, by force, now is it? Care to drop a name or two?"

"Not particularly, Hrolf, and you should know better than to ask. However, I can appreciate your interest in this matter, and I value your support as much as Einar will, so if I tell you that Onund, who now owns Hrafnkel's farm, and Gizur the Dane, came to see me earlier - on a quite unrelated matter, you understand - you might take that information and draw your own
conclusions from it. On the understanding that you might still get it completely wrong, of course…"

Hrolf smiled. "I see - or rather, I think I do. Wasn't there some question over how Onund came to be master at Hrafnkelsby in the first place? I don't know Gizur myself, he lives further out than Eyvind did, and it's not the road I use if I'm heading for Chester."

Oslac shrugged. "He's alright, I suppose, if a bit easily led. But they both have fields and woods that border on Einar's land, and they'd be strange not to want a little more, after all."

"Think they'll cause problems when Einar claims his inheritance, then?"

"I doubt it; but just to be sure, I've suggested to Einar that he offer some sport to his new neighbours and friends: perhaps a ball-game, or a horse-fight, just to make a few bonds between them and start him off on the right foot in these parts."

"That sounds a good idea; I'm all for games. I'd sooner have ball than horses, since I don't have any that fight, and so there's little I could put into it. But if he chooses the ball-game, I'll see who wants to play from my men, and offer our support to Einar. I've got to witness his claim on the farm anyway."

"Good man; I knew I'd get sound words and deeds from you." The lawman stood up. "My thanks for your hospitality, Hrolf; now I'm off to find your other shipmate, and see if I can extract the same from him. Or is Snorri intending to come to our Thing this year as well?"

"I've not seen him since we were at Eyvind's burial, and I don't remember him saying either way. I think he might come though, even though he lives beyond your boundaries, what with the change in our own circumstances. He knows what's going on, after all, and he's not stupid." Hrolf thought for a moment, then smiled. "He'll certainly be here if he smells a fight brewing!"

"In my official capacity I would have to frown on such unruly ethics, but it would be useful if he were here, I suspect. No doubt he would stand with Einar as solidly as you do, and the bigger the front ranged against Onund - for I suspect it is he that's principally behind all this - the less likely he is to do anything." He leaned closer for a moment. "Do you think Einar's holdings would be well enough guarded in his absence?"

"You saw as well as I how many men are there now, and he's had some of them with him for years. They won't let him down, and all of Eyvind's old hands know the way to your steading well enough, should they need help of any sort."

"Hmm. Well enough, I suppose. I dislike it when people get restless in my jurisdiction, and if Onund does wish to take it further, he'll have to go through me as well." The lawman sighed. "No rest again; no rest at all." And with that, he stumped off into the twilight.

Hrolf watched him go, with a crease in his forehead and a slight frown around his mouth. Like Oslac, he did not relish the idea of warring neighbours: it meant being called upon to support one side or the other, and that meant legal costs, in both time and money. It also might well involve getting his weapons out, arming some of his men (few of whom seemed either keen
or capable when it came to fighting) and throwing his military weight behind Einar. Along with Brynjolf and Eyvind, Hrolf, because of the nature of his business, was one of the most well-equipped men in the district, and in a little outbuilding to the side of his hall sat enough spears and shields to man the Felag's ship three times over. He had no idea what Einar's war-strength was, but he suspected it would be equal, at least, to his own; Eyvind had always been well-appointed in that regard, too. Should he, Snorri and Brynjolf have a need to, they could, between them, raze Onund's farm to the ground

and slaughter everyone in it, without even working up a sweat. It was a daunting thought, and for reasons of politeness, none of the Felag-men had ever made much of their armed strength in public. It was equally certain, however, that the sons of Ingimund were aware of it, and would wish to intervene in any dispute long before so much armament was seen in the field that their own positions felt threatened.

More pressingly, much as he loved the idea of a few days of sport after the Thing, Hrolf knew that the summer was moving on. He had a ship to launch, and trade to conduct. Much as he disliked doing it, he might have to leave the seeding of his fields to other hands and eyes this year. As he headed to bed, he found himself echoing Oslac's parting words: "no rest, no rest at all…"

CHAPTER EIGHTEEN

Einar duly stood before the assembled Thing- men the following day, his bright blonde hair trimmed, his beard cut close, and wearing a shirt of fine, pale blue linen under a long scarlet cloak. Showing the token, he declared his inheritance of Eyvind's farm from his dead uncle. He had clearly been spreading his money where it would do the most good, for all the witnesses whose marks were on the token were present to swear the truth of Einar's words. Around the crowd a bit from where Hrolf sat (being one of the principal landowners in the district, he got to sit as one of the principal justices), Onund could be seen, with Gizur the Dane beside him. Neither man looked particularly dangerous to Hrolf's eyes, but he quietly and discreetly pointed them out to Brynjolf, who had the bench next to him.

"Oh, I know Gizur a bit," said Brynjolf after taking a sideways look. "He's not a problem. Oslac asked me if I could have a quiet word with him."

"Fine," replied Hrolf. "That should be the death of anything Onund might be planning, then!"

Hrolf just happened to be at Brynjolf's tent later that day when Gizur walked in.

"Ah, Gizur," began Brynjolf, "I'm glad you came by."

"Your… messenger… was very insistent," replied the Dane. Brynjolf looked crestfallen.

"Oh dear, that's not how I intended matters at all! Do sit, have a drink, and we can talk properly." He settled himself onto rather an ornate stool before continuing. "I wanted to sound you out about your new neighbour, see if everything was alright. I may have some influence with him, you see, and as your farm is close to both mine and his, I thought I might ask if I could help with anything. Bad business, Eyvind coming off his horse like that."

"Indeed," said Gizur slowly. "I got on well enough with Eyvind, although we weren't close friends; the first I saw of Einar was today, when he declared his rights to the farm and the land on it. He looks a well enough man; we'll see how things go, I suppose. Clearly the Lawspeaker has no problem with any of it, and I'm not about to argue with the likes of him."

"The man beside you, Onund was it? He didn't look too happy."

Gizur grinned mirthlessly. "Onund is rarely happy, and altogether too eager to lead other men into his arguments. Don't worry," he added, "I'm not going anywhere with him! I know you two gentlemen better than to try."

"Hmm." Brynjolf considered for a moment. "Have you ever sailed with us, Gizur? I don't remember you, but…"

"No; my viking days are long gone. But I remember what's involved, and what my ship-master could do against people that annoyed him. Leave Onund to me, lords, and I will
handle him for you. Keep him out of your way, so to speak. He's not a bad man, but he works hard and gets little for it. I think it's going to his mind a bit, after so long."

"I understand, Gizur; thank you. You won't find us ungrateful," Brynjolf continued, putting a silver ring on the empty stool beside Gizur, "and, if things go well, maybe Onund's luck will change too, if you follow me?"

"I follow you entirely, sir. And I can promise I'll try to make Onund see, too."

"From what you say, he deserves a little luck," observed Hrolf. "It would be fitting if we could send some his way. And I rather suspect that as the years go on, Einar will prove to be a good friend to be in with."

CHAPTER NINETEEN

Einar somehow contrived to arrange his games to happen before the last day of the Thing; neither Hrolf or Brynjolf could remember Oslac ever permitting such an occurrence before, and putting their heads together, concluded that Einar's silver was finding its way even into the Lawman's pockets- albeit with beneficial effects, since all the serious business was, seemingly, already over, and everyone fancied a bit of sport before turning the Thing-place into the local market and then heading home. So, leaving Grim and Solmund to attend to campsite matters (since they were both either too creaky or too old for games), Hrolf took Erlend and Arnkel across to the field below the Thing-site. It was just as well that this was the Summer-Thing, since by autumn, the land here was usually heading rapidly to swamp. Var decided to follow with the children, primarily, Hrolf thought, to deck Elle out in her best dress and parade her for suitable matches to see. Kendrick was more likely to join in the ball-games and take out people's kneecaps with his bat, a potential problem that his father was not entirely sure how to deal with, beyond giving all the players his usual warning about it.

Einar was in fine humour when they found him, surrounded already by a good crowd of supporters, among whom was Gizur. Onund was not to be seen, either in Einar's camp or the knot of men who were slowly forming the opposing team. Hrolf was happy to see Oslac among the latter, and guessed that he was their leader, thus preventing any escalation of play into bloodshed.

"Einar," said Hrolf when he reached his new shipmate's side, "this is Var, my wife..." he got no further as, once formal introductions were over, Var took matters into her own hands, and was soon leading Einar away arm in arm, with Elle and Rowan in tow.

"Well, there goes our captain," laughed Gizur. "Lord, do you think she'll let him go in time to hit a ball or two?"

"Well, if she doesn't, there's an ale-cask half-full by my tent that I'm sure would be easier to carry home were it empty."

"Seems like a fair proposal," agreed Brynjolf, "ah, no, wait, he's escaped! Damn, that means we'll have to run around all afternoon instead."

"Look on it as extra training for later," suggested Hrolf, without much sympathy.

Two sides quickly formed up in the middle of the field, with a home-post rammed into the ground at either end of a loosely demarcated pitch, and a straggle of spectators around the edges. Einar and Oslac both made short speeches on the broad themes of friendship, the value of good neighbours, and the unspoken threat of what could happen to anyone who disturbed the peace of the Herred. They very conspicuously shook hands; the ball was thrown in, and the game began.

Hrolf had never really enjoyed playing ball: he preferred his violence to be rather more one-sided, with the advantage all his. Here, everyone had a long stick with which they attempted to hit the small leather ball - or anything else that came within range. Strictly speaking, the stick was never supposed to be raised above the knees, but that was yet another of many rules that went by the wayside within a few minutes of the game starting. When he had proper notice of a game, Hrolf frequently dug out his father's storm gear and a resilient leather-and-wicker hat he had; it was considered bad form to wear iron helms and mail on such occasions. Today, he was completely unprepared, and thus had to fall back on basic skills such as anticipation, premonition and the exercising of eyes in the back of his head. He also asked fervently of any unseen beings in the vicinity that all his fellow-players recognised him before dealing out any serious blows.

Staying away from the ball was another good tactic, but today, the thing seemed intent on seeking him out no matter what he did. Neither team had any identifying mark on them, so
Hrolf just tended to hit the ball away from himself, towards anyone who appeared to be running in the same direction as he was. He preferred to send it to people he knew were on his team, but he just didn't know everyone who was playing.

Reflexes long-forgotten began to return: he found himself jumping over incoming bats, and turning his shoulder towards any incoming players. Across the field, he could see Einar, grinning hugely, encouraging his team forwards, and it seemed to be doing some good, for they did appear to be gradually pushing closer to the opposing home-post. At a point when Hrolf was looking the other way, a cheer went up as one of Brynjolf's men, within reach of the post, grabbed up the ball and touched the wooden stake with it. The activity on the field gradually subsided into knots of men, resting their hands on their thighs, gulping in desperately- needed lungfuls of air, red-faced and sweaty, exchanging quips and comments with those around them. Oslac's bondsmen carried buckets of water around the field for those that needed it; once he had got his breath back, had some water and the world had stopped spinning before his eyes, Hrolf noticed his family weaving through the crowds towards him.

"Well, husband, I'm sure you feel all the better for that! At least you remembered to take your best shirt off before you went rolling in the dirt this time!"

"Thank you for your support, dear; did any of our local young men take the bait?" he added, grinning at his daughter.

"There's a nice lad lives over beyond the Irish farm," she replied, shyly. "Mother says we might visit later this summer."

"That sounds good. Any word from Solmund or Grim yet? Are we packed and ready to go? We don't have time to stay for markets this season if we want to get the ship out before winter comes again; I must find Brynjolf and Einar before we leave, and set a day for them to come." He turned back to Var. "How long to get the house ready before I bring the ship-men in?"

"Give me a fortnight, perhaps a night or two more. Will that do?"

"Yes, I'm sure that will be enough for them, too. When Erlend and Arnkel come back, I'll arrange to send someone to Snorri so that he knows, too."

"I can do that for you," put in Einar, coming over to them. "Fine game, Hrolf; well played." He looked around the field. "I think it did some good."

"I'd say so," replied Hrolf. "Fourteen nights, then, 'till we meet at Liscardr, and get the boat in the water at last. Bring everything you need; you won't see your wife or your new farm again before autumn."

CHAPTER TWENTY

By the end of the fourteen stipulated nights after the Summer Thing, it was so far into spring that there could not really be any argument about the time of year. When the Felag gathered at Hrolf's steading on the rocky hill that overlooked the marshes and the sea, it also became one of the rare times of the year that Yngvar really earned his place in the kitchen, staying in the little outbuilding for day after day as the guests arrived, feeding the fires, stirring the pots and generally running around to ensure everything went well. Even so, Var sometimes thought when she looked around and he was not to be seen, that he might be better placed elsewhere, where either she *could* always watch him, or he could be safely left to his own devices, harming none but himself if he slacked. Thurbrand seemed to be shadowing him, too.

Brynjolf, Snorri and Einar all brought in a share of their cargo: timber and cloth began to fill the shed Hrolf set aside for the purpose, along with barrels of dried fish, salt and bars of iron acquired from the Mercians. It had been a bad year for driftwood, which was Hrolf's usual source of timber, and so he had needed, reluctantly, to order a few trees cut down atop the ridge of the drier hill. The visiting hauldar also brought a share of the crew with them, to work the oars of their twenty-bencher and provide a few extra hands besides. Einar in particular brought a large contingent, but, as he explained, not all would be sailing with them.

"I have more men than I can use," he began, stating the obvious as far as Hrolf was concerned, who had seen the farm he had taken over. "So, as well as bringing my share of the crew, I had a mind to ask if you wanted any of them to stay here and help around the farm in place of your own people. If you'd rather not - I'm aware that you must have managed without extra help all these other years - I can send them home again without any trouble."

"Not likely!" replied Var. "Good hands are always welcome- they *are* trustworthy, I assume? I mean no offence, but I don't know you - or them."

Einar smiled. "Your caution is fine, my lady, and having heard about you from Eyvind, I take no offence. They are among my best; I grew up with most of them. Anlaf in particular is one I trust more than many. He does not sail, though, and so is an ideal foreman, if you have a mind to make him so, over my other men at least."

"That sounds good," put in Hrolf. "Then I can send Solmund over to Gytha with a clear conscience. Can you feed them well enough?" he asked Var. She nodded, a confident smile on her lips.

"Splendid," added Brynjolf genially, "everyone can go round and round in circles at home, while we go round and round all at sea!"

"What of the ship?" asked Snorri. "Are we set to sail?"

Hrolf scratched his beard. "We've done what seemed needy to do…but the weather's been bad since I returned, and other matters have needed seeing to, so it's not in the water as yet. But it looks as if the rain might ease perhaps tomorrow; so before all these extra men go home, I think we should put them to use and haul it out as soon as the day is dry."

"Fine by me," said Einar, rubbing his hands.

Snorri peered at him closely. "You're getting eager," he observed. Einar grinned.

"Yes, I'm keen; if you had heard the tales I had from uncle Eyvind about his Felag-men, so would you be! I've been on Viking trips before, since I was around ten years I think, but never so successfully as you men have been. Eyvind was proud to have sailed with you all; I can only hope I remember enough sea- craft not to disgrace him."

"Sounds a bit as if Eyvind ...*selected*...his tales rather carefully," said Brynjolf. "For instance, I bet you never heard about the time Hrolf steered us onto a sandbank in the middle of the river... by the side of the local brewhouse..."

"Or how Brynjolf pulled us away from a mooring and brought half a forest along in the mast-top?" countered Hrolf with a smile. "With all the things we've done to it, I wonder the ship even floats these days." He looked up and smiled again as Var and Elle poured more ale. "Drink well, friends, and soon we'll see how well Yngvar has done in the cooking- house.
Tomorrow we haul the ballast- stones out, and walk the ship to the sea."

CHAPTER TWENTY- ONE

Hrolf looked out of his doorway the next day - up before his wife for once - and gazed over the mists that covered his fields at the base of the cliff. Far away, he could see the grey, hazy shapes of the Welsh mountains, and that was enough to make him smile, for if he could see them, it meant a fine day ahead. Truly, it was time to be getting the ship afloat once more,
and the Gods had clearly agreed. So, with a lightness in his heart and his spirits buoyed up, the Lord of the Rock went back inside and spooned porridge out of the night-ember pot for his children. He even allowed them some of the precious salt sprinkled over it, although he
noticed Elle eagerly eyeing the cream-jug and wondering if she dare ask for some. He stirred the fire back into life, ready for the day, just before Ymma came in with the other poker and a bag of kindling.

"Honing your skills again, husband?" came Var's sleepy voice from the bed-closet. "I can always tell when ship- time is on us, you go all domestic and helpful." She swung her feet out as he straightened and looked for ale-cups, and smiles passed between them. "I take it the weather is better today, then?"

"Yes, I can see the hills into Pawl's country." Having found cups, Hrolf began a search for the jug; the house was only saved from total destruction when Ymma fished it from a bucket and filled it for him.

"Where's my top-dress..." murmured Var as she took a few first steps, blinking in the smoke. "Ymma, I'll need an apron, go find one. You too, dear, and a cleaner dress..."

"This is my night-shift!" protested Ymma.

"Well go and change, then! The children are fed, go feed yourself, I doubt there'll be time later on, not with a house this full. Where's Hild? And have you seen Yngvar yet?"

Hrolf knew when to retreat, and did so with speed. Here, Var was the chieftain, for all that he held the lands and the titles to Walea and Liscardr, and the marshes round about. His place today was at the river, and the boatsheds, but his stomach rumbled and convinced him that hard work on just a cup of ale was no way to begin the day. So he sat in his high-seat, and waited quietly until his guests and the rest of the household arrived for the day-meal, served once their morning chores were done. He played each of his children in turn at Tafl, and marvelled at how well they learned the game: he lost to Elle and Rowan, and only won against Kendrick by the skin of his teeth. Einar's friend Anlaf came over and told them stories, and all the while the porridge warmed, the bacon sizzled, and the smell of new bread grew ever-stronger.

By the time all his bondar had arrived, bringing the house-guests billeted with them, it felt to Hrolf as if it were long past morning; but, he reflected, this was unlikely to be so, as Var hadn't started loudly deploring the sluggishness of the servants yet. He had woken early, as he always did at such times of high excitement, and he had to remind himself sternly that there was actually still plenty of sunlight in the day. As if sensing his thoughts, Var came over with the ale-jug and a murmur in his ear of "patience…"

As soon as the other Felag-men had settled in their places at either side of the high-seat, food was served. Hild and Ymma ran to and fro with bowls and plates, ale-jugs and cups: even Yngvar came to help, chiefly with the bacon, which seemed to diminish whenever he was holding the bowl. Bread came in, still steaming from its oven, and the sound of talking grew ever louder. Eventually, Hrolf judged the moment right, signalled Hild for his ale-horn (the one that only got used for special occasions, as it couldn't be put down safely), and rose to his feet. He waited patiently as the chatter slowly ceased around him, and smiled.

"Friends, fellow ship-men, it is summer again! Time to be going, making the silver we all enjoy so much, making the stories we all endure next winter… today, work in the fields can wait, all hands are needed at the noust. We have a ship to float."

Snorri led a straggly cheer; it was the sign for tables to be cleared and put away, and the men, closely accompanied by most of the women and children on the steading, followed their ship-master down to the boatshed. Hrolf fished the padlock key from around his neck, and opened the small landward door that gave access into the noust, and from there onto the river that
nearly made Walea into an island. Small compared to the waters on either side of Wirhalh, it was still

big enough for ships to travel on, and it led into the northern river at a point sheltered from its more fierce currents. As an alternative, Hrolf reckoned a ship could be portaged overland in the other direction, and taken straight to the sea. After all, he had walked the distance easily enough to meet Kol and Arne, and although the way was marshy, it was pretty flat, too.

"What orders, ship-master?" called Brynjolf from the depths of the shed.

"We need to get the ballast-stones out first of all, so five men aboard, the rest to form a line and carry them to the river's edge."

The chain was quickly organised, and to the sound of singing, the rocks made their way out towards the river. As this task ended, Hrolf directed some of his workers out of the line, and sent them to either side of the hull. In the meantime, he passed a couple of strong, plaited walrus-hide ropes through a hole at the rear of the keel, sending them forwards to groups of
men kept back for this task, and directed yet others to get the oars out, and then pass them back

through their ports to form a row of handles along both flanks of the vessel.

"That's the last of the stones," called Einar from the door of the shed.

"Fine," answered Hrolf. "Next, take those split logs by the wall and lay them as a gangway. Kol, Arne, do you have what you promised?"

"Aye, lord!" The two brothers came out of the crowd, carrying buckets of foul-smelling fish livers, which they proceeded to empty over the logs in front of the ship. That done, the men under the sides were instructed to brace their shoulders against the timbers; the other gangs took hold of the ends of the oars, and braced themselves for the lift. On Hrolf's shout, the gangs lifted and the rope-men hauled: and so, slowly at first but then more swiftly as the keel hit the fish slime, the ship moved towards the river.

As the stern-post cleared the shed the gangway suddenly sloped downhill to the water. Hrolf stopped the work just as they reached this point, and had bracing timbers propped against the prow while the men rested. He also took the opportunity to put extra lines around the bow, and count off further teams to haul on them as a check to the ship's speed down the slope.

"That was well- timed," said Snorri. He looked back up the hill, to where the ladies of the house were bringing beer and baskets of fresh bread.

"Couldn't be better," agreed Brynjolf.

Snorri took his share of the ale gratefully. "Thirsty work, this," he commented, leaning on his spear and surveying the dusty, sweaty men around him.

"Careful," replied Brynjolf. "We wouldn't want you overdoing it, or you'll work up an appetite as well…"

Once the rope-crews had reassembled, Hrolf again gave the order to pull: the aft-crew heaved, the fore-crew took the strain, and the Felag's ship slid gently and easily down the slope and into the river with only the gentlest of splashes. Spare hands, including those of the owners, hurried to pile the ballast back in and stabilise the vessel before it had a chance to roll and capsize; gradually, the hull settled down in the water, and the wild rolling motion lessened.

Einar looked the ship over for his first time as the crowds of men stood back; Hrolf and Snorri both took lines from either end and made them fast to stakes hammered into the riverbank. Jon and Arnor then waded out to the vessels and somehow clambered up the side and over the rail; once aboard, they pushed the gangplank out to the bank where it too was secured.
Others hastened up to join them, bringing buckets to begin the baling that was constantly required until the timbers soaked and swelled shut after their dry winter in the shed.

"Well, that's a good day's work," commented Brynjolf as they made their cheerful way back up the hill in the last of the sunlight. "I reckon we've earned our ale tonight, eh?" Behind him, Snorri sniffed disdainfully.

"Undoubtedly," said Hrolf. "I'll send a fresh gang down tonight to bale and sleep on board, and then tomorrow we can get the stores brought over, and the sail back on." He grinned broadly at his fellow owners. "We'll be away in a day or so; if you want to send messengers back to your homes, now is the time!"

"No need," answered Snorri. "The goodbyes are all said, including ours to Eyvind. Let's see if he passed his good luck on to you, Einar, along with the farm and his oar-bench!"

The newest member of the Felag smiled. "I would hope he has, but he didn't say. And if it turns out I don't have his luck, we'll just have to get rich without it, I suppose. I'm sure
your collective luck will be worth more than mine anyway."

"I have every confidence," announced Brynjolf. "After all, any man who can inherit an estate like Eyvind's, keep it safely, and befriend our lord Oslac into the bargain, has got to be possessed of all the good fortune we'll ever need."

CHAPTER TWENTY-TWO

Almost the whole of the farmstead followed the crew down to the ship on the following morning; looking back at the waving, cheering crowd from the middle of the river, Hrolf knew full well that little work would be done until they were out of sight. Even then, he guessed, many eyes would follow them from the top of the hill as they rounded his land's edge and headed for the Mercian coast to the south.

He left Snorri to call the oar-stroke, saving his own concentration for the feel of the steerboard's long handle as it quivered and tried to turn in his hands, guiding the vessel through the ever-changing patterns of silt and weeds on the riverbed. Beneath him, the planks of the small aft deck twisted with the long, snake-like form of the ship, and every once in a while there was a gentle scraping sound as the keel slid through the topmost peaks of little sandbanks. Along each side, getting used to the feel of benches, oars and the motion of the vessel, the crew rowed slowly, gently, more intent on the orders shouted from stem or stern than on getting up any sort of speed. Up in the prow, Kol, Arne and Grim crouched over the rail, watching the patterns of the water intently, calling out instructions, and taking frequent soundings.

Grim did not sail, but he had a deep love of ships for all that, and for reasons that escaped Hrolf completely, he had an uncanny feel for this particular river. So, every year, he travelled with them until they ventured into the faster-flowing, swirling waters of the big northern river. It was no problem, once free of the main currents, to swing the ship shoreward, and to let him off on the gentle, muddy slope of the riverbank, from where he would squelch ashore to drier ground and wave his own farewell. A few hard shoves of the forward, landward oars
would see them out into open water again, where there was enough breeze to allow the men to ship their oars inboard, and raise sail for the first time. Those closest to the gently pointed
ends of the ship pulled their oars back in on Hrolf's command, and, leaving their benches, took hold of the long lines that ran up the mast and then back down to the ends of the yardarm, where it sat, along the length of the ship, on a high pair of solid wooden rests.

"Haul up!" called the shipmaster. Arms tensed and heaved; lines grew tight and shed little sprays of water. But with every jerking pull, the sail and its yard lifted clear of the rests and began the climb to the top of the mast.

"Arghh!" spluttered Jon, from his bench by the mastfish, as the woollen mass began to unfurl and crawl upwards, "it's still wet!"

"Stop moaning," grinned Snorri, "it'll dry out soon enough." He too got up from his seat, and took one of the ropes sewn into the bottom of the sail. "Look quickly, lads: don't let these lines flap loose! Take 'em up, tie 'em off on the rail there."

He stood with hands on hips, swaying gently to the rhythm of the ship's movement in the waves, satisfaction in every inch of his body. "Ah: I couldn't have missed this for the world!"

By tradition, only the Felag-men got to choose their places in the ship; everyone else drew lots. As the sail filled and the lines grew taut, they stowed what little baggage they had - any
spare clothing they could find, and their weapons, all wrapped well against the inevitable damp and

salt - under or around their benches. Food was packed under the small areas of fore- and aft- deck, whilst the cargo shared space with the ballast in the body of the ship, all covered against the spray with a thin, patched, second-best sail and the ship's tent spread out as far as it could be made to. The benches themselves were a part of the ship, being those timbers stretched across the tops of the ribs from one side of the ship to the other. The more experienced men brought out cushions from their packs, and lashed them in place with their cloaks or odd lengths of rope. And so they settled into life aboard ship, their home and workplace for the next few months. For the first day, eyes kept careful watch on the seams between the strakes, testing the withies that tied the ribs in, looking for signs of rust around the nails and their roves. But, it turned out, the ship had wintered well, and there was no more seepage than in any other year. It was still enough to fill a bucket or two every day, but easily contained, and everyone took turns at baling.

Crossing the mouth of the Mercian river was fairly straightforward, merely a matter of following the Wirhalh coast until they passed behind Hilbrey and rounded the western corner. Then upstream into

the river just far enough (before the wind died off and they needed the oars again, for preference), before tacking back across the current, which gently took them
over and towards the open sea again. If the steersman did it right, this manoeuvre would carry the ship beyond the point at the corner of the Mercian coast, which more or less marked the boundary between the Englisc and the Welsh lands. If he got it wrong, it simply meant rowing up the shoreline for a while, but the loss of reputation would be mortifying. This year, Hrolf was lucky: the tide in the river was strong, and it sent their ship well out into the bay on the power of the sail alone. He got a cheer from his shipmates for it, and the happy thought of an easy start to the next day's travel. The ache in his arms from holding the steerboard steady in the outbound current was nothing to complain about in consequence. As soon as they had cleared the Mercian point, Hrolf leaned the steerboard over, felt the bite of the ocean upon it, and took them into the shore, where easy beaches would allow them to stop for their first night. As they neared the land, Hrolf ordered the sail down, and the oars out. They rowed the final half- mile or so, and wedged the prow of the ship snugly into the sand.

Hrolf and some of the others were aware that people lived a short way inland, people who had moved here out of Ingimund's land-holdings, out of Mercia, and even out of the deeper parts of the Welsh lands, and who now shifted their allegiances to Mercian, Norseman or Welshman as the borders and fortunes of their more organised, more powerful neighbours

shifted around them. The ship-men didn't care who they were currently loyal to, so long as these people were willing to sell them food and the local news. To ensure their willingness, it was the Felag's custom to send a small, but well-armed party into their settlements as soon as they had beached. To a small cluster of farmers, four or five men wearing costly iron helmets and carrying spears was as good as an army when it arrived amongst them; to make an even bigger impact, Snorri and Einar offered to wear their mailshirts as well. Brynjolf opted to stay with the ship and oversee the erection of their tent, and so the rest of the Felag-men pulled out their gear, chose a companion each, and set off over the dunes, shoes kicking through sand and loose, light soil, shields thumping against their backsides and their swords (those who had them chose to wear them for this sort of thing) slapping against thighs.

Those not rich enough yet to have swords carried axes, most of them from their household woodpiles; all took a spear.

It was only a mile or so to the nearest of these little settlements, and the day was cool enough that not even mail and helmets caused any great discomfort. The farmers had, of course, seen the ship land, and had guessed that it was the same vessel that put in almost every year. As a result, they came out to welcome their visitors; negotiations were soon in hand for extra
provisions, and the senior men sat down together to exchange the gossip.

"What news of Pawl?" asked Hrolf after a while, quietly hiding his maimed hand. "Has he stirred after the winter yet?"

"We've had no news," answered his host, one Starkad. "He's sent no men to us, to tax us or otherwise, although I've no doubt it's only a matter of time."

Snorri rubbed his beard. "Could it be because the Mercians are feeling bolder this year?"

Rhodri shrugged. "Had no word from Chester, either. But there was talk of armed men seen further back up the river, earlier in the spring. Make of that what you will; I don't know where they were going except that it wasn't here."

*

"What do you think?" asked Einar as they made their way back towards the coast in the evening twilight. "Does any of what these men said make a sort of sense?"

Hrolf thought for a moment. "You've not been here before, of course; I'll explain. Starkad used to have a farm on the edges of my lands, but he always found it hard going, mostly marshland, not very good. He got fed up that the Mercians had all the best patches, even though they were there first, and more of them, then, than our people. I remember Dubhnjal saying that.

"Starkad was one of those that listened most eagerly when Ingimund gathered all the hauldar together and suggested they demand more of the Mercian king. When it all fell apart, he ran,

along with a number of others, and all around this area you'll find them making a living and giving their oaths to whoever is strongest around them. It's a funny sort of place, this: lots of
people without the full share of courage or wit any more, after the hiding Ingimund led them into; lots of land empty still, and there to be taken. Even I've got a bit, closer to the river shore, though I've never done anything with it. But this situation does give its people a good sense of what's going on around them, and if they say nothing is happening, then it's most likely true. We pay them well, and never impose; they've no reason to lie to us."

"Any danger of them sending runners about us to this Pawl, or the Mercians? What's the story with him anyway?"
Snorri chuckled. "The story of our involvement with Pawl the Welshman is carved on Hrolf's hands! They might tell him we called, I suppose, but I get the feeling that Starkad, at least, sees us as friends of a sort." He shrugged. "Doesn't mean I'd ever trust him, mind. Shifty, unreliable little type."

They recounted what little information they had gleaned to the rest of the crew, and spent the evening getting comfortable in the tent and cheerfully drinking. Towards the end of the alehorn, Einar asked, "What next, ship-master?"

Hrolf was aware of his fellow owner's eyes upon him, and guessed that Brynjolf, at least, was thinking back to the words spoken in his hall earlier in the year. To the trade-routes, or to hard knocks and the chance of weregeld? An interesting choice, and one that could split his fellow-owners, if it were left to them. He was also aware, however, that for now, the two courses were as one: they had to follow the coast westwards at least until Ormsness, whatever they did; after that point came the decision, really, but having said that, Hrolf always preferred such matters decided well ahead of time. It was at least two days to Pawl's lands, on the far side of the channel between the mainland and the island, but only one to the settlement in the bay, on the Anglian Isle. That was where at least one good market was, and that was where they ought to head. He had said to Brynjolf that he wouldn't press the matter of Pawl and his finger; so he ought to hold to that promise.

"Ongle-sey," he announced, "that place up on the cliffs, above the beach that looks back towards our

homes, where we always sell well. After that, we'll see, but having gone so far
towards Ireland, it would seem foolish to go right around the rest of the island and come back again. Unless, of course, we are sent that way."

"Suits me," answered Brynjolf. "We can decide on the next step afterwards; better, I think, to get somewhere first."

"Indeed," agreed Snorri. He yawned. "But even sooner, to bed."

CHAPTER TWENTY-THREE

On a clear day, it was possible to look out to sea, a fraction out from the line of the coast and, from the Felag's campsite, see the dark, solid mass of Ormsness pushing out into the waves and the sky. It was obviously a landmark, but also a useful spot to aim for, as once around it, it was a quick cut across more open sea, right into the bay Hrolf was aiming for. Sadly, today was not that clear, and all that could be seen was mist and low, dark cloud. The tops of the waves showed white through the murk, and the water itself was a deep, uninviting grey.

"Can't see any rain yet," said Snorri, "so that's good news."

"A good day for hot food and warming ale!" laughed Jon. He was stirring the fire back into life as he spoke, whilst Erlend was unwrapping one of Var's sausages from its cloth and coiling it onto the cooking-stone.

"Well said, that man," agreed Brynjolf. "Food before anything, although from the look of things, once we're away from the shore, it'll be sail up for the day. I can't see us needing to row."

"Where do we think the tide is?" wondered Hrolf. "Going out, or coming in?"

They stood at the water's edge and watched for a while, before deciding that the tide was definitely going out. By careful examination of the pebbles and other debris, they were able to
find the high-tide mark and see how far down from this the waves currently were, which in turn gave an idea of how long they had until it turned back again and drove their ship onto the
beach instead of away from it as they would prefer. Snorri and Hrolf, who had more ship experience and interest than the other Felag-men, reckoned they had long enough to cook an early day-meal, and then eat it once aboard and free of the beach. On a day like this, hot food was a definite advantage.

Whilst Hrolf's men cooked and fed the fire (also putting a good stock of trimmed branches into the ship for next time), Einar set his to dismantling the tent and stowing it and the other gear away. Brynjolf and Snorri set a man each to stand guard over their work, and put the others into preparing the ship for departure. By the time the sausage was done, and bread cut and warmed, the ship was pushed out and floating free of the sand, tethered only by a couple of lines back to shore. The last up the ladder were Erlend and Jon, who shared out slices of meat and passed round baskets of bread. Those who wanted beer had to leave their bench and go aft for it, to where the barrel stood, lashed between two ribs on the steer-deck. Erlend brought Hrolf his share, and filled his master's cup whilst Hrolf pushed the steerboard round, the oars bit into the grey water, and the ship pulled away from the shore. The thrall waited until the immediate task was over and when the sail bellied out, full of breeze, and then asked permission to speak.

"What is it, Erlend? A problem, or a question, or an opinion?"

"A question, sir. Are we going through the Island channel this trip?"

Hrolf swallowed ale before replying. "I assume you ask because of what lies beyond the straight?" Erlend nodded.

"I'm not surprised at that. No, the plan is to head for a settlement on Ongle-sey, as I said last night,

where we have done business before. After that, I would think it most likely
we'll head towards Dubhllyn, and perhaps cruise along the coast in whichever direction looks to offer the best pickings. I've said to my ship-fellows that I won't press the matter with Pawl this year, but this is out of respect to them, not due to your being here."

He sighed. "They're getting old, Erlend, and new men are coming in. It is not a good year to go looking for fights, I think."

"I understand, sir. I was sad to hear Master Eyvind was dead. He was good to me last year. But I think, if I may say so, that Master Einar's coming feels like a good thing. He is very energetic, and very keen for everything - like you, sir. Master Brynjolf and Master Snorri are not young men any more, as you have said, and perhaps Master Eyvind has given them things to think about in his death. It is indeed a time of change; even I can see it, who only met you last year. I don't mean to speak out of turn, sir, or offer any insult, by this."

"That's alright, Erlend, I don't take it as such, but I won't speak for the others." He threw the hard crust of his bread overboard, and reached again for his ale. "It may be a good thing to keep silent in front of them, and see what turns out."

Erlend nodded. "As you say, sir. I have no wish to cause any trouble."

Not after our last few meetings, thought Hrolf as his thrall returned to his bench. But he also wondered how long the man's good intentions would last.

CHAPTER TWENTY-FOUR

The arms of the bay spread wide, welcoming the shipmen inwards on a heavy tide that crashed and hissed onto smooth, broad sand. Beyond the beach, the land rose steeply; beyond this rise, out of view to those at sea, lay the outer earthworks of a large and well-organised settlement.

"I can't tell if it's my eyes playing tricks or not," murmured Einar to Brynjolf at the prow of the ship, "but there seems to be a lot of glinting metal on that hill."

"I wouldn't doubt it for a moment," replied the other. "We aren't the only visitors these people get, and not all of them are as friendly and well-disposed as we are. So, friend Einar, trust your eyes and sharpen your wits; you'll need 'em all once we get up there. If it's been a bad year so far, they'll be touchy."

As they headed for land, it became clear that not only was the ship being observed from the safety of the ramparts, but as they came ever-closer, men descended the cliffs and stood ready on the beach as well. Men with shields held across their chests, ready for trouble should any arise, and with the fine shine of spear-points high above their heads.

Brynjolf hurried aft, and once beside Hrolf, he turned to his shipmates. "Listen to me," he said, in a loud voice that even Einar could still hear clearly. "It looks as if our friends in this place have had a hard summer already. We don't come here to fight; they're too well defended for that, and we've done good business with them in years past." He fixed each man in turn with a strong, hard stare. "So unless they start the weapon-play, you don't make their summer any worse, you hear? I don't want you fighting them, chasing their wives, getting too deep in their
ale-casks, or doing anything else that you won't do in your own lords' homes. We've come here to sell our stuff, cloth and wood and so on. If you want something from them, you buy it. You do *not* just take it, and you keep your weapons on the ship. *All of them.* Do you understand?"

There was a chorus of "aye"; content with that, Brynjolf nodded his thanks, and turned his attention back to the shore.

With a few furlongs to go, Hrolf ordered the sail down and the oars out. Brynjolf returned to the prow, pausing only to pull his helmet and spear from beneath his bench. He rose and spoke something to Einar, who nodded and also retrieved his wargear. Thus, as they came to ground on the sand, two armoured men were visible in the very front of the ship: just enough to check the advance of the men who awaited them, and prompt a more friendly opening dialogue between ship-men and shore party than might otherwise be.

"This is a good thing to do," observed Snorri, coming aft.

"What is?" asked Hrolf. "Besides not just laying into each other, that is."

"Having Einar and Brynjolf to do the talking as we land. Brynjolf does it very well, got a good way with words, and doesn't go rushing in like an idiot. Einar, I would bet, is a fast learner."

"He's having to be; but he seems to be taking it all very well."

"Oh, indeed," replied Snorri. "Eyvind left us a good replacement, in my opinion. It's all working out very well. What of your two hopefuls?" he nodded forward, to where Kol and Arne had sidled to within earshot of the prow.

"They aren't used to keeping much company, and they're not used to being ordered around," answered Hrolf. "That said, though, they're keeping their eyes and ears open - as now - and their mouths shut. They're learning fast as well. I think they're likely to be invited along again next year, if their behaviour keeps up."

"Good," said Snorri, but there was a faraway look in his eyes. "I like them; they remind me of me."

Hrolf looked over at him. "You speak as if you won't be here next time; as if you're looking for replacements."

"Gytha's words keep going round in my head, for all that I'd rather ignore them."

"Ah. Well, I'll say to you what I said to Brynjolf, who was thinking of not sailing this season far more than you were when I visited. There would be no shame in selling your bench; you've done well from your voyages, and you've been doing it a long time, longer than any other I know, now that Eyvind is dead. If you wanted a rest from it all, there's none could say you haven't earned it."

"Would you buy?"

"I might, though I'm not sure I could fill your share of the crew every spring. If you think Kol and Arne might buy… well, I don't know for sure how well-off they are, but I do know that they don't maintain any sort of household to find crewmen from. Perhaps we could share that part of the duty between us all; Einar certainly has men to spare, he proved that." Hrolf rubbed his beard. "I'm sure we could do it; it's really just a question of whether you want to or not."

"I don't *want* to, Hrolf; but I'm starting to think I may *have* to."

Hrolf grasped his friend's shoulder. "Not an easy choice, then." He looked up as Brynjolf whistled and waved from the prow, motioning the Felag-men forward. "In the meantime, it looks as if we have a ship to unload."

CHAPTER TWENTY- FIVE

Once the initial danger of hostilities had been avoided, the people of the bay proved as keen to trade as they had ever been, and escorted their visitors up the narrow twisting path that led to their gate. Within that barrier of timber and soil, most of the compound was filled with lean-to's and flimsy sheds, but a fine paved roadway led across it to a cluster of more solidly built houses set close by the inner face of the rampart. Even Einar, who had never seen this place before, was driven to wonder what must separate the dwellers in these buildings from

the rest of the community; his colleagues, however, were more interested in how the smaller, seemingly seasonal structures had proliferated since their last visit. Clearly, something had changed, but what that might be was harder to tell. Some things looked the same: the farmers still grew their oats and wheat in fields on the higher ground to the south, and the sound and smell of livestock permeated the place. The people of the bay had never relied entirely on the whims of passing trade, for all that their lords, both resident and absentee, seemed keen to promote the idea and make themselves amenable to visitors.

For reasons the bay-dwellers kept to themselves, the Felag's small supply of timber was snapped up for an extremely good price, setting Hrolf to wonder if the Mercians had been
campaigning around the narrow channel and thus cut off the tracks into the mountains of the Welsh, which held good numbers of cheaper trees in their more sheltered valleys. Their hosts appeared very keen to acquire iron, too, which was not unduly suspicious given the numbers of blacksmiths they supported; yet, on a seemingly innocent stroll around the centre of the village, both Snorri and Einar had noticed a lot of spear- and arrow- heads piled in baskets around the forges. Their customers were not as interested in bronze or silver this season, for all that these makers, too, were busy over their fires and crucibles. The smoke from their endeavours wafted continuously across the settlement.

Hrolf and Brynjolf spent more time in the main building at the landward edge of the rampart, in the company of men who were either the lords of this place, or the agents of the king's hall further west (Hrolf could not fully make out which it was; perhaps it was both), conducting the majority of the business. It was both easier and safer, under the prevailing laws, to do all the deals through the same set of people, with the same set of witnesses. And so they sold timber and iron, and bought cloth (they already had ells and ells of their own produce stowed in the belly of the ship, but the Welsh cloth was different, and so worth adding to the stock), honey, and metals, bronze and silver, worked into intricate designs around everyday objects. Used as they were to finding animals in most of their own decorations, the preference of the Welsh and Irish smiths for straightforward geometry, devoid of heads, tails and claws, baffled the Felag-men somewhat. But it sold well in most of the places they were likely to visit, and it took up very little space in the hold. Apart from any artistic considerations, silver was silver, and good currency in any form. Hrolf privately considered that buying silver with surplus iron was about as good as it got.

By the end of the second day, it felt as if business had been pretty much exhausted. The big men of the settlement had done their deals; all that was left was small-time bartering for little items, at which level it was safe to allow the members of the crew to strike their own deals with whoever wanted

their meagre stocks of goods. By keeping their own people near them,
the Felag-men were able to avoid disputes, and head off trouble by a friendly (or sometimes not-so-friendly) word in the appropriate direction.

"It's been a good stop," commented Snorri at the eve of the last day. He was counting silver coins (their hosts having a preference for coinage over raw silver) into a bag; once done, he scratched the number on the edge of the table and divided it by four, getting a feel of their profits so far. That done, he sat back and looked over at Hrolf. "Are Kol and Arne in for a share yet?"

"They've not bought in, to my knowledge," put in Brynjolf.

Hrolf shook his head. "No, they aren't Felag-men, they're part of my crew share. So, like the others, I pay them out of my split."

"Fine; I just asked to be sure."

"Are these people always this friendly and helpful?" asked Einar. "Considering how many weapons they appear to be making, they seem very respectful of a handful of swords."

"They have dealings with the Mercians too, remember," answered Brynjolf. "They view these things differently. I went out and bought my sword as soon as I could afford it, and there was nothing to stop me having it." His hand strayed over the pommel of the weapon as he spoke, caressing the bronze wire, wearing it down still further, if imperceptibly. "The Englisc see matters otherwise. For them, if you've got a sword, you're important. They've even got laws about it in some parts, or so I'm told." He shook his head. "It all seems a little strange to me,
but it's certainly worked to our favour here."

"Hmm," agreed Hrolf, watching Brynjolf's actions with some amusement. His own sword lay on the table of their guesthouse before him. "But I think we're done here, pretty much. I would say we pack up and go on the tide tomorrow, before we become a nuisance." He stretched, and smoothed back his hair. "I'd like to be gone before anyone thinks to try out all these new spears and arrows on us."

"That said," replied Snorri, "I'd like to know who they *are* planning on using them against."

"I haven't seen any ships," said Brynjolf, "so it can't be to raid our lands. I'd bet on the Mercians, if what Starkad told us had any truth in it."

"Keep your money," grinned Hrolf. "That's a bet I'll not take." He looked down at his maimed hand. "All the same, if they marched against Pawl, I can't say I'd be sorry…"

Brynjolf snorted. "As if! We've been sat in a hall with their chief men for two days, and even if you weren't listening to what they said between them, I was. Not that I could understand much, but your man Erlend could. Have you asked him yet?"

"No, I haven't."

"You should: he's very useful. He has, shall we say, been quite informative." He shrugged. "The gist of it is that Pawl sent them messages last year, offering friendship and better ties between them. Then the Mercians pushed west again earlier this summer, and that sort of clinched the deal. The leading men in the hall on the westerly side of this isle would,

I'm sure, prefer to battle Englisc than their cousins hereabouts."

"Pawl not subject to this mysterious king then?" wondered Snorri. "I find that rather odd. It can't be true; if I were king around here, I'm not sure I'd want anyone as strong as Pawl that near, and not under my thumb."

Hrolf shuddered at Brynjolf's words. "What he says may well be true, but I would advise getting too close to Erlend. He's turning out to be a bad investment, and trouble besides."

"Now I'm curious, Hrolf. Come on, what's the story here?"

Hrolf frowned, and wished things hadn't come to this. He would much rather have dealt with it in his own way, in his own time, and not had to air his failures before his peers. But there was nothing else for it now; Brynjolf had asked the question, and so he had to answer.

"Erlend has fallen for that handmaid Asa brought to my hall last spring. He went to your farm when you needed help in the harvest month, mainly to try and be with her. Only this year, he begged to come with me when I visited, and when we changed our plans and went on to see Eyvind, I felt it best to send him back home before I left your hall, so he could not try any tricks. He was trying to ask if I'd buy her off you - for him! I broke his nose for his presumption, the bastard. Wish I'd not spared him last year, now…

"And now, he's worming in to you. He's not mentioned this to me, by the way." Hrolf's frown deepened. "I've told him that I value your friendship far above his life, but evidently he doesn't believe me yet. It's not my place to tell you how to conduct yourself, but it is my duty to warn you about men I'm commanding, if there is need. And it seems that there is that need; so be wary of his friendship. There's a price attached."

"And a bloody high one, from the sound of it," commented Einar into the silence that followed. "The cheek of the man!"

"It is often the way, that the highest prizes bring the greatest cost behind them," added Snorri.

"Ah, don't worry," said Brynjolf eventually. "Just telling us his plans has pretty much defeated them, I'd say. The Gods alone know what Asa would say if I tried to take her maid away!"

"More seriously though," said Snorri, "is he likely to become dangerous to us if he doesn't succeed in this?"

Hrolf shrugged. "I don't know. How much damage can one man do? Although, having said that, he was high in Pawl's confidences, would have to be since he was in his hearth-troop.
Maybe I should just take him out and kill him?"

"Can't see him standing still for the blow, somehow," said Brynjolf. "And doing it now would cloud our luck this voyage, maybe." He went to the barrel and got another drink. "Leave him be for now; if the rest of us can't keep him under control, there's really no hope for us!"

"Hael to that," said Snorri. "So, what next?" He smiled, with a glint in his eye. "Isn't there a colony of priests around the other side of this island? Wonder how well-stocked they are?"

Hrolf waved him quiet, before rising quietly to his feet and putting his ear to the door. The walls of the guest-house were not unduly thick or heavy, being just wattle in the Irish style, and if they were to start discussing raids in the area, the last thing Hrolf wanted was eavesdroppers. For all that the people of the bay ran their own lives pretty much, there was another hall elsewhere on the island, rumoured to belong to a king of these folk or some such, and he felt no need to trust to his host's silence regarding such matters as raiding and bloodshed. He slowly circled the room, peering through cracks in the wall, listening intently for sounds of anyone on the other side. Finally, he returned to his bench.

"I can't hear anyone outside, but that doesn't mean they aren't there. I suggest we keep this talk for tomorrow, once away from here." He grinned suddenly. "All the same, I'm in favour!"

CHAPTER TWENTY-SIX

The people of the bay fort sent their guests away with fresh supplies and promises of friendship when they came again; for their part, the Felag men gave them gifts of silver rings and bronze cloak-pins in the Irish style, with equally warm assurances of friendliness and honest intentions whenever they returned. There was no duplicity in any of this: the Felag had never raided their settlement, the geography being against any such action, but also, the fort in the bay had always been a good market, and no sensible businessman would wish to upset such an arrangement. As for the island people, their view was that one ship was not enough of a threat to worry about, but, if kept friendly towards them, might be a useful asset in times of danger from elsewhere. This was a time when threats could come from any direction, and when friends only stayed that way for as long as it was in their interests to do so.

To reach the monastery Snorri had spoken of meant sailing around practically the entire island, in either direction. If they headed south, their course took them through the narrow straight separating the island from the Welsh lands proper. The currents were strong, and the passage difficult, not only because of the need for vigorous rowing the whole way, but also because on the landward side it became the estates of Pawl, and men there would undoubtedly be watching. Once through the channel, they then had to steer north-west, going against the tides that swept into the big bay between island and mainland, and come upon the monks from their southern shore. Before they reached that goal, however, they would need to sail unchallenged past the hall of the Welsh king, and Hrolf was not even certain just where that lay. It certainly wasn't visible from their ocean- path.

Alternatively, they could head out to sea, going roughly north, and cruise around the ocean side of Ongle-sey. This would take them around the top edge of the island, and with a
final fast approach across the smaller northern bay, they could reach their destination much easier. As for landing-places, there was one, and one only, on either side of the monk's little
headland in the western extremity of the Angle's Isle. No watchers to worry about, but lots of potentially dangerous seaways, and an uncertain anchorage at the end of it. Hrolf was thinking long

and hard as the ship pulled away from the beach, the waving and cheers of their recent hosts mingling into the sounds of surf and swell. The sky was cloudy but the wind, once clear of the cliffs, was strong and steady. Finally, when they were far enough out, he made up his mind and pulled the steerboard over, sending them northwards, around the top of the island.

"Harder sailing, less rowing," he explained to Einar, who was sharing the aft-deck with him at the time. "The southern way takes us through the narrow channel, and it's a fight on the oars all the way. If we go around the top of the island, the wind and current do most of the work for us - if we get it right. Ship the oars!" he shouted forward. Brynjolf and Snorri waved acknowledgement, and gave the command. Twenty long, wet oars rattled aboard, and were stowed lengthways down the spine of the ship, with a minimum of fuss or confusion, Hrolf noted with some approval. As soon as the last oar was down, the crew turned to the ropes, and once again hauled the yard to the top of the mast, jumping clear as the sail shook itself open and grabbing at the loose lines in order to tie them off and put some wind into the woollen field. He turned to Einar again. "Want a turn at the steering?"

"I'd love to," he replied, so Hrolf stepped aside and relaxed on the rail as Einar planted his feet wide and got a feel for the vessel. By the mast, Snorri looked over and grinned encouragement.

Hrolf reckoned they could do this trip in a day, taking advantage of good winds and no upsetting currents to worry about; providing they kept the ship well away from the shore,
the chances of getting caught in a bad tide were minimal as well, and any watching eyes would assume they were heading out to sea in the direction of Ireland. All well and good; as an added bonus, it meant they were likely to arrive at the monastery in a reasonable state to do their work straight away, and not have to risk waiting around for unwelcoming local levies to arrive. So they sailed on; there were enough men in the ship to be able to take turns at the sail-ropes and the steerboard, while the others rested, mended gear, and ate. As the land veered away to the west, Einar turned the ship to follow, shouting changes to the sail-men of the moment in order for them to tack the sail and keep the wind filling it. As they sailed further and

further from the direction of the wind, Hakon fished out the *beitiass*, and fixed it into its sewn socket in the sail's bottom corner. The other end was manhandled into the side of the ship, wedged between the strakes and the nearest rib, and once in, it kept the sail taut without the need for further tightening of the ropes.

The coastline of Ongle-sey slowly changed as the ship went on, becoming more convoluted and filled with little inlets, bays and cliffs that rose straight out of the sea. Waves became something of a danger to any vessel that strayed too close to their feet, pushed against the rock by the full force of an open ocean. But Einar was proving to be a good steersman, whose lessons from earlier trips had not entirely deserted him. It was only with some difficulty that Hrolf persuaded him to give up the oar, in order to rest and prepare himself for the *strandhogg* ahead. All the Felag-men would be leading this expedition, so Hrolf put one of Snorri's followers, older even than his master, at the steersman's place.

"We'll lose the wind as we head into the north bay," called Hrolf to his colleagues, "so we need to be ready on the oars. Strong, fast men, the best we all brought."

"No help if it tires them too much for walking," observed Brynjolf.

"Nothing else for it," came the reply. "We need a fast cruise over that water, or the monks will see us coming in time to get away."

"Providing they leave their silver behind, does that matter?"

Hrolf shrugged. "Perhaps not; but running to our friends across the island, or to this king's house, to say what we've done, isn't such a good idea. Let's compromise," he added, to forestall any further discussion, "and put a mix of the lads to work. There aren't enough spare to make much difference anyway, when we're rowing. Pick one each, your weakest of those you want to take ashore, and he doesn't row. That way, they should all end up around the same!"

All the Felag- men appreciated the need to keep a guard over the ship when engaged in this sort of

business, and of a total crew of thirty- two, only twenty were needed to row. One
more steered, another kept watch at the prow; with the ship's owners excusing themselves from most duties on the grounds of their position, that left just six to juggle. Hrolf wanted Kol and Arne on the raid, to find out just how experienced at such work the brothers really were; Jon would go without any doubt, and Erlend was probably best kept on a short lead for now, as well as being useful for translating. If they each took their best five, that would leave eight on ship: probably enough to ward off any local trouble. So, one more for his share. After a little thought, he decided on Hakon, a nimble, wiry character who seemed likely to be useful in tight places. For the rest of the year, he was a hunter and trapper in the scrubland of Walea, and, in all probability, he went much further afield. At any rate, he turned up for the chance of ship-duty every spring, and usually brought bribery for the kitchen with him.

Soon after they broke out the day-meal rations, Hrolf saw the headland approaching that marked the tip of the northern bay. He strode aft to speak with old Otkel, who listened intently and then followed the ship-master's instructions exactly, turning the ship to follow the waves parallel to the shoreline. As Hrolf had predicted, the wind that had taken them along the top of Ongle-sey began to fade away; before he could even call the command, Einar and Snorri had the oars out, and the men set to rowing.

The coastline they followed actually formed two bays, a wide outer stretch, and a much smaller inner one at its base. From the far side of this inner bay, the men aboard could see their landing- place opposite, a small patch of faded gold in a face of grey, wet rock. The settlement they were intending to visit was above them, beyond the top of the cliffs, and set some way back in order to collect fresh rainwater rather than sea-spray. This was an advantage for the ship- men, as it meant the inhabitants were unlikely to be watching for them.

The mouth of the inner bay was easily crossed, cut off as it largely was from the force of the ocean proper. A final dash on the oars and a push on the steerboard found them just aground on the little beach, enough to float off again when the time came, but firmly enough not to drift away. As a safeguard, however, they ran a line ashore and secured it deep in the sand.

That done, the chosen men gathered their weapons and followed their chieftains ashore. A few final instructions to those left behind, and the shore party set off towards the path that wound upwards into the cliffs.

CHAPTER TWENTY- SEVEN

In the lowering light of the afternoon, twenty-four men trod quietly up the path towards the flat, green sward that topped the cliffs of the monk's lands. Weak sun shone through clouds on the grey iron of spears and the round bosses of shields. Mindful of the impression it could convey, their four leaders had all put on their mailshirts and iron helmets, and carried swords at their sides; but now, in that oppressive heat of wet summers, the sweat was already soaking into their shirts and breeks as they plodded onwards.

"Keep the strongest fresh and ready, you said…" panted Brynjolf.

Hrolf chuckled. "So I lied…"

"Nonsense," put in Snorri. "You just didn't include us in that command! My men are well enough, look at 'em."

"It's a bit early for grumbling, surely," said Einar. "We aren't even in sight of the place yet."

The Felag had visited this place before, but that had been when Eyvind was still with them. For all their complaining, none of them was that out of condition - the lifestyle of their time precluded such luxuries as excess fat for most - and they knew very well exactly where their target was. The monks of this place had chosen to build their houses right on a cliff-top on the far side of the land to the northern beach, but having said that, it was a fair march from the other one as well. Clearly they valued their isolation, which would go ill with them since it also placed a low value on lookouts or warning beacons. It was not a particularly wealthy establishment, especially not when compared to the great houses of Northumbria or Ireland, but it was the largest monastery in this part of the world, and that made it worth "visiting" every few years, since even the Welsh were very aware of the necessity of keeping in with those who helped their souls to heaven. Hrolf had been in churches, sometimes even on legitimate business, but despite being signed over (purely for the purposes of trade), he had never really understood how this idea of paying other people to keep cleansing your spirit was supposed to work. He imagined it was like having house-thralls, but he didn't remember ever having to give *them* money for their work. But then, he wasn't entirely certain he had a spirit in the sense that the churches claimed he did. Hrolf remained convinced that when he went to the God's realms after his death, all of him would be travelling together. How could it be that only bits of the church-followers went somewhere else? What was supposed to happen to the rest of them? Maybe that was where the stories of corpses coming out of their mounds had started. He didn't know, and perhaps more importantly, he didn't much care. By the time any of this became important, it would be too late to wonder about the mechanics of the process, after all. In the meantime, monasteries were for pillaging; he could use their silver far better than they ever did. There might even be thralls for the taking, which would make Dubhllyn an obvious next stop. There was always a thriving market for such things in most of the *longphorts* along the coast of the Irish Sea.

It took them no time at all to walk the intervening distance, and before very long, the low, stone-and-turf built chapel and huts of the settlement appeared over a low rise. The ship-men were approaching from upwind, but Hrolf did not expect the monks to be able to smell them. They might hear, though, unless he and his fellows were careful. There did not appear to be anyone about in the small fields outside the narrow wall, so he supposed they were all either eating or praying at this time.

"Swiftly then, to the gate there," whispered Brynjolf, evidently thinking along the same lines. Gathering up their weapons, the men ran towards the rampart, looking for any sign of an accompanying ditch. Sweat ran from under the brow of his helmet into Hrolf's eyes, little trickles that stung and blinded. He shook them out quickly, and led his men on.

Twenty-four bodies hugged the wooden uprights of the outer wall, not so much a defence as a demarcation, even after having been attacked in previous years. The wall was barely even a man's height, nor was it very thick; there was no ditch. The Felag had left the place alone last summer, partly to let them restock their silver, but mainly because the business with Pawl had required a hasty rethink of their plans. The year before, they had gone north, to Mann and the islands beyond, along the Galwaeg coast. Two years was a long time in anyone's memory, and Hrolf was aware that the monks had wine and beer to cloud their minds just as they clouded his on occasions. So, all in all, it was likely that the Felag had been forgotten since their last visit.

That suited him fine.

He sent Arne to peer round the edge of the gateway, and was pleased to see his half-brother Kol guarding the rear as he went. Brynjolf and the others waited impatiently for a report; after what seemed forever, Arne waved an all-clear, and they went forward as a group.

"From what I remember," said Hrolf in a low voice, "there is a kirk straight ahead as we go in. The working buildings, kitchen and such, are to the left; the little houses the monks live in are scattered to the right. Who wants where?"

"I'll take the houses," offered Snorri. "Are we collecting useful ones?"

"Yes, if there aren't too many of 'em. We'll have to feed 'em, remember."

"Not if I go to the kitchens," said Brynjolf. "Einar, if you go with Hrolf and see what they've got in the kirk…?"

"Gladly. Are we ready then?"

Hrolf and Einar both sent one extra man to go with Snorri, it being likely that most of the monks not at work or prayer would be in their separate little cells, small grass-covered houses set into the hard ground of this place, so that from the gate they resembled little oblong grave-mounds. Hakon and Bard waved a quick farewell as they headed across the yard behind Snorri; Brynjolf went next, to cover the other flank. Then it was their turn.

"Keep close," whispered Hrolf to his companion as they sprinted towards the church door.

Once by the walls of the solitary stone building, it became clear that most of the community was indeed within: praying voices could be heard through the high, narrow slits that served as windows. Hrolf quickly looked over the faces of the men around him.

"We go in, we knock them aside, we finish them if we need to - or if you want to," he added as an afterthought, although he doubted many of his crew, taken from their farm chores and workshops, would care for such cold slaying. But you never knew. "We want their silver, gold, any treasures you can find. If there are any youngish men, who look able to work, try not to
batter them too much, alright?"

"And if they fight back?" asked Arnfinn.

Einar shrugged. "I know you, you enjoy a fight as much as any man! Just finish it quickly, is all."

"Come on, then," said Hrolf. He pulled his axe from his belt, and swung it idly. "In we go." His hand was already on the iron latch of the door; he pushed it open as quickly as he could, plunging in after it. Einar followed, so close he could hear his breathing, then the others, making more noise. Heads turned at the sound of the door; men in rough everyday clothes, the shorter shirts and ankle-length trews of the field-worker and the very poor, gathered at the far end of the room, began to take in what was happening and looked for a way out. There was none: Jon and Steinar had taken the job of blocking the door as their mates surged forwards. Hrolf brought his shield up, not to defend himself but to act as a battering ram to the furniture around him. Candles toppled. A middle-aged monk made as if to fight, bringing huge, soilsmith's fists up into view. Hrolf swung the shield into his face, which ended the argument, and strode towards the apse, the little alcove at the far end where he knew all the most precious things were kept. By this time, the other members of the community had scattered; there were only a dozen or so, and none of them carried more than a little table-knife. They were no match for even a handful of men with spears, and they had nowhere to run to. So, whilst Jon and Steinar continued to hold the door, Kol, Erlend and Eirik pushed them all into a corner, and jabbed iron at any who tried to move.

Einar brought Arnfinn and Thorbjorn over to join Hrolf and Arne. "That was simple enough; is this where it all happens?"

"Never been in a kirk, then? Yes, this is the place where they do whatever it is they feel they have to." Hrolf looked around at the paintings adorning the walls. "This table is the centre of it all... usually there are chests around it, and stuff on the top. Like

this," he said, picking up a silver goblet and a tray. "Anyone got a box, or a bag? No? Well then, we'll have to see if
the others found anything useful." He pointed at the huddle of monks. "Get 'em outside, lads, and let's see if they're worth taking with us."
One of the prisoners said something in a haughty, defiant tone. Hrolf looked enquiringly at Erlend.

"He says he'd not expected us to return, sir. He seems surprised we are still alive; I take it he means you, sir, and any others who came last time."

"Hit him, and tell him to shut up. Clearly we are stronger than whatever wyrd he was invoking against us." He motioned Einar and Jon to him. "Jon, keep a few men here and help Erlend with this lot. We're going to see how Brynjolf and Snorri have done so far."

He sent Kol off to look for rope with which to bind their captives, and, leaving the others in the yard, headed over towards the storerooms with Einar. The door to the building was barred from the inside, but since the wall of this building was only wattle-and-daub, Hrolf used his axe to smash through that instead. Once inside, they found dried food, firewood and a few small barrels of something: Hrolf guessed it was drinkable, and made a mental note to send someone for them afterwards. Farming tools stood in one corner, but of treasure there was no trace at all.

"Could it all have been in that chapel?" wondered Einar. "it looks a pretty poor place all over, to my eyes."

"Hard to argue that point," agreed Hrolf, albeit reluctantly. "Snorri won't be happy if he's brought us all this way for so little. Maybe Brynjolf can still make it worth the trip, eh?"

The Master of the Burgh had indeed had better luck, for adjacent to the kitchen he had stumbled – literally - upon a step leading into the abbot's own quarters. Now he sat, rubbing a
twisted ankle with one hand, but running the other through a little box of coin.

"Ah, you got here then," he commented as his man Harald led them through the doorway. "Not only food to spare, but this pretty find, too. Got a spear?"

"Here, sir," replied Ljotolf, handing his master a weapon that scratched the top of the little cell. Brynjolf nodded thanks and hauled himself upright on it.

"Might be a good idea to look under his bed and in his chest. I haven't searched it properly: too busy trying to sit before I fell. Bloody stupid place to put a step…"

The abbot's chest contained better clothing than he would ever need in this place, and a small amount of silver ornaments, which were quickly added to the coinage. The kitchen had yielded a spare bag, and the proceeds of the raid were deposited within it. Other sacks were filled with food: mostly smoked or dried, which would survive for longer than the fresh bread Olvir had rescued from the oven. Hrolf decided to take that as well, on the basis that such things were a rare treat aboard ship, and they might have extra mouths to feed.

Back into the courtyard, where they found Snorri waiting for them. Most of the cells had been empty when he went in, and so he had just scooped up whatever he could see, and was now busily examining it all for items of value. Those few huts with inhabitants were now also empty, and their occupiers stood with the captives from the chapel. The man who had spoken earlier seemed about to do so again, but on catching sight of the bags carried by Brynjolf's men, he appeared to change his mind, his shoulders sagging imperceptibly.

"What's the story with him?" asked Brynjolf, catching sight of the gesture. "Is he the head man here, or what?"

Erlend asked the question; the man in question nodded, and uttered a brief sentence in return.

"He is the abbot, sir," translated the thrall. "He says his name is Daffydd, and that he has some worth to one of the noble families in Powys. That's a place further south, I believe, sir."

"Not enough worth for us to wait around, though," muttered Snorri. Hrolf tended to agree with him.

"Erlend, ask him if he has any other stuff here to buy his life with…"

This seemed to have more of an effect on the other monks. Some shook their heads sadly; others

looked as if the life had already left their eyes. Their leader answered, and even the
Felag-men understood entirely what he meant. There was no other treasure to be had.

Hrolf stared hard at the man. He did not believe him; the answer had been too quick. An idea began to form.

"Einar, Brynjolf: indulge me. Take these others outside, and take Erlend with you. Ask them again, away from him."

"You and Snorri going to finish him, then?"

"Don't know yet." He scratched his nose, which in an iron helm with a bar over one's face, is not the easiest thing to do. "Depends on what he does or says next, I think."

Brynjolf looked unhappy with the plan. "Who's going to talk for you? You don't know enough of their tongue to catch it all, especially not if he talks quickly."

"Ah, but I don't want him talking, I want him showing! Now go; we're losing the light."

Brynjolf nodded. "I'll post someone to listen for you, and I'll sort out some torches."

He and Einar set four of their followers to herd the captives out of the gate; Snorri and Hrolf both sent men back into the buildings, to search them more thoroughly. That done, Hrolf motioned the abbot to sit (two other men remained behind him, however), then took off his helmet and sat on his haunches, looking into the Welshman's eyes. A steady, fearless gaze met him.

"My use of your words is not good," Hrolf began, using the Welsh tongue, "but I can say enough. You think that I will not kill you because you are of good birth and family. Is that right?"

The abbot nodded, but did not deign to speak. Hrolf stroked his beard, then continued. "You also think that I will not kill you if we do not find the rest of your gold and silver?"

The abbot thought for a moment, then shook his head. "If there is not enough for you to take, whether I hide it or not, you will kill us all."

"Yet we did not kill you all last time we came, did we? You at least remember us."

"Yes, I remember you. Or your kind. Perhaps last time, you had enough to satisfy your lusts and greed."

"So it would be a good thing, then, would it not, to bring out your other things: your books, and your staff, and the big cross that sits on the table... then, from what happened last time, you and your men would not be killed. My friends are asking the others where all these things are, even as we speak here, because *I* think they would not say in your hearing, if you had told them not to. And then, when we have these things, and we go away, you can send word to your family that you are alive, but that you need more of these things, to replace what we have taken from you. There is no shame in that; there was nothing you could do to stop us, after all."

The abbot frowned. "There was so much shame for me last time, that I was hardly able to bear it. I could not bear it again."

Hrolf sighed. "Then I will be obliged to kill you. You are too old to sell…"

"I have already said that I have worth in Powys."

Hrolf laughed. "I'm hardly going to wait around for your noble family to bring a ransom, now am I? No, sir, I am afraid that it ends here, for you… unless you show me what I want to see." He stood up, and reached for Ragnar's spear. "This is your final chance."

True to his word, Brynjolf had posted his best man as lookout, one Asbjorn, whose sight and hearing far surpassed any of his fellows. Although he could not follow what was being
said between Hrolf and the abbot, he could hear the tone of the words, and when Hrolf stood up and took Ragnar's spear, it was as clear a sign as could be. He whistled, catching the attention of both Felag-men. Hrolf stopped, and looked to the gate; Brynjolf, for his part, left Einar to instruct Erlend in what to say, and strode back into the yard, meeting Hrolf half-way.
"Any joy?" he asked hurriedly.

"He'd rather die than reveal anything. And you?"

"I'm hoping that Erlend is putting the question now. There's a couple of 'em might be worth the taking, but none outstanding."

Hrolf looked around him. "Hardly suprising, in a place like this." As he spoke, Einar appeared through the fences and waved them over. "Ah! What's this?"

"They cracked when Erlend told them their abbot would be killed," explained Einar when they reached him. "The good bits are kept in a stone box, under the floor of the chapel, in that little alcove, I think." Erlend nodded agreement.

"Right then; the abbot can live, I think - unless he suddenly turns nasty on us, but I somehow think he's past his fighting days. Take out the ones you want to go with us, and head 'em towards the beach. Einar, Erlend: with me, if you would?"

They headed back in, taking Snorri along with them, and heading for the church. Hrolf threw Ragnar his spear back as they passed, and grinned triumphantly at the old man still sitting in the dust. Once they had pushed the altar-table over, and exposed the floor, the lid of the cyst was plain to see; Einar fetched a candle-post to use as a crowbar, and between them, they got the slab off easily. Sure enough, inside was a good sized bag of fine woven wool, which clanked promisingly as they lifted it up. Within it, even in the dim light of the chapel, the sheen of precious gems and metals was plain. Snorri chuckled, and clapped his hands.

"Worth coming for, then, yes?"

"Indeed," answered Einar. "There's enough there to keep us all well-fed over winter, I'd say."

"You're not wrong," agreed Hrolf, "not wrong at all." He stood up. "Well, I think that now we are finished here. One final sweep through the kitchen, and away."

"Then to Dubhllyn?" asked Snorri. "We could do with offloading those extra bodies as soon as we can."

"Dubhllyn sounds good, if the seas will let us. They ought to; it seems we have luck on our side. A good treasure and no need for fighting; what more could we ask?"

CHAPTER TWENTY-EIGHT

As they would with sheep, the men of the Felag herded the remainder of the monks back inside their fences, before following the captives and their escorts back towards the ship.
Their victims made no attempt to follow, or to prevent their leaving; what would startled, unarmed men do against such a force?

Night was soon upon them, making the going dangerous down the cliffs as shadows grew and merged into an ever greater darkness. Fortunately, the men left aboard had had the foresight to light a torch on the prow, and this was just enough to guide their ship-mates back to them without any more harm than wrenched ankles and grazed knuckles. Arnfinn managed to lose his knife from its sheath, but it was a small price to pay for not drowning in the surf.

"If it was any brighter, I'd say to pull away and find another mooring," announced Hrolf as he came aboard, "but in this darkness, it would be courting disaster to do it." He frowned. "We'll have to stay put for tonight, friends, even though it goes against all sense."

"Oh, I'd think we'll be alright," opined Jon. "After all, if it's this dark, nobody's going to send for help either, are they? I didn't see any horses up there, and there's no boats here."

"He has a point," added Brynjolf. "I say put the tent up on deck, and open a barrel. We did well today."

"Yes, we're owed a little celebration," agreed Hrolf, "there's no argument about that! Alright then: my men, get the awning up, and uncover the fire. Get some food on, someone? And enough for these," he added, pointing at their captives huddled between the bench-tops. "Are they still tied? Put a line around their ankles, and string it between them; then we can let their hands free to eat. I'm not feeding them like children!"

Eager hands sprang to the tasks. Soon the yard-arm was turned on the mast, and set on its stands; then the tent-sheet was hung over this, to cover the heads of the ship-men, and a pot was set to simmer on the flames of the firebox. They made free with the supplies taken from the monks, an irony that did not go unnoticed by their captives, who, as soon as food was brought to them, began chanting over it before they would touch a morsel.

Brynjolf looked over at them in disgust. "If they're going to make that racket all the bloody time, then throw them overboard, they ain't worth the trouble!" he spat. "Erlend, tell 'em that, would you?"

Hrolf's thrall conveyed the message, and the singing abruptly stopped. Satisfied, Brynjolf went back to his meal.

*

From their mooring, it should only be a two, perhaps three-day crossing to the numerous Norse settlements that dotted the eastern coastline of the Irish lands. Hrolf and Snorri were agreed that, if conditions and luck were with them, Dubhllyn would be the landing of choice. Hrolf had relatives there who had proved friendly in the past, and this fact of previous visits to the place of the black pool made their welcome more predictable. Not that they were totally unknown in other places: they had traded well in Cork one year, and had visited Water Ford on occasion. But Dubhllyn held a special appeal, and so it was with this in mind that Hrolf set their course the following morning.

Pulling away from the little beach under oars, the men had to row them a long way out of the northern bay before there was even a trace of a wind. When it did finally come, it blew from the west, rather than from the north as before. Snorri clambered back towards the steer-deck, looking worried.

"This will take us back towards the Welsh!" he called, totally needlessly as far as Hrolf was concerned. Then he remembered that Einar might not have realised yet. "We can't take the ship into this wind head-on!"

"If we veer north, we might catch enough of it to make some sort of headway," answered Hrolf, "but it's likely we'll miss any sort of haven we know. We'll have to head to the south, until it changes. Hopefully that'll be before we hit the Welsh shore again. It makes Cork more likely than Dubhllyn, though." He looked absently down the length of the ship, barely seeing the cargo and the prisoners sitting atop it, the men ranged along either side, or the ominous turning and flapping of the sail as Brynjolf and Einar oversaw it's raising.

"Thinking of Pawl?" asked Snorri.

Hrolf shook himself. "Not really; just trying to decide what's our best course here." He creased his brow in thought. "It wouldn't hurt to pour a little beer over the side, I'm thinking."

Snorri nodded. "Good idea! Always best to have the Gods on our side, especially with those aboard." He nodded towards the captive monks, who were looking at the surrounding waves and murmuring to each other. Snorri went forward again, taking one of his men with him from the benches, and dipped a cup into the ale-barrel when he returned. If he said any words, they were lost in the wind; but the beer went over the rail and was devoured by the sea. Hrolf caught Snorri's eye, and they both silently hoped for a break in the weather.

CHAPTER TWENTY-NINE

The ocean-god was clearly not in the mood for ale: the wind got stronger, if anything, and the tides around the tip of the monk's isle threatened to put them into the rocks at any moment.
Hrolf found he needed Thorhall's extra strength and muscle on the steer-board simply to keep the ship safe, and the oars made as much headway as the sail. The waves grew larger, sending water into the belly of the ship, and pitching it from side to side almost constantly. To add to their concerns, from watching the coastline alongside them, it was clear that they were being driven back towards the lands of Pawl the Welshman.

"I thought you said you wouldn't press this matter!" shouted Brynjolf with a laugh.

"Don't blame me, just find out what Thor and Aegir are wanting for their day-meal, before we get smashed to bits!" joked Hrolf in return. He looked forwards. "Are they wailing again?"

"We could ask Erlend to tell them to be quiet, if it helps..."

"Or," said Snorri darkly, "we could enquire whether the Thunderer has a taste for meat today."

Einar looked over at him. "Is it that desperate already, that we talk of throwing good cargo overboard?"

"Not really, I suppose, but that chanting is beginning to get on my - and Brynjolf's - nerves a bit."

Einar grinned wryly. "I won't argue there."

The captives themselves had quietened down during this exchange, and Hrolf began to wonder if one of them at least could speak his own tongue. His eyes narrowed, and, leaving the steering to Thorhall, he carefully stepped his way towards the mast.

"You," he growled, pointing at one of the men, "you understand this, don't you?"

"I know some, sir." Came the reply. Hrolf nodded with a cold smile.

"Do you know enough to understand what we have been saying?"

"That the old one and the big man want to throw us to the sea? Yes, I understood that much." He looked at his companions. "Your killing us to appease these spirits you worship will make no difference to the wind or the waves. We do not fear death; our Lord awaits us."

"I don't doubt it, but if you keep up that sort of annoying noise, you'll be going to him sooner rather than later." A further thought suddenly struck Hrolf. "Are you by any chance calling this lord of yours down on us, as well?"
There was no answer beyond a stubborn silence and a defiant stare.

"Well, we'll see," said Hrolf. "My money is still on our getting out of this without any real damage. What will you do when that happens, hmm?" And with that, he returned aft.

The wind continued steady but not dangerous - but it continued to blow them south and a little east for the rest of the day. After a while, the crew got used to the conditions, and the mood lightened somewhat. The first clear sighting of the Welsh coast was greeted with a degree of derision and good-natured joking in the direction of Hrolf's missing finger by his fellows, but the captives amidships appeared to be less happy with their lot, and their presence escalated from mere prayers and chanting to actual interference with any crewman who had to go near them. When Olaf headed towards the rear, one of the monks managed to trip him, and he came up with a blooded nose from the fall. Unsurprisingly, he lashed out at the nearest, sending the man sprawling just as he had done. As one of Snorri's crewmen, it was his master's task to drag him away, but the old man soon joined his fellow owners at the steer-board.

"We can't allow that sort of thing," he said, with real anger in his eyes. "They're becoming too much of a liability now. If they try that sort of trick here, out in open sea, how will we ever get rid of them in any civilised market?"

"Sad though I am to lose the chance of the money tied up in them, I agree," said Brynjolf. "If we have to beat 'em nearly to death just to keep 'em quiet, what's the point in keeping them at all?"

"How say you, Einar?" prodded Hrolf.

Einar shrugged. "I don't want my men near them, and their wailing is becoming more annoying every time they start it up, so if we choose to ditch them, I'll not complain."

"That makes us all agreed, then. Thorhall, stay and steer; we'll take one man each, and send them to the fishes. I'm agreed with you, friends, but as always in our fellowship, we lead, and we always go in front. So it's up to us to heave them over the rail."

The monks saw them approach, of course, and even if they did not speak the same tongue, they undoubtedly guessed what was about to happen. The one who had spoken before looked suddenly haggard and tired; the other two, somewhat younger, were getting scared. One tried to fight, but a fist to the skull put an end to that; as soon as his limp form was thrown overboard, however, his fellows appeared to decide they too had nothing to lose by fighting. The other young man broke his bonds and leaped for Einar, leaving deep gouges in his face and arms from nails and teeth. But to no avail; the remaining shiplords closed in, and between them, he too went over the side. The old one stood tall and defiant, but gave nothing but spit and words in the faces of his executioners. And so they were dispatched, one by one, until all three were small specks in the waves far behind. The ship sailed on, uncaring as to their fate, as driven by the wind as before; and still that wind pushed them ever-nearer to the lands held by Pawl the Welshman.

CHAPTER THIRTY

"This weather's getting up again," murmured Brynjolf to Hrolf some time later that day, "it has the smell of rain and trouble in it. What do you want to do? It'll be dark sooner than later, from those clouds."

"I've been keeping an eye on the shore, as well," answered Hrolf. "Not much has changed since last time. There are any number of places we can put ashore for the night, without too much worry about visitors."

"I'm all for putting in for tonight," added Einar, joining them at the steer-board. "We need good seas for crossing to Mann, or Ireland, surely; better than this, at any rate." He sniffed. "I think we may be guests of the Welshmen for a few days."

Hrolf shrugged. "This is Pawl's holding, although I think we're towards the north of it, so going ashore doesn't hold any great fears. He may be on the move this early in the year, but I've not seen any fires to suggest his men are watching for us, and we did well enough on the Island that I'm not expecting them to send messages about us. Jon, go and let

Snorri know, and I'll put ashore on the next cove with a beach."

The bay the ship eventually sailed into was small, but cut well into the coastline, affording a small degree of shelter. It was deep enough to bring the vessel nearly to the tide-line, and so they threw the anchor-stones overboard and ran extra lines onto the beach itself, to provide a little insurance against the coming storm. Einar's men fashioned a windbreak from debris lying around, which allowed a small fire, set deep in a pit of sand, over which the cauldron was set to boil. After that, it was merely a matter of putting up the tent, bringing the weapons and blankets ashore, and waiting to see what the night would bring.

CHAPTER THIRTY-ONE

It was not the night, but the next day that brought a hint of future problems. Walking along the beach, away from the ship, and trying to judge the strength of the wind further out, Brynjolf's lookout-man, Asbjorn, spotted smoke coming from a short way inland. The country rose steeply into cliffs beyond the beach, so he could not tell if this smoke was from a beacon or a dwelling, or even a wild fire, but it was enough to decide the Felag-men that it was time to be on their way. Long years of experience began to tell, now: apart from their shelter, very little had been brought ashore apart from weapons and shields, and it was all easily carried back aboard. Looking to seaward, the clouds still loomed dark and dangerous, but the promised storm had so far not appeared, much to everyone's surprise.

They did not hurry their departure: here was a ship of capable, well-armed men, quite able to deal with any trouble that might come their way. So when an arrow whizzed into the sand a short way ahead of Brynjolf as he stood surveying the scene with his men, he was somewhat taken aback. He stooped, and retrieved it, looking up to the cliffs to see from whence it had come.

On the heels of more arrows, a knot of men appeared from a gully at the top of the beach, two with bows and the others holding long spears. None wore helms, and only three had shields. Clearly these were local men, come to see who their visitors were, and what they wanted.

"Want to pay them for their arrow?" Hrolf asked Brynjolf, who was still standing where the first shaft had landed, and staring up at the newcomers.

"Not particularly: they missed, after all, and from the way they hold those bows, I reckon they'd have got me if they wanted to. Do we know any of them?"

Hrolf shrugged. "Can't tell from here. They don't look especially noteworthy, do they? I'd be surprised if this was any more than the local farmhands and their boss - him in the bright green shirt. Even Pawl turned them out better than this."

"Maybe he had a leaner winter than us."

Men were looking towards them for orders: to load the ship, or come back with weapons. Hrolf looked around for Erlend, and motioned him over.

"Do you know any of these men from your days here?"

Erlend shook his head. "You and I met a bit to the south of here, sir; this is not my home country either." He squinted up the beach. "It's too far to really see their faces, sir, but I don't expect I would know them - or them me."

"Yes, I thought as much. You know the language, though, better than we do. Tell them we were just going."

Erlend shouted the message, but the men did not give any sign they had heard. So, he walked slowly towards them, Olaf beside him with a shield, until about a third of the distance had gone. Bows were raised as he drew nearer, but no arrows came, as he repeated the words. Hrolf did know quite a bit of the Welsh tongue, and at times, certain words struck him as similar to some of his own language; he had followed more of the talk on Ongle-sey than Brynjolf had appeared to think, and he had known enough to get what he had wanted from its inhabitants. But on the whole he preferred to leave such tasks to those who did them best. His turn came when they reached the longphort at Dubhllyn, for not only did he know *that* tongue very well, but he also still had family there.

"What did they say?" he shouted, as Erlend headed back towards him. The thrall shrugged.

"Nothing, my lord; not a word that I could hear."

"This is odd," opined Brynjolf. "Clearly they're not hirdmen; clearly they don't want us going any closer to them, but in that case, why not at least exchange pleasantries and keep us happy? If we chose to, we could charge straight over this little gang, and never even notice them. I'd think they'd either be fighting us by now, or running off; and yet there they stand. What's going on?"

"Forget them," advised Snorri. "Let's get the loading done, and be away."

"Maybe," countered Hrolf, groping dimly for understanding. "If a ship beached on your holding, what would you do?"

"Me? Go out and meet them."

"And if there were only you and a handful of thralls at home when they came?"

Comprehension dawned. "I'd send a runner to you, and Einar, and all my other neighbours; and in the meantime, I'd go and watch 'em like a hawk."

"Yes," Hrolf nodded, "they're waiting for company to arrive, and we aren't meant to get away."

"Hard to see how they're going to stop us," murmured Brynjolf. "Are we loaded? Come on, then, let's be off for better profit than we'll have standing around here."

They walked back towards the ship. The men watching clustered into a knot, seemingly talking amongst themselves. No doubt, Hrolf thought, this had not been what they had expected to happen; what an anticlimax, to come out so bravely and have your opponents just walk away! He could hear snatches of their talk as he reached the bottom of the ladder-pole, and started up it; suddenly, his side was full of sharp, searing pain, his foot slipped off the rung and he tumbled face-first into the rail.

Above him, he heard voices, louder than the Welsh, although they seemed clearer too; hands grasped his arms and pulled upwards, over the ship's side, and he landed in a heap on the foredeck. Jon and Eirik pushed him flat against the timbers; Olaf was holding a shield up, guarding him from further injury. It seemed to be his task for the day. Hrolf's head began to clear, though his side still hurt abominably.

"Lie still," muttered Einar, crouching beside him. His bony fingers prodded and pushed. Finally, he grunted. "Not deep; very long range. One of 'em is a fine shot, at least."

"Wonderful," came Brynjolf's sarcastic reply, "it's nice to know we're fighting men of decent quality for once."

More pain, followed by someone pulling his shirts up around his chin. Hrolf managed to roll an eyeball downwards, and saw what looked like a river of his own blood welling out of a hole in his side where the pain had been.

"Looking for this?" asked Einar, holding out the arrow.

"I knew I should have packed my bow," joked Jon. "Look on the bright side; it isn't a mail-piercer, and it isn't a hunting head either."

Einar went aft to his usual place, and pulled a length of thread from his satchel, intending to sew the wound closed. Hrolf, meanwhile, once he was certain he wasn't about to die, started contemplating vengeance for such an insult. He tugged from his prone position on Brynjolf's hose until the other man bent to speak to him.

"What are they doing now?"

"Coming closer, bows ready and spears to the fore. Erlend, I need you up here to listen to them, I can't follow a word of what they're saying." He grabbed the thrall by the neck and hauled him to the rail. The Welshman listened intently.

"They are waiting for more men to come, in response to the signal Asbjorn saw earlier, my lords.

One of them has spoken the lord Pawl's name, too. They're wondering if they've killed you, sir."

"I'll soon put an end to that... I need to stand up. Jon: you may have left your bow behind, but I didn't. Go get it, string it, and wait for a good shot from the other end, where they won't see you. Soon as you get sight of the head man - shoot him." Jon grinned, and was gone.

Snorri was looking the crew over. "We're alright for a long while like this," he called. "So far, you're the only injured one, and that's not enough to kill you, from the look of it. There's, what, seven? - of them, and thirty-two of us, and I suppose we hold a sort of high ground, too." He sat back, turning his helmet over and over in his hands. "I can't see them causing us any serious problems."

"I can if their mates are on their way," winced Hrolf, "and while they hold the beach shooting arrows at us, we can't push the ship off, can we? We need to end this, and quickly, or we miss the tide and then they'll just wear us down over time. Where's my spear?"

"I doubt they're in range of that," said Brynjolf, "and we may need it later…"

"I'm not throwing it, I'm leaning on it!" Strong hands helped Hrolf from the deck; as his blanched face appeared to those below, their talk increased, with angry overtones. As he had guessed would happen, their apparent leader stepped forward to take another shot - but Jon got his in first, and the green-shirted man fell to the ground. His companions chose to retreat, rather than stand within bowshot and demand vengeance; the jeers of the ship-men followed them back up the strand.

As soon as he judged it safe enough, Brynjolf sent most of the crew over the side, to stand guard over an attempt to push the ship off the beach. Einar sewed Hrolf's side, whilst Jon got a silver ring for his marksmanship, and fine words of praise from all the Felag-men. But the ship would not move, and so they guessed they had missed the tide after all. Rather than be caught unawares on the beach, the men put the awning up over the deck, and prepared for a night on board. But in all the excitement and bustle of these new preparations, none saw the clouds in Erlend's eyes. More importantly, none noticed when, having gone onto the beach to attend to the ropes, he slipped away into the darkness.

CHAPTER THIRTY-TWO

Erlend's absence only became apparent when the pottage was cooked and everyone lined up for their share of it. Whilst freely admitting that the Welshman was nothing like as greedy as Yngvar, Hrolf could not recall his difficult slave ever missing a meal before. Perhaps of more immediate worry was the fact of a couple of knives and an axe not accounted for.

"What do you think's going on?" asked Snorri. Hrolf, who had not been moved from his place at the bow of the ship, attempted a shrug, but carefully, so as not to disturb Einar's stitches.

"I don't know what he's up to, or where he's gone: I wish I did, then at least I could plan what to do with him when the little shit gets back! If he comes back, of course; no reason why he might not have just taken the chance to bolt for home, and try worming back into Pawl's graces. But somehow, I think that might be too simple for Erlend."

"Expecting complications then, are you?" enquired Brynjolf on his way aft to the ale-cask.

"Why spoil the pattern of the winter?" Hrolf sighed. "Friends, I have, through my own lack of foresight, brought us into a messy business, which may yet cost us dearly. For this, I ask your pardon, and also that you put off any lawsuits until next year, when we've all got home and had time to weigh our losses more carefully."

Einar snorted. "Don't look for trouble from me, Hrolf. I'm the new man here, and up to now I have no complaints. You manage your men well enough, but I think we could all tell this
Erlend to be a handful. He wasn't always in thrall, was he?"

"No, we picked him up last year, near this very spot," answered Snorri, forestalling Hrolf's own reply and letting him get his breath back. He grinned. "That was a good fight! Hrolf here lost a finger - he seems to act as the gatherer of injuries for us - and, when Pawl backed away and ran, Erlend stayed, and put his spear at Hrolf's feet. Maybe he thought it was good payment for the wound. Maybe," he added, looking over at Hrolf, "now he feels he has discharged any debts to you."

"How so?" asked Hrolf. "What did I miss, that he did so well today?"

"He talked for us," mused Brynjolf, coming back in time to overhear Snorri's words, "and he was among those who pulled you up onto the ship, once you were shot." He rubbed his head, thinking. "And then you gave silver to Jon for his archery and we all gave fine words - and Erlend got hauled back to the side to talk and listen some more, without a thought for his own life from any of us, and thrall or no, that was poor behaviour from men such as we." He frowned, and settled down beside them. "Well, if he's gone, he's gone, and I suggest you declare him freed at the next Thing we're home for, and leave it at that."

Hrolf nodded. "That's well said, and right enough. I can see it would be more of a problem if he comes back, though."

He leaned back, resting his head on someone's rolled-up cloak. His world was one of discomfort, cold wood beneath and behind him, the ever-present dampness of shipboard clothes rubbing wetly on his skin, and the blinding, unceasing agony of both his wound and the sewing that now held it shut. He winced as he moved, every time he moved, and clenched his teeth against the pain. "I'd feel happier if I knew what he was doing."

CHAPTER THIRTY-THREE

Partly to make sure they were not surprised in the night, and partly to keep an eye out for Erlend should he return, the Felag-men posted a watch, from which only Hrolf was exempt on account of his wounding. Before he went to sleep, Einar looked over his sewing, and declared it clean and likely to mend well. Hrolf was far from certain that he would be able to sleep, but warm food and a few cups of ale soon had him snoring gently in the shelter of the foredeck.

All too soon, it seemed, he was gently nudged awake again. Arne and Kol's lean faces were crouched over him; behind them, he could hear the rest of the crew awake and quietly gathering weapons.

"Are you awake, lord?" whispered Kol. "Lie still; we'll tell you what goes on. No need to move about yet, sir; save your strength."

"What *is* going on, then?" asked Hrolf, somewhat testily.

"We were taking our watch when Erlend - or it sounded like Erlend - came back to the shore, sir. He shouted to us – must have seen us against the sky - and then came closer. Once we could see his face, it was Erlend. He is on the sand, sir, calling for you."

"We woke the other ship-masters first," added Arne, "and then came to you."

"Right," answered Hrolf, shaking sleep from him. "Is there anyone else with him?"

"We saw nobody else, sir, and he claims to be alone."

"Hmm. Brynjolf? Snorri? Einar? I'm not keen on taking men down to him in this light; if he does have any friends with him, we'd be easier meat on the strand. What say you to bringing him up here?"

"I can't see there's a lot of choice," replied Brynjolf. "He *is* still one of your men, I suppose, and you're in no fit state to go down off the ship. Let him come. Someone fetch benches for us, and uncover the firebox again, so we can see each other."

Stools were produced, and Hrolf lowered onto one, his fellow ship-owners ranged to either side. The ladder-pole was put over the side for Erlend to ascend, and once aboard, he knelt before his master.

"Very well Erlend," Hrolf began, wondering how to start this on the right sort of direction. "Where have you been, and why did you go without asking my leave?"

"I saw you wounded for the second time today," began the thrall, "and, as last time, I didn't think that wounding was right or fair. Knowing you to be occupied, I chose to act for you, and avenge this." He put a hand inside his shirt, and pulled out a little bag on a cord, which he passed to Hrolf. "In here you will find the truth of my word, lord. In this bag is a silver ring, taken from the hand of Pawl the Welshman. He is dead, and it was I who slew him, this night, in his own bed."

CHAPTER THIRTY-FOUR

"By all the Gods, Erlend, what have you done?" Hrolf's face was still pale from his wounds, but his thoughts sent it whiter still. "How badly did you want your life last year, that you forsook your lord and settled for servitude to me in order to keep it; and how badly now do you want out of that deal - a deal *you alone chose to strike* - that you would creep away from here and do this sort of a deed to the man you've already betrayed once before?"

He sat slowly, carefully, back on his stool, resting his back against the side of the ship and pulling a fleece around him for warmth. "All this last year you have been a bad bargain,
Erlend, for all I thought your war-skills worth having with me. All this last year I have closed my eyes to the deeper signs, which is my fault alone." He sighed, and winced from the pain. Brynjolf passed him a horn, saying nothing for the present.

"If anyone here had reason to slay Pawl, it was me. Me! I'm the one who lost a finger to him; I'm the one who's owed the blood-price here! Not much chance of collection now, is there, thanks to you. Now we have far worse to deal with than my intent of calling him out and demanding my wergeld could ever have brought on us; now we have a thrall who has gone out, in the night, and *murdered* a Thegn of the Welshmen. Don't interrupt me - you went under cover of night, so for all that you came here and declared the deed, it is murder, and payable as such. I bet you didn't wait around to declare what you did to his own bench-mates, did you? So a murder it most certainly will be counted. And don't forget, we're well beyond the dyke of the Mercians here, so it's their own laws they'll do you under – if they don't just come howling out to slay the lot of us." He wearily rubbed his face with his free hand, and sat staring into the firelight for long, long moments.

"I went out to seek a fair price for your wounds, lord," muttered Erlend, "and after the work I did for you earlier, I thought this enough to have met the price you put on me. When I was Pawl's man, this was often the way to further matters when they had reached a stalemate, and great would have been the thanks due me had I taken your head to his table."

"That," said Snorri harshly, "is because Pawl was the lord here, and we are less than welcome visitors.

Had he been sailing up to my shores, and his thrall had killed me without his leave, just to force a gift from him, would you have expected him to be grateful to that thrall? Hardly! You are a fool, Erlend, to think otherwise. From a tale worth the telling, this has descended into a desperate and dangerous hole for all of us… and all thanks to one idiot thrall who couldn't see beyond the end of his own nose!"

"It's not his nose that's the problem," sighed Hrolf. "As I told you on the island, friends, this has been brewing all winter. Erlend, I warned you that no good would come of taking you on a visit to Brynjolf's Burgh, and now we are at a cliff-face with few ways back from it. However, we are going to have to find one. So; we must mend this to our best advantage, and quickly, and then be gone from here just as swift, or at least prepare to fight off Pawl's household again 'till we can get away. I wouldn't mind betting there are still more of us than them, and they are without their head for a while. But you," he grated, staring hard at Erlend, "can expect little mercy or friendship from me for this. Yours was not the place to avenge me for my wound - Jon had already done that, and with far more skill – and this would not have been the way to do it even if that place had been yours. All our laws, be they from Dubhllyn or from the Mercians, say life must be paid for with life, eye with eye, or the money equivalent. No doubt the Welsh here have something similar. You have no money, so there is only your life for you to pay with.

"If you had only done this in the daylight, in plain fight and in sight of men and Gods, Pawl's men might have taken geld for their lord. But I can't see it happening for this sort of act. Not only did you creep into his hall and murder him, but they missed you doing it, and *that* stain will have to be paid for, too. You of all men must know that, for you were one of them! That debt can only be paid in blood, but the shame is theirs, so it's their lives that are shadowed. Pawl's house- men *will* come for us, they have no choice now, especially not after their deeds towards us earlier. If they discover it was you, their old bench-mate, who killed him in his bed, they won't rest until either they have you, dead or alive won't matter much, or they all lie dead at our hands - and then the forces will gather against us from even further afield. And I, for one, would rather be gone on the next good tide. I think our trip is over for this summer, on this coast at least."

"And with precious little to show for it, either," added Brynjolf. "Perhaps we can cut back across and try for Ireland again, if the storms have passed."

"Take the chance, I say," said Einar, "what do we have to lose? Better a good death than this messing around with wergelds and wagers." Brynjolf and Snorri nodded their agreement, and further out of the firelight, their men murmured assent.

"Right enough then," said Hrolf, "go we shall, on the morning tide. Are there enough of us fit to row? Remember how we were offered that forty-bencher in Cork that time, and how we argued over whether to take it or not? I'm glad the wiser heads prevailed, eh?" He chuckled. "Ah, it could be worse, we're none of us dead from this – yet - and if nothing else it may stop Pawl's sending for more spears."

"And what of your man here?" asked Brynjolf quietly.

Hrolf drained his horn, and held it out towards Jon for another. "How well do you trust me, Brynjolf?"

"You? I trust you completely. You're a Felag-man, and you lead us, by and large. Him, though, I trust not at all, and if you're about to do something daft because of him, I may revise my opinion of the pair of you."

"I'm assuming that none of you want him back aboard with us, if it can be helped? So, then; nor do I, particularly. But at the same time, it is true that Erlend did good service earlier today, and I only wish I had paid him for it then. But I'll pay it now, and have my own vengeance on him for this last act also. Help me up, someone."
Arne and Kol lifted Hrolf to his feet, and put a spear in his hand before letting go.

"Erlend!" The thrall looked up from the fire, still on his knees before his master. Hrolf motioned for him to stand.

"Erlend, for your help to us all earlier today, I should have given you reward. For your deed tonight, I should have your head, but that would be to disown the earlier event, which would reflect well on nobody.

"Therefore, in thanks for your defence of me, I release you from me, as you have wanted for so long. I free you from your thralldom; I hereby give you silver, this ring from my own hand - not Pawl's, you witness - that you may buy tools and the means to make your living. I give you this knife, that you may have the mark of a free man upon your belt for all to see. The facts that you stole it earlier and then did a murder with it make the gift all the more ironic, do they not? And I also give you a hide of land, that you may have dwelling and soil to work, to earn your food, since from this time forward, by these witnesses gathered, I am not obliged to feed, house, or clothe you."

He leaned forward slightly, to stare into Erlend's face. "And this is my doom on you for this deed, that I am no longer expected to provide for you - but never forget, I can still have your service should I need it. Get to your place now, and come morning we will start taking you to your new home."

Erlend looked surprised. "My land is not in Walea?"

Hrolf smiled grimly. "Oh no, not in Walea, not where you might cause me any more problems. Your hide of farmland, my fine freeman, is on this coast - on the Mercian side of the dyke. You can be my eyes on Pawl's lands, and if you want to keep 'em, you'd better be the first tongue to shout when they decide to avenge their master."

CHAPTER THIRTY- FIVE

Two days later, after rowing with the hard currents through the narrow channel between Welsh lands and the Angle's Isle, they left Erlend - who turned his back and walked up the shore almost as soon as his feet hit the ground – and slowly, by muscle and skill, headed back out to open sea and enough wind to make it worth putting the sail up. Hrolf's side hurt too much for him to take the steerboard, or to row at a bench, so Snorri held their course steady, and Hrolf rested grumpily at his feet on the aft deck. The sky had cleared of storm, and in the distance the clouds piled over Ongle-sey were plain to see.

Brynjolf and Einar came aft to talk; as they sat and got comfortable in the lee of the ship's side, Snorri motioned one of his own bondar to take the steerboard, then joined the other Felag-men.

"You did well with Erlend," began Brynjolf.

Hrolf shrugged. "I could have done better. Since he first saw that woman of Asa's, he has been nothing but trouble, and had I a sensible head, I'd have got rid of him earlier, one way or another. Had I left him anywhere near either you or I, we'd have seen him again, mark my words on it. On this coast, I doubt he'll last the winter, but his debt is paid, and mine to him. And there it can end, I think. I'm not aware of any family who'd want to take things further."

"Oh, there's no argument there," answered Snorri. "It's not always easy to see what other men are thinking, until they've done something to show you. And as soon as you knew, steps were taken."

"I'm happy they were the right ones," added Einar. "Hmm," grunted Brynjolf, presumably in assent, although Hrolf later thought there might have been room for doubt, "I wouldn't even grumble too much at your keeping it quiet from me for as long as you did; no doubt you had your reasons. I can't think what I'd have done about it in any case."

"I can," muttered Hrolf, "and for myself also, and it involves the biggest axe I could lay my hands on."

"Just be glad we all came out of it with little more than scratches." advised Einar wisely. He grinned. "There's still a good story in it, and after a few nights in the mead-hall, even the pain will go away!"

Hrolf watched the seabirds overhead. "Ah, yes, now there's a thought... although I think that even twenty years from now, if ever I find a skald to tell it, I'll not want it told too often." He shook his head before looking up again. "Ah, enough of it! Tell us, master steersman, is it Dubhllyn or Mann?"

Snorri got slowly to his feet; they all heard the joints in his back creak as he moved, and perhaps for the first time, Hrolf felt a little of Gytha's worry take a hold. But the older man straightened, followed the line of the gulls, peered over the side, and sniffed the wind theatrically, before announcing that, as they were still far to the south of Mann, they might as well head straight for Ireland. "But I'm not promising it's Dubhllyn that we reach," he added earnestly.

"It had better be," smiled Hrolf, "since none of us has family or friends in any other phort in that land. And I think we've all had enough hard knocks for one summer. We're almost back where we started out from, after all, so a gradual drift southwards as we go ought to put us in reach of the phort."

"Out to the west it is, then," said Snorri. He added wryly, "it's got to be an easier passage than north to Mann, and I reckon that's what we need."

CHAPTER THIRTY- SIX

Dubh-Llyn, the settlement of the Black Pool, sat, or perhaps squatted, on the wider section of its river, just before it opened fully and ran out into the sea. It had attractive features: long, easy-sloping banks for getting ships up onto, even at full tide; from the riverside, large open areas allowed visitors to set up temporary homes and market areas without crowding the permanent settlement further up the hill. A short way upstream, there sat a developed series of wooden-fronted wharves and jetties within the town proper; from these, winding, crowded streets led to good markets, a prosperous population who seemingly spent little of their wealth on their housing, and, probably most importantly, a good, solid set of defences, built to protect the town both from jealous fellow-exiles, and also from the natives further inland. Hrolf always had mixed feelings when he saw this place: being too young to recall it in detail personally, he remembered it more through his father's eyes and words from later days, before the old man had died. Stories mostly about blood, and fire, and anger, that ended in lists of friends who had not got out when the native clans had risen and joined against the Foreigners. Just occasionally, in better moods,

Dubhnjal had provided names of other friends, who had either stayed and weathered the storm under the protecting eye of the churchmen - always strong among the Irish - or returned to wreak havoc and vengeance in later years, before scores were finally settled, funds finally gathered, and a kind of order restored just last summer, under Sihtric. As most kings of any sort tended to, this Sihtric frowned upon lawlessness and random plundering - unless he was the instigator, of course, which seemed to make it acceptable somehow.

Not that Hrolf could actually see very much from the steersman's aft deck, as he was still unable to stand without assistance. The cold and wet had got into his bones, it seemed, and no matter what he did, it wouldn't let him go. The waves had not been easy, and he felt sure that his body carried more bruises than it ever had before. Snorri had been right to be wary of promising his landfall; after a run into a strange squall, it had taken the ship another day of tacking back up the coast to get here. So now Hrolf shivered in his cloak, propped against the stern-most rib of the ship, and waited impatiently for news and comments from his shipmates. At least, he reflected, he wasn't leaking blood all over the deck-planks any more.

"Church still stands," grunted Snorri, with clear disapproval, as he leaned the steer-board over still further.

Brynjolf chuckled. "Bet you'll still be going for your blessing, though."

"Of course I will: it lowers the prices. Doesn't mean I have to like it, though, does it?"

Hrolf spat. "I wonder how this new lord, this Sihtric, feels about such things. My bet is that he's done a deal with the Irish princes hereabouts, keeping their churches in return for being left alone awhile. I can't see how else he can have come out of nowhere to being king of Dubhllyn within the space of a year. He certainly wasn't here last time around."

"That was over two years ago," Snorri reminded him. "Things can change a lot quicker than that."

Brynjolf shrugged. "It doesn't bother me, I've had Mercians for neighbours too long to care any more. It would make sense, though: I'd heard that Sihtric hit 'em hard when he first came in - remember that ship-man I lodged last winter? He told me all this, he reached the Water-ford about the time we were sailing home from the *Suthreyjar*. The Irish have got a reputation for holding grudges, after all. You can only keep fighting for so long, especially if you're trying to drum up trade in the place."

"Hmm," murmured Snorri. "I wonder how much his empty war-chest had to do with it?"

With Einar and Kol guiding from the bow, they drifted towards a patch of dark, wetly muddy beach just inside the rim of the defences. They were expected; the town's governing Thing-men kept lookouts as far as the coast, as did all the 'phorts and towns around the coasts of Ireland, and so none of the Felag-men expected their arrival to come as any surprise. As if to confirm this, a handful of men could be seen riding slowly, carefully, towards their landing- place, staying at the top of the mudbanks and trying hard to keep their horses from sticking in the mire; from further upriver, smaller boats began rowing quietly towards them. Feeling the current against the steerboard, Snorri gave the command to drop the sail and ship out the oars.

Seeing this move, the men on the shore hailed them, asking names, lineages, and the nature of their business. Snorri held the oars at the ready and let the ship drift slowly backwards in the current briefly, before ordering the oars dipped into the river to halt the movement. Brynjolf, having the loudest voice, took it upon himself to answer, although Hrolf found it highly amusing when one of the shore-men, recognising him, enquired where their usual ship-master was. Satisfied with the answers, the ship was given leave to beach, and with a few hard strokes of the oars, the keel pushed up onto the shore, sending mud in all directions. Willing hands caught ropes, shoulders were pushed under the curve of the hull, and long before dark the ship was fully out of the water. Thankfully, the tide was out, and the bank was sodden enough for the ship to sink lower into the mud, so there was a chance of keeping it upright by itself: the local men charged extra for supplying posts to do the job. Brynjolf sent a number of his own men ashore to attend to fixing further lines against the rise of the river later on.

The king had apparently ordered his representative to come aboard straight away, and so Einar, heading aft, escorted him to where Hrolf sat, his fellows gathered around him.

Greetings and the standard courtesies were exchanged; beer was brought out, and the small box that held their stock of silver. Both parties produced a set of scales, and the taxes for their arrival, "protection", and trading licences were calculated to everyone's satisfaction. Then on to the more delicate matters.

"I am assuming, sirs," began the Reeve, a tall, rangy, dark man named Dagfinn, "that you are all baptised - or at least signed - in the sight of Our Lord?" He sighed, as if in apology, although to hold his position he must of necessity be a follower of the new Christ. "The laws grow ever stricter about such matters; the natives beyond the town are more and more demanding, and, to be truthful, we grow ever more dependent on them."

"Burning a few of their houses would soon cure that," murmured Snorri with a smile.

"Don't even think it, sir; not with things how they currently are. We've had the answer to that within living memory, after all, and Sihtric's grip on things has to be loose for now." He leaned forward to whisper. "He can't afford even a decent hearth-troop at the moment, let alone an army."

"It bled him that much to come back, then? No wonder he is so keen to have you come and do your business as soon as we beach," said Hrolf.

Dagfinn spread his hands. "I am just as keen to see you about your business, sir! You bring us news, and fine things to buy, and you spread silver around the seas. It is all to the good, I say."

He stood up. "I wish you a comfortable stay, sirs, and good fortune in our town. I can't see any objections if I attend to your permissions straight away. Though it would be as well to present yourselves to the church, and to Sihtric, as soon as you can. Things are still far from ideal here, and friends are still worth having."

"Funny remark," mused Hrolf, after Dagfinn had departed.

"Which one?" replied Brynjolf.

"About having friends."

"What of it?" asked Einar.

"Just that I'd never considered otherwise; it sounded as if some around here had."

"You're among the Irishmen again," answered Snorri, "I'm surprised you even had to stop and wonder about it."

CHAPTER THIRTY- SEVEN

Hrolf's distant kinsmen had also seen his arrival, and were not slow in coming out to greet the visitors. Kraki had seemingly mobilised all his friends and neighbours, and once the business with Dagfinn had been concluded, the ship was pushed back into the water as soon as the tide had risen enough. With the keel still bumping occasionally on the bottom, Kraki guided Snorri to a better landing-place, a long stretch of open ground on which they could set up a tent to hold most of their cargo. He had also managed to rent the cluster of buildings at the top of the

slope: a day-house with a hearth, a night-house that was smaller, and a storehouse to the rear. The more valuable things were transferred up the hill, and the Felag-men appropriated the night-house for their own use, leaving the rest to sleep either on deck or in the tent.

Knowing the importance of local contacts and knowledge, each of the ship-owners thought it appropriate to find gifts for Kraki and his family. He accepted cloth and silver gladly, and toasted his visitors from an ale-cask he had provided with the lodgings. "Fine things indeed," he said, "but I hope you have more like these. You'll need 'em."

"Why's that?" asked Einar, stirring more life into the fire.

"You've not been to see Sihtric yet," was the reply.

Brynjolf shrugged. "I can't see anything unusual about taking a king a gift to get his protection while we're here." His eyes narrowed. "What's going on that we haven't been told about?"

"I'm not talking in riddles for the fun of it," answered Kraki, "and I don't really see it's my business to tell you how to conduct yours, if you follow. But it's likely that Sihtric will want more than the usual sort of thing from you."

"We know his coffers are empty," put in Snorri, "his man Dagfinn said as much. But he can't expect one ship to fill those for him, surely!"

Kraki frowned. "It's likely to be something other than money he's after. Rumour is, Njal the king in Tara is not as beaten as we thought he was. There is talk of him massing another army. Sihtric's not going to stand for that, not after smashing him only last year - but he's not only short of cash. He's short on men as well." His bright green eyes turned cloudy in memory. "It went hard last year, even though Sihtric won the fight in the end."

"Oh lovely," muttered Hrolf, "as if things haven't turned out poorly enough already, now we're going to get dragged into another war." He frowned, and stared moodily into the flames.

"There's only thirty of us, Kraki, surely he wouldn't even notice what we could provide?"

The Dubliner shrugged his wide, burly shoulders. "Who knows? I suppose it depends on how desperate he really is. I'm only another free craftsman here, remember; I don't get to talk with the high and mighty who run the place. But visitors do; Sihtric looks out for 'em, and you can bet Dagfinn has already gone back and told him all about you - and your cargo, and your weapons. He'll be back for another chat before long, I shouldn't wonder."

"Who is this Dagfinn, anyway?" put in Brynjolf. "I don't remember him from last time."

"Oh, he's new to the company of kings, but an old face in this town. Gall-Ghaidhil, they call him: Dagfinn the halfbreed. Went away with his heathen father when Ingimund was driven out; the churchmen wouldn't let them stay, any of 'em who wouldn't give up the old ways. But his mother was Irish, and a kirk-goer. The Irish have been that way since the Romans were around, or so it's said. He was baptised when born, and everything, but he turned away from it, and threw in his lot with our people. Anyway, he came back with Sihtric, and has been rising ever since."

"But for that to happen, surely he must have embraced the kirk?"

"Him and Sihtric both, as well as all their hangers-on. That was one reason they were able to pull an army together last year to deal with Njal, albeit one that was more Irish than any other race." Kraki's mouth twisted into a wry smile in his ruddy beard. "How much is true belief and how much is just lip-service and the manoeuvring of kings is anyone's guess. Nobody with the choice would trust such a turncoat. The rest of us just keep our heads covered and go to Mass when we should – and keep our thoughts to ourselves."

"Including you, kinsman?" asked Hrolf.

"Including me. How else do you think I was able to get these houses, except through the priests?" Kraki looked around at his guests. "This isn't the town it was even last year, as you've already said. Tread warily. Mind your tongues in the markets. And if trouble does find you, for crying out loud, don't go dragging me or my family into it if there's any choice in the matter."

"Can we expect anything more from you than bad news and advice, should we need it?" asked Snorri. The disdain in his voice was plain.

Kraki shrugged. "You can dislike what I'm saying all you want, it doesn't change what's true. My place in this world's not the same as yours; I have no men to command, just a family and a lone thrall, and my own lord commands me when he has need. I see the world from a little house and a tree-smithy; I talk to my neighbours, who are all the same as me, and who watch the doings of kings and lords from as far away as possible. It's a view you men don't always get to see, but in this town, it's one worth having, I'd say."

"That's well spoken," admitted Snorri, "and I'm sorry if you are upset by my words. We owe you enough not to insult you. But," he added, with a faint smile in the firelight, "you still haven't answered the question."

"I can give you the gossip from my neighbours, and I can have eyes all over Dubhllyn, to see what's going on. But if Sihtric wants to take you off to war, I'm hardly in a position to stop him, now am I?"

"You've found us lodgings, and you gathered men to help unload," said Hrolf, placing a restraining hand on Snorri's arm. "It would be ungracious of us to ask more."

"Nevertheless," answered Kraki, "if I can give more, I will."

CHAPTER THIRTY-EIGHT

The town of the black pool was a fascinating place to explore. From the riverside wharves, the main street snaked back, around the open market-areas, and up a gentle slope towards a rather more grandly built house, where Sihtric and his cronies currently abided. Mostly, the town was rough wattle-walled buildings around simple four-posted frames, with windproofing provided more by the other houses around each one in the hundreds of little snickleways and courtyards, than by the inclusion of anything more than bracken and moss in the walls. Plots were frequently divided into further sub-areas, but the average household comprised a main building fronting the street, a separate sleeping-house, and optional workshops and storehouses behind. The street itself was paved, albeit only here and there, with a random mix of split logs or wattle panels – usually where an adjacent wall had collapsed and nobody had been bothered enough to clear away the debris. Whichever one happened to be walking on at the time, the mud persisted in seeping through. Rubbish and debris piled up with alarming speed, and the seemingly ceaseless rains and mists kept everything damp and smelling faintly of mould.

Good shoes were therefore at something of a premium, and looking at his own footwear, Hrolf wondered if Yngvar had been caught leatherworking yet.

Dagfinn's comments about the longphort's reliance on the native population were clear enough as the Felag-men entered the markets of the place. Irish traders and craftsmen were everywhere, calling their wares and products out in their own local tongue. Around them, the buildings all clearly showed a native origin in their rounded corners and their four-square roof-posts; of Norse-based, or even Norse-derived, business, there was very little. Small wonder, then, that Kraki had thought their arrival would be eagerly welcomed by the new king, and
when the reeve's man had arrived early the next morning with their tokens of permission, Snorri and Brynjolf had nodded quietly to each other. All through the town, as they sent out the initial overtures to invite business, they could feel the tension underlying the alleged economic boom. After a quick discussion, the ship-owners decided to restrict their own men's activities within the town, as they had on Ongle-sey. They were clearly going to have to tread warily enough as it was, and none

of them felt inclined to add further potential problems to their worries. The men grumbled, as well they might: it meant they stayed cooped up, thirty-two men in all, either in a cold, damp tent by the shore, or in a small, draughty house that elsewhere would only hold around a dozen. There was the option of going out to the sleeping-house, but that was smaller still, and had no hearth. It also rapidly took on an odour all its own, in spite of a pre-emptive round of baths. The storehouse was naturally taken up by the cargo from the ship, although one or two voices wondered about bedding down amid all that cloth. Brynjolf sweetly suggested they take a few of the ballast-stones with them, preferably one on either side of their heads; he even offered to apply them in person. To cap it all, the smoke-hole in the roof of the main house was not even in line with the hearth, and the wind whistled between the wattle strips without respite, bringing a fine and pervasive mist of rain along with it.

To alleviate the potential tedium, a few of the crewmen suggested that, as they had a door to the street, those with usable skills could set up shop for the duration of their stay. A quick survey of their number revealed a blacksmith, Jon, who clearly could not ply his trade in such cramped quarters, but a couple of leathersmiths, Thorkel and Steinar, took up the idea, quickly arranged a table and got Kraki to point them in the direction of the nearest tanning pits. Kraki also offered the woodworkers among the crew space in his own workshop, in return for a share in their profits. Eirik had some skill with antler and bone, and so went along to the tanners and the shambles with the others; all in all, the Felag looked well on the way to becoming a thriving little business sector all by itself. Rather than cramp their own quarters, Hrolf and Brynjolf decreed that, as soon as it was feasible, the workshops should move out to the ship, where there was perhaps less comfort, but considerably more space.

And so things settled down, and the Felag-men briefly thought that Dubhllyn would be a good place to stop for a fortnight or so, whilst goods were traded, deals struck, and their supplies restocked in preparation for the trip homeward, well before the autumn storms began. Sihtric, however, proved to have other plans, and for now, in his town, it was Sihtric who held the ear of the Gods.

CHAPTER THIRTY-NINE

Sihtric was reputed to be an imposing figure, every inch a leader of men - and there were a lot of inches to go around, wherever one cared to look. This news did not, however, sweeten the mood of his visitors, roused as they had been at something earlier than their usual getting-up time, and certainly before their morning drink. Somebody in the king's retinue appeared to be aware of how such things should be done, however, for seats, food and ale were soon forthcoming once they had entered the king's lodgings, and his steward, one Ingjald, assured the Felag-men that there would be time to eat before he took them into the royal presence. He even included their bodyguards in his generosity, which came as a surprise to Snorri's hearth-men.

Once alone, however, Snorri sniffed disdainfully. "Bloody rude, I calls it. I can't see how dragging us out of our beds is intended to turn our favour towards this new king."

"This stew's not so good, either," added Einar, pulling gristle from between his teeth for emphasis.

"Wonder what he wants, that it can't wait until a civilised hour?"

"Kings never wait on other men, even insecure and bankrupt ones like this," replied Brynjolf. He looked around at the solid walls, wooden in here instead of the loose-woven wattle of their own lodgings. "And if anyone's listening," he added defiantly, "I hope your tongues are as good as your ears!"

Hrolf sighed and sipped his beer - which was better than the food, he had to admit. His side still hurt enough to colour his whole mood, but he was, at least, able to move about largely on his own by now, albeit cautiously, and this early tramp through cold, damp streets had irked him as much as his companions. But his own natural wariness was coming back to the fore, and he was, by now, more curious than annoyed by the king's actions. "Come on, brothers, Kraki told us pretty much what to expect. The Irish king isn't as dead as he ought to be, and Sihtric is looking at another fight, sooner rather than later. He needs money, he needs men, and we, like every other ship that puts in, can give him a little of both."

"I didn't see any other boats," commented Brynjolf darkly.

"So either they got out before Sihtric got worried, or we are the first of the summer," replied Hrolf. "Either way, I don't see much to worry about."

"How's that?" asked Snorri.

"Well, if it's soldiers he wants, we have thirty men, in round numbers. Hardly an army, and only we four with any real war- skill, or experience, except for your lads, and Jon. We've already heard how he relied on native men last year; he may be able to pull the same trick again, in which case we might find ourselves as captains over them. Then he could call on our
money as well, legitimately, rather than just taking it from us – if he could. Seen any signs of a strong hearth- troop yet?"

"Nothing we couldn't flatten in an instant," came Olaf's answer. Ragnar turned to look at him.

"Does that mean we have to stay sober, then?"

"I'm not inclined to play at love-taps with the Irish, or to part with my share of our proceeds," said

Brynjolf. "Short of piling back aboard and running for home, what can we do?"

"It may already be too late for that - we're in here, and his reeve knows where the ship is - and where the rest of the lads are, come to that," observed Snorri. He rubbed his eyes wearily. "This is a corner of the tafl-board I never wanted to see."

"Like it or not, here we are," said Hrolf. "After everything else we've got through, if we can find our way out of this one, it really will be a tale for the long winter nights. But I have to agree; it's not easy to see how, just yet. We may have to go along with matters for a while, and just wait for our moment."

"And what if he demands oaths from us in the meantime?" asked Einar.

"Swear it on whatever you hold least value in," advised the shipmaster, "and promise everything stronger that you'll do better next time."

"Of course, we could be getting all worried for nothing," suggested Brynjolf. "He might just want to wish us a good morning, and share a horn with his visitors."

The only response he got was a raised eyebrow from his bench- mates.

CHAPTER FORTY

The king's hall was not, perhaps, as great or as large as it might have been, but Sihtric filled it well enough, Hrolf thought. He sat in his high-seat as the Felag-men entered from a door in the gable-end, smiling as he saw them, and beckoned them closer. The day was still early, but he had put on a fine shirt of blue linen edged in purple and silver thread, to greet them, and the fire had been made up enough for it to be seen; there were a lot of mutton-fat lamps set on iron brackets in the roof-posts to either side of him, too, making his seat the brightest spot in the room by a long way. His voice came from deep in his belly somewhere, and rolled out and around, filling the room.

"Hael, friends from Wirhalh; come, sit, and share a horn. Tell me of your doings, give me your news and rumour, and in time we shall see what I can do by way of payment for your presence in my realm, hmm?" Suprisingly, perhaps, his smile reached right into his eyes as he spoke - or maybe Hrolf was becoming more cynical about such things than he cared to admit.

As was the way with kings (not that he had ever met any others, but so Hrolf had been led to understand), Sihtric appeared to know quite a bit about them already. He greeted Hrolf, Brynjolf and Snorri by name, and surmised that Einar must be some relative of Eyvind simply by virtue of his being in their company. There were only a handful of his retinue in the room, and they waved Snorri's men over to share an ale-jug, well out of earshot from their masters.

Seeing his guests settled, Sihtric turned back to Hrolf.

"Did I see you favour your side, shipmaster, or is last night's ale still working well?" After that, there was little choice but to declare the wound, which in turn required the tale of how it had been won. The king looked sympathetic. "The Welsh have long been a thorn in many a side, so to speak; much like my own neighbours here, in some ways." He stroked his long beard, a sheet of pale whitened gold that ran all the way down past his shoulders - as did his hair - and looked thoughtful. An awkward silence settled.

Brynjolf finally took the bait. "Yes, we'd heard from people in the markets that the Irishman you thought dealt with is on his way back." He narrowed his eyes slightly, and took the plunge. "The word is, you're looking for spears and silver to have another go at him."

Sihtric chuckled. "Well spoken, my lord; my position here is tenuous enough that I can't afford the luxury of ignoring the truths behind it. Yes, I am poor by the standards of kings, and poorly served, too; but," and here his eyes went steely, and his voice warmed, "this is *mine*. I am Hauldr here, something I am sure you can all appreciate. Our people won this place, made it - there was nothing here before the longphort, you know – and now the native men want it back, now it's worth having." Hrolf noted the king's knuckles were white and strained around his horn. "I thought I'd made my claim well enough last summer, but now, as you have heard, it begins to look as if I may have to do it all again. I lost good friends last time."

"A difficult thing to face," said Hrolf. "Have you decided what to do about it?" To one side, he heard Einar's intake of breath.
"Ah, shipmaster," smiled Sihtric, "I might have known that dealing with sea-men would not be so easy." Hrolf found himself wondering whether he

and his companions stood any chance of just getting up and walking away at this point in the proceedings. It seemed unlikely, he had to admit.

"You are, by your own admission, battle- hardened men, used to the whims of chance around you," Sihtric continued, "and so your skills are of immense use to me. I am prepared to be… generous… in my friendship, shall we say, if I could persuade you to throw your support behind me…"

Brynjolf coughed uncomfortably. "I'm not entirely sure how much generosity thirty spears would call for, but I'd hazard a guess at not much…"

Sihtric stroked his beard. "Oh, I think you'll find more than that at your command, my lord."

Snorri cast a quick sideways glance at Hrolf, his mouth tightened in a frown.

"Let me be sure I understand, sir," replied the ship-master. "Your idea is to put us in command of other men than our own? Forgive me if I seem unconvinced, but is this such a good idea? Surely the natives you presumably plan to enlist - as we heard you did last year - will have their own men to lead them? Men they know and trust? I can't see that they'd take kindly to following us, any more than my folk at home would be happy with, say, Gizur the Dane to lead them."

Sihtric waved a hand dismissively. "The Irish need strong hands on their necks, or nothing gets done without them fighting over it for three months. Oh, they have their own chiefs and lords, but if they lead, how can I trust them when it comes to the test? There is nothing to tie them to me when the sword- play begins, and they're as likely to run off into the mist as do anything else. No, friends, after last time, my mind is set on this. *We* shall lead, and they shall follow."

"We?" queried Snorri.

Sihtric chuckled. "Did I forget to say? Your pardon, friends, the minds of kings wander many paths. Your cargo is bought, Dagfinn attended to it only today. There are fine gifts for all of you, as a seal of our friendship. You'll go home wealthy from this visit."

"So, then," said Hrolf, "we are indebted to you, and gifts should be matched between friends."

"And all I ask," said Sihtric with a broad smile, "is that you spend the summer with me."

CHAPTER FORTY- ONE

Thunder had settled on the brows of the Felag-men as they sat in their own lodgings once more. Dark looks and smouldering anger permeated the room, along with a chill that was far worse than any that whistled through the walls. Around them, their crew sat quietly, nervously, aware of the morning's events but still looking to their lords for guidance and command. Death had suddenly come a whole lot closer, and while even the church-followers among them still had no real fear of what came after this life, none of them saw any particular value in hastening the event.

"It is well said, that men would do wisely to stay out of the gaze of kings," said Snorri eventually, from between his teeth. "We walked straight into that one, and no mistake."

"Never mind how we got into the mess, what about how we get out?" answered Einar. "We can't lead our lads into this: they've got farms, wives… rents to pay…"

Olaf looked up from his place in the corner. "Don't include me in that, lord, if you please! I've been hearth-man to Snorri more years than I can count; I'm not running out on him now. I'm sworn to protect him, to fight for him, to die beside him. And that's just what I plan on doing. If you take us away from this fight, you shame me and my mates here – and yourselves, if I may say so."

"I'd rather you kept your mouth shut," retorted Hrolf angrily. "If you're so keen to get into the fighting, run along to Sihtric and put your sword in *his* lap. You have nobody to think of but yourself, Olaf; we don't have that luxury. Einar is right, we have you lot to think of as well, and you, my friend, are in the minority here. Most are farmers and servants, not hired spears. And for all that we have silver to spare, thanks to Sihtric, it'll do us precious little good if we're not alive to get it home. He won't send it on for us."

Olaf looked ready to argue further, but Ragnar's hand on his arm was enough to hold him back. Hrolf glared at him a moment longer, before turning back to his comrades.

"I'm out of ideas, friends; the raven-god is not giving out craftiness today. Perhaps he has a greater plan in mind."

"That's comforting," growled Brynjolf, "I can bet it has Sihtric in it somewhere. No wonder he outmanoeuvred us so easily. The next raven I see, remind me to stone the bloody thing." He refilled his cup and drained it in one swallow. It must have been the fifth cup that morning, at least.

Hrolf couldn't see any reason not to join his friend at the bottom of the ale-cask. His head hurt and his side ached; he couldn't think. The walls seemed to be closing in around him, even as he had walked painfully back through open streets, and the world looked a whole lot darker. The frown seemed to have settled into his face just as it had on his fellow-owners. The king had, as Brynjolf said, cut off all their options, and pulled their world out from under them.

"We could always just leave…" suggested Snorri, but there was no conviction behind the words. Running now meant they could never come back to Dubhllyn, even if Sihtric were no longer king. Towns have long collective memories, and nobody would welcome, or trust, a ship-master who had not honoured a friendship, or repaid a gift, in the past. And word would travel. This was not like raiding a church for treasure, or trampling over peasants for food or slaves; now they were dealing with kings and aristocracies, and the rules had changed. In this company, they were the underlings who got trampled on, and Hrolf for one did not care for the sensation. He liked it least of all because there seemed to be nothing in his power that could make things better for them.

CHAPTER FORTY-TWO

The view had not improved by the following morning, and, over a new barrel of ale and a mountain of bacon, the shipmen grudgingly agreed that they had turned from sailors and traders into fighting-men, with a responsibility to get their men as familiar with the implements and tactics of battle as they could. They took a quick head-count, and then a slower, more measured assessment of each man's experience and skill. This turned out to be a good idea, psychologically at least, as the number of potential *stallar* began to unexpectedly grow. Mulling over the findings of the morning, Hrolf was forced to conclude that his crew of genial, unskilled farmhands was a great deal more war-crafty and capable than he had perhaps wanted to admit.

The four Felag-men, by virtue of their position in the world, all had war-gear, and the training to be able to use it all. Even among them, though, there were differences: he and Snorri had a deep love of sharp, shiny edges, which expressed itself in a selection of knives, axes and swords. Brynjolf, by contrast, even whilst proudly wearing his sword, scorned anything other than the longest spear he could find for serious business, and could probably do more damage with this than Hrolf and Snorri combined. Einar, to nobody's real surprise given his family, demonstrated a skill with every weapon they could find, including the bow, and he knew uses for a shield that the others had never dreamed of. It was a rapid learning-curve by anybody's standards.

Snorri's own hearth-men, Olaf and Ragnar, were equally adept, if not more so; considering that fighting was their chosen occupation, this came as no surprise. Olaf was the more solid, a bulky, muscular, red-faced man who virtually lived in his mail-shirt, and the obvious choice for the tip of a boarsnout. Ragnar was thinner, rangier, springy on his feet and totally unpredictable. With a little more effort, Hrolf thought, he could have been a *berserkir*. But Ragnar was well- known for his easy-going approach to life in general, which made his choice of career all the more remarkable.

From his own men, he knew Jon had fought before, usually by his lord's side, but the rest were strictly ship-duty men, so that although they could use a spear, and probably an axe (since they handled these tools every day), Hrolf did not really want to rely on them in a proper fight. Fleetingly, he missed Erlend, who would have been a useful addition in this change of fortune, but then, he reflected, the thrall would probably have had more sympathy with the natives here - or he would have tried to strike another deal to secure his loyalty. No, they were still better off without the troublesome Welshman, even in this circumstance.

He knew nothing of Brynjolf's men, and neither, it seemed, did Brynjolf. Hrolf had assumed that they were, like his own contingent, mostly farmhands and woodsmen, and so it came as something of a shock when, in the wide yard between their buildings and the shore, a large amount of weapon-skill became evident among them.

"Don't look at me," said Brynjolf to Hrolf's questioning look, "I didn't teach 'em any of this."

"Very wise," commented Snorri, "I wouldn't want a rebellion on *my* doorstep, either."

Hrolf stroked his beard, deep in thought. "So, then, old friend, if you don't know they're this capable, I have to ask – are these your men, or have you been selling the bench-places?"

"I'm impressed, in an odd sort of way," commented Snorri. "I hadn't thought of doing that."

"I have *not* sold benches to strangers," protested Brynjolf, "these are my men." He held up his hands in bafflement. "I just didn't know they could do this stuff this well!"

"And you never thought to ask?"

"Why should I? We've never *needed* to ask before..."

"Look on the bright side," advised Einar, leaning on the corner of the store-house, "we're better off for having them this good." He waved an arm to include the whole crew in an expansive gesture. "Any of 'em could lead a gang of men, and hold their own; even if that doesn't happen, they'll make bloody good *hersir* by themselves. Friends, this adventure begins to look better than it might have; some of us may even come out of it alive enough to claim our silver from Sihtric."

Hrolf grinned at the thought. "That alone makes it worth doing, doesn't it? Alright boys, there's our

aim in all this – to come out alive and claim our price from this manipulating,
greedy, tight-fisted arse who calls himself a king! We'll fight for him in his mad little war- although to be honest, I can see his point. Our forebears made this place - earth and stone, walls and houses, and a good many of 'em are buried up the hill there, outside of these new walls. Sihtric is right: this place should be ours, not in the hands of these grubby little natives who can only see the silver that flows through it. But mark this: we fight for him only – *only* - because he's cornered us into it. He has promised us riches, yes, he has arranged to buy all our cargo – but the goods have been taken, and the silver for them has not come back yet." He paused, and smiled even wider as the irony of it all pushed into his mind. "Lads, friends… we have extended credit to a king! So who's to deny us if we levy a little interest along the way, eh?"

CHAPTER FORTY-THREE

Days passed: se'en-nights, that drew on into fortnights. The Felag- men found it harder and harder to keep their crew's attention on any given activity, be it weapon-skill, dealing in the markets, or making their little stock of wares to sell from the doorway; the rain still fell, though not perhaps quite as much, and the wind still blew through the walls of all the houses, if with less might and a little more warmth in it as summer went on. Through Kraki and his extended family scattered around the town, Hrolf and the others were able to keep an ear out for gossip and news, for none of them trusted Sihtric to tell them more than he absolutely had to on any given subject. The king kept in touch, with various members of his retinue paying
"casual" visits from time to time, and an open invitation to attend him "whenever they had need or time to"- which was correctly interpreted as an expectation of their presence in his hall, if only to demonstrate that they had not fled port. Not that the ship was likely to leave: the payment for their cargo continued to be conspicuous by its absence, and Hrolf was by now in no mind to abandon it for the sake of mere personal safety. As time dragged

on in Dubhllyn, the mood of the Felag turned from anger and frustration at being conned, to a resigned acceptance of whatever was to come next.

"I don't see how much longer we can wait on this king," said Snorri one day, though, while most of the crew were out in the town. "He said to stay the summer with him, and that we've done. It's got to be heading for winter soon; before much longer the days'll be shortening. And the wind's getting colder." As if for emphasis, he reached out and put another peat on the fire around which they were huddled. "If we don't go soon, we'll be here for the winter as well. I for one don't fancy the storms at this time of year."

"I won't argue that," nodded Brynjolf. "Question is, how do we tell him? He still owes us for a cargo, and he's as likely to claim he can't pay until next year as give us the money. It's coming to the end of the season, as you say, and if he hasn't collected enough from the town to pay his debts, what's he going to do? If he can't pay us, he can't pay an army, can he?" He furrowed his brow in thought. "Come to that, if we do sit out a winter here, can we afford to pay for our lodgings, if Sihtric doesn't pay *us*?"

"Hmm," mused Hrolf, resting his chin in his hand, "I can't help thinking that lack of money won't stop him; he may send word to Ragnar over in Jorvik, ask for a loan. They're related, I understand from the gossips around here, so it might happen. If anything does hold him indoors, it'll be the weather. Marching in an Irish winter won't be any fun." He looked over to the chest, the only one the Felag owned, and where they kept their ready cash supplies. "I think we can last until spring, especially if we can keep the lads working and selling."

"We might have to march, if we're not for starving," commented Arnfinn, as he came back in with Bard and Harek. "The markets are near-empty; there's hardly anybody out anywhere."

"Alright," said Einar, "come, sit, and tell us the full story."

Damp cloaks were draped over the tripod that usually held the iron kettle over the fire, and hung from the hooks over the roof-beams; beer was brought, and the fire stirred up a bit. Once the men had warmed, Arnfinn took up the tale.

"You sent us out for food, lord, so we headed first to the riverside to get fish: we've come to know a few of the boatmen there, and the catch is usually pretty good. That wasn't too much of a problem, but even they said there had been one or two ships not about today, either in the haven or out at sea. Bad weather today, by the way; not good for sailing in. So we got fish, both fresh and dried, and carried on back up the hill to the places where there's fruit and herbs and such. Most of those who sell these are natives, with farms and plots outwith the town. Maybe something's going on, but there were a lot of barred doors and empty baskets today. We started to wonder, what with the news about the missing boats and such, and thought we had nothing to lose by poking around a little more.

"So, we found a place where a lot of the other traders go to drink and talk, and just sat and listened for a while. Metalsmiths, treesmiths, house-builders... they're all wondering where some of their friends are today. It seems some have been gone for days, but nobody thought anything of it at the time. Now, it's just sort of... well, people are noticing, now more are away from the place." He shrugged apologetically.

Snorri looked thoughtful. "So, how long has this been going on, do they think?"

"Nobody really seemed to know," replied Harek. "The sellers and market-people come and go all the time, like they do anywhere else. What appeared to be unusual was that none seem to be coming in, rather than that they went in the first place. People have regular habits, especially if they're growing plants or meat for selling. Something seems to have broken those habits, for some of the natives around here at least."

Hrolf stroked his beard, a frown on his face. "I can only think of one reason for a seller to desert his usual market - he's found another one more to his liking. Friends, I think it's time to attend the king again. He should hear this, I reckon."

Brynjolf looked hard at his shipmaster. "You and I are thinking alike, I would say. Are you thinking that this Njal of the Irish is on the move? I am, and I'm betting he's moving towards us rather than away." He sat back, shaking his head in admiration. "If Sihtric guessed this was coming, then we really have misjudged him. He won't need to march an army through the countryside; his enemy is coming to him! He's waiting to see how many of his rats desert him, and then he'll put the rest into his *hird* to defend their own town. Brilliant; there's no other word for it."

"*If* that's what he's done," countered Hrolf. "Either way, we should go tell him, and quickly. If he already knows it, he'll praise us for keeping up with events, and if he doesn't, he'll thank us for telling him what's going on so soon." He stood up. "Kol, Arne, Jon: to me. Where's my sword? Grab a spear each, and a shield, quickly now." Around him, the other Felag-men called for weapons and men, and the house quickly dissolved into a chaotic mass of stumbling, writhing bodies as the crew sorted itself into some semblance of order. Arnfinn and his companions of earlier were left to warm by the fire; the Felag-men and a handful of picked companions went out into the rain to make their urgent way up the hill to the king's hall.

CHAPTER FORTY- FOUR

They squelched up the hill in the rain, huddled in their cloaks, mud seeping through the seams of their shoes. Dubhllyn was never a place known for its vibrancy and colour; on a day like this, it took on an even gloomier cast. Few of the houses bore any paint, and in the rain they pushed through the water, at the edges of vision, all a uniform dull grey-brown. Not even the turf on some of the roofs looked green any more, and the sky was leaden, heavy with yet more rain.

As they tramped onward, Snorri edged closer to Hrolf and Brynjolf, who were walking ever so slightly ahead. "How sure are you of this?" the older man demanded. "Out here in the cold and wet, it suddenly seems like one huge leap, getting to this idea just from what we were told."

"I don't see that it matters if we're right or not," Brynjolf replied, "the important thing is that we're seen to be doing something. As it happens, I don't think it's that far a stretch, really; can you think of any other reason to abandon your usual markets? It comes down to being either scared or greedy, really."

"Scared of being caught in the wrong place, like here, or greedy for the chances for profit from an army on the move?" Snorri shrugged, and immediately wished he hadn't, as the rain went down his neck. "It's reasonable, I suppose."

"Anyway," added Hrolf, "if we go and tell Sihtric what we think, he's much better placed to prove it true or not. And in the meantime, we can sit around *his* fire, and drink *his* ale for a while. I bet his walls are drier, and his roof warmer, too."

Snorri grinned. "That'll do for me!"

As the ground grew higher, and further from the riverfront, the main street was better paved - which meant fewer gaps between the logs, and fewer fallen walls being recycled. There were probably good views to be had over the town, but the Felagmen had their heads down, tucked well inside their cloaks, and only paid attention to where they were putting their feet. Even with that amount of care, the moss and damp collecting on the split wood had all of them slipping and sliding at almost every step, and spears were more useful as walking-sticks than as weapons.

Sihtric had developed the habit of keeping a door-watch at the entrance to his hall (Hrolf suspected somebody had told him it was a Kingly Thing to do), and as they made their slow, painful way towards his hall, this worthy ducked into his porch and sent word inwards that visitors were heading towards them. By the time Hrolf and Brynjolf were within comfortable hailing distance, Ingjald was standing just within the dry portion of the porch to welcome them in.

"You choose an... interesting... day to come visiting, my lords," he began. Their men dutifully piled the weaponry into the corner, as custom demanded (one *never* went armed before a king, if one wished to walk out again), as the Felag-men pulled off their cloaks and, in the absence of pegs, draped them over the reluctant arms of nearby retainers.

"It's not out of choice that we come to drip rain in the king's hall this day," Hrolf replied. "We have news that he may or may not already know, but we felt it prudent to come and tell him as soon as we could, regardless."

Ingjald frowned. "This sounds serious, my lords; I'll walk you in directly."

The steward was as good as his word. No waiting in side-rooms this time, no time for ale or mediocre stew while they waited on the king's pleasure, but straight into the royal hall they were taken. Sihtric was talking with men the Felag did not know; he looked up, waved them over, and dismissed his other guests with a curtness that bordered on the downright rude.
Hrolf concluded that they were townsmen of no great consequence; that, or Sihtric was too big a fool to have ever survived as king.

Sihtric began a smile, then saw the expressions of his visitors, and stifled it. "Friends, this is unexpected, and from your faces, I wonder if it's all that welcome. Sit; we'll have ale brought, and you can tell me what brings you here through the mud and the rain with such grim expressions."

"The ale would be welcome, sir," began Hrolf. "What brings us here is news we have had from the streets of the town, news we did not know whether you had or not. So, we thought it best to come and share it with you as soon as we knew, as I think it may have bearings on your plans for the coming months.

"We sent our men out for supplies today - we do it every few days or so - and they came back saying that many of the usual faces were gone from the streets. Native men, these, not of our people. It seems to be pretty widespread, from the gossip heard over the ale-cups. We could think of only two reasons for men to abandon their livelihoods: either they are running from
the fight, or they are gone to sell to the other faction hereabouts."

Sihtric sipped his ale, his eyes steely grey, full of flint and iron. He was silent for a long while. Finally, he spoke.

"You think Njal is on the move, then."

Hrolf shrugged. "As I said, lord, we could think of no other reason for what we heard. It's the only thing that would explain it, for either reason. He's coming here to challenge you, it seems."

Sihtric smiled and settled back into his high-seat. "He'll find us ready."

Brynjolf shifted slightly. "Since we last talked, sir, we have been drilling our men as best we can. They are better than we thought they were."

"That's good news, lord Brynjolf, since my plan is still to put those who are best suited as leaders over the rest. Be assured, I'll spread the loyal ones as widely as I can, for anyone
would be hard-pressed to keep these natives in line for long when the spear-play starts. But we have an advantage, if all the dodgy ones are running for cover this soon, eh?"

He leaned forward. "I must send people to verify what you say, lords; it's not that I mistrust you, or doubt you, but I have to know for myself." He beckoned over the heads of the Felag, to men unseen in the shadowy corners of the hall, before turning his attention back to them. "Stay a short while, friends; finish your ale, have the day-meal with me, while I send others
out into the rain, to see if they can find Njal and his rabbles. It will take a day or two to get the news back, I expect, but the least I can do is give you time to get dry again after your walk here. Somebody, get Hrafn in here: he knows a few sagas from the

old lands. We'll have some inspiration while we wait."

CHAPTER FORTY- FIVE

Sihtric evidently got his confirmation of the Felag's intuitive leap, for within a few days his men were to be found everywhere within the town. Mainly, they were requisitioning food and other supplies, but as a sideline, they were enquiring into the weapons each man had in his house, and how often he trained in their use. Those found wanting were taken away for
further instruction, and most returned without more than superficial bruises.

The man who led Sihtric's paltry hearth-troop went by the name of Svein Thorsteinsson, and he made it his business to come and speak with the Felag-men personally at almost every opportunity; just why, Hrolf was not at all certain, since Sihtric himself knew all about them already and there should not have been very much they could teach Svein about soldiering.
Perhaps he was nervous about organising an army; possibly, Hrolf mused, he might not have done it before, for all that he was a paid sword in a high position. The ship-master tried to remember the exact circumstances of how Sihtric had got his crown in Dubhllyn; there had been a fight, he knew,

and he had just assumed that Svein had been in the thick of it - where he should have been. He didn't know what this sort of circumstance required; perhaps Snorri or Einar did. He went to find them and ask.

"Hmm," said Snorri when Hrolf broached the subject, "we're talking ancient history, nearly legend, if you're asking me about such things."

"Does that mean you made up all those stories, then?" interrupted Brynjolf with a wicked smile. Snorri ignored him.

"I have fought in a king's army, but it was only a little one, and it was long ago - and we got badly beaten, too, which is why I don't talk about it much. I was one of the youngest — my father took me with him when the summons came for him - and I spent most of the fight under my shield, so I didn't see a lot."

"All very interesting," cut in Hrolf, "but I'm interested in how it was organised and pulled together. I don't think this Svein has much clue what he's supposed to be doing."

"Don't look at me then, I've never organised more than a gang of farm-hands for harvest-time! How about you, Einar? Your uncle Eyvind had a lot to do with this sort of thing, and from what I've heard, so did your father. Did they tell you aught? Or have you done it for yourself?"

"I've heard a bit, and done a little," answered Einar with a smile. "I've not got a great deal of trust in this hird-man either. He talks too much, to my mind, and somehow never really says anything! But I think we may be stuck with him all the same.

"I'd say we can probably get him to dance to our tune, rather than us dancing to his. Svein has the job of organising his lord's forces, from what I understand, so he'll be wanting good men to put over the native fyrd-men. He hangs around here so much because Sihtric has told him to look out for the likeliest of us. If we can find 'em first, I say we march 'em up to the king's hall and just present them as captains for him. Then," he continued, leaning closer over the table to the others, "*we* have organised the army, and *we* can keep a closer eye out for our own lads. 'Cos Sihtric'll just throw 'em away if he feels he has to, and he'll do it without a thought. And I'm not standing for that without a fight."

"Well said," murmured Brynjolf. "That's a good plan, and no mistake. Time to get off our backsides, then, and start making some choices, yes?"

They ambled out into the yard behind the storehouse, where some of the crew had set up posts and boards to use as practice targets. Already the wood showed scars from spear and axe, which Snorri and Einar thought encouraging. Hrolf privately suspected most of the damage had been inflicted by Olaf, Ragnar and Jon, as they competed among themselves at a higher level than the rest of their bench-mates. As their lords appeared in the yard, those of the crew present stopped their practice, or rose to their feet if waiting their turn at the posts. Brynjolf nudged Hrolf, and with a small twitch of the head, suggested he do the talking.

"Here's what we know, or think we know, all mixed up together," began the ship-master without any preamble. "King Sihtric has sent his hird-master, one Svein, to look us over and fit us into his lord's plans for defending his crown here. Njal the native lord is on the move - your news from the markets

was proved right, we hear - and so we, soon, will be fighting for
Sihtric's kingship in Dubhllyn. It can't be helped: we're here, and he hasn't paid us for the cargo he bought yet, and even if he had, this service would be the gift we give him in return for his generosity.

"Now, as I say, we happen to know something of Sihtric's plans. He doesn't trust the native men - last year, he had trouble from them, as I understand it - and so he's looking to put any of us with *any* war-skill as leaders over them. Those of us who've not done much in terms of weapon-play will be in with the natives...

"So the plan is to get as many of us as high up in Sihtric's army as we can; that's why we've had you knocking lumps out of these posts for so long. Now, though, we take the posts down, and play with each other."

He paused, and looked at his fellow-owners for acknowledgement. "Those of us who *have* fought before, and who have the wargear, will test the rest. Olaf, Ragnar, that means you as well as we four. Jon - I know you can fight, go out and see if you can find mail, or a good war-shirt of some sort.

The rest: sort yourselves into gangs to go up against us. How many can write their name, or make a mark? Someone go find some bark and charcoal."

Hrolf's initial idea of dividing up the crew proved impossible within the confines of the yard, and the Felag-men were agreed that going elsewhere for training would only attract unwelcome attention. So they all clambered, wriggled and swore their way into their mail-shirts, jammed padded caps and iron helmets over their heads, and unwrapped their weapons from the heavy, oily, unwashed woollens in which they had travelled so far. This done, five of the six sat conserving their strength whilst one began the process of testing the men. Each was evaluated, and a score put by their marks on the birch-bark sheets. When the first tester became too tired to carry on, the next took over. It was a punishing, gruelling necessity: in the sticky wet heat of a Dubhllyn summer, even Olaf soon wearied from the constant movement and exertion required. Shield-arms numbed and ached from holding the big round boards above the shoulder, and soon they began to droop lower - and then, that shoulder got hit, again and again, as spear and axe leapt over the shield-edge to bite at the exposed joint. Axes became harder and harder to swing; spears began to wander and miss their mark more and more; eyes misted and became blurred by sweat as it ran in rivers from every pore. And so it went on: it *had* to go on. Lives depended on it, on getting over this aching in limb and muscle, on being able to hold that shield up for longer and longer, on being able to send the spear-tip just where it ought to go, even when your arms felt as if wrenched from their sockets. Over the next two days, each of the crew was tried out at least twice, and by at least two of the examiners. The scoring was a bit hit- and-miss, but with all six of the armour-wearers in the yard, a degree of validity somehow worked its way into the proceedings. Jon was not forgotten, and was pushed into the line of waiting men whenever he appeared. There was no mail to be had anywhere, it seemed. Brynjolf for one was not surprised.

"You've not asked at Sihtric's door, though, have you?" he asked scathingly. "That's where it's all gone, you mark my words."

"Think there's any chance if we did go and ask?" wondered Einar.

"Could be," answered Snorri slowly. "Fancy taking a walk with me, and finding out?"

"If we go in all this lot, we'll set some tongues wagging."

"Ah," replied the older man with a grin, "that's the idea. Also, it shows we're serious, and that we *are* men of worth."

"If nothing else, it might put Svein in his place," commented Brynjolf. "And that may not be a bad thing at this stage."

"Go, then," agreed Hrolf, "go and bait the bear in his den. Take whatever he offers you, and who knows what we'll get out of him."

"Think we should take Jon as well?"

"I'm happy to go," answered the smith. "I've not seen inside a king's hall before."

"Don't expect too much," warned Snorri. "I'd rather judge him by the quality of his armour-hoard at the moment."

He turned to Hrolf. "What do we tell him if he asks what we want it for?"

"Give him the truth - that we're making men to lead his *fyrd*, as he wanted us to, with armour and weapon-skill to spare." Hrolf smiled to himself. "Let's see what he has to say to that."

CHAPTER FORTY- SIX

"Sihtric's answer is very clear," announced Einar on his return. "Jon can have his pick of the wargear - after the king's men have plundered the hoard of course - and his lordship will be pleased to see us in his hall yard three mornings hence. Oh, and he's sending us some extra spears and shields, too."

"Anything else?" enquired Brynjolf darkly.

"Mmm... ah, he likes what we've done by way of getting the lads up to scratch..."

"But he hasn't seen 'em!"

"... and is sure they will make fine *stallarar* on the day, for that is how he intends to deploy us, as he's said so often before." Einar looked around the dark and crowded day-house, whose only illumination came from the fire and the daylight streaming through the cracks and gaps in the flimsy wattle walls, and comparing in his mind the heat of that fire to the damp and wet outside. "And there, my friends and bench-mates, is what the lord of Dubhllyn tells me, and I pass it on as best I can, given the interruptions from the corner there!" He grinned at Brynjolf.

"Make of it what you will."

"Oh, how I wish we could just get paid and get out of here," grumbled Brynjolf in answer. "I see nothing but trouble in this business, and I truly think we'll be lucky if we all come out of it alive. I know we've driven the lads hard, hammered some weapon-skill into them… but they're still untested where it counts, and they'll stay untested until Njal's own men come howling out of the marshland at 'em!" He shook his head slowly, the frown on his face echoed deep in his eyes. "I have no great wish to be buried here, and that thought clouds all others at the moment."

Hrolf refilled his cup before answering. "None of us wanted this, but we've got it now. If we ever want paying for that cargo, we have to go along with Sihtric, the bastard. And, moreover, we have to make a cheerful face of it." He sighed. "At least we've had a hand in keeping our lads out of the worst of whatever comes next; captains can lead from behind if they need to."

Snorri laughed. "You think you'll get any of this lot skulking behind the others? They were bold enough before all this, and now we've put even more wolf-talk into their heads, and skill into their hands! My advice would be to make the best of it, and take with good heart what's been served up for us. This could make our fame far more than any number of trading trips would."

Brynjolf looked up. "It's a trade-off, I suppose, and if I'm being honest, it's probably not that much more dangerous than sailing over oceans in an open ship." He frowned in thought. "It just *seems* a dodgier option, and my stomach turns at the thought of it."

"No argument there," agreed Einar, squashing onto the bench beside him. "But, as the shipmaster says, we're stuck with it. It's only three more nights here, and then we're out under the stars. I wonder if Sihtric's got any tents?"

CHAPTER FORTY- SEVEN

"There are mounds and howes to the west of our longphort here," said Sihtric from under the carved bronze brows of his iron helm. "and the remains of what look like monkish buildings, atop a long ridge with water on both sides. One of those rivers is the same that runs past us here, but where I speak of, the tide doesn't reach. My understanding is that all this marks the site of the first settlement, the one that our fathers were driven out of, so who can say if all the ghosts are within the soil, eh? The point is, friends, that in places around the ruins, there is still the remains of a ditch, and a wall of sorts – a palisade, or the roots of it by now, I should think. My idea is that it's a good place to stand and wait for Njal: it's far enough out of the town here to keep our homes safe, but close enough to fall back should we need, and close enough also that nobody could get around us and into our walls without being seen and stopped. Close enough to get food out to us, too."

He paused and surveyed the leaders clustered around him. The rain had abated, although the skies still held the promise of more to come, and the soil underfoot was slowly creeping higher up their shoes as they stood motionless, digesting the king's words. The walls of his residence loomed around them, the eaves of the roofs just above their heads, in contrast to those in the town below and around Sihtric's hall. But even here, paved roads were a joke: stones and wood alike just sank slowly into the mud, leaving nobody any better off for their ever having been there.

"Nobody have anything to say, then?" Sihtric joked after a silent moment or two.

"Your pardon, sir," said Brynjolf slowly, "I wasn't aware you were wanting advice on such matters."

Sihtric's smile seemed to harden slightly. He cocked his head a little, fixing an appraising gaze on the ship-man. "Feeling out of place, my lord?" he enquired at last.

Brynjolf shrugged. "I'm fine, sir; you presented an idea, and hadn't asked for suggestions on its merit. If this place is where you want us, then there we go."

"Fair words; perhaps we're all a bit twitchy today. Could do with more ale, and hotter porridge. Ah well. Let me speak further: are you all happy to follow me to this place of ghosts and memories, or do any know - or think - of a better move to make?"

"Anywhere with fortifications, however decrepit, is a good start," said Snorri. "And I'm sure the ghosts will be with us in this business."

"How good are your men? You've driven them hard into their weapon- skill, I hear."

"They'll not disgrace you, sir," answered Hrolf, "but for all we've pushed them, they're still farm-hands and seamen. Any shelter and advantage we can get for them would be useful.
Does this place have a name? I don't remember Dubhnjal ever calling it anything beyond Dubhllyn." Sihtric shrugged. "Not that I've heard, but then perhaps I've not been here long enough to hear it." He grinned suddenly. "If we do well, I'll give it a name; better still, I'll let the hero of the battle - if there is one - give it a name. Njal's- howe would suit me well."

"Fair words, as you say," murmured Brynjolf under his breath. Hrolf shot his companion a wary look, a slight frown on his lips. The morning seemed suddenly colder.

For all that his goal was nearby, Sihtric seemed eager to be on his way. Hrolf and Snorri marshalled the crew into some semblance of order; to one side, Svein bossed his own bench-mates as they formed their own, habitual, marching lines without much attention to his words. Further out, the townsmen, the real, untested bulk of Sihtric's forces, milled about in the way that only the timid and confused ever really can. Einar spotted them, and beckoned to Hrolf.

"Before this lot break and run, do we want to send some of the lads over to form them up? I'd lay money on Sihtric wanting to make a speech to 'em before we set out."

"Good thought. Olaf, Ragnar, Jon: get over there, and turn that rabble into three columns, will you? Put yourselves at the head of each; take a couple of our better lads each to put in the middle and behind. That should stop 'em running too readily."

This measure had the desired effect, and reminded Hrolf somewhat of the times he and Jon had been required to make similar impressions on tenants who were owing rent or service.

Faced with three men who clearly were happier carrying their weapons, the townsmen shuffled into line, shields were adjusted better onto shoulders, and spears stood a little straighter in untrained hands. Just why those hands had been allowed to be so untrained was a different matter; Hrolf considered that, living where they did in times such as these, *everyone* in the town should have been practising their war-skills regularly. The king had been lax, he suspected, basking in his recent victory and enjoying his position maybe just a little too much. Hardly surprising, and hard to blame - until now, when the weakness of it showed up all too readily. He sighed, and pushed his own helm more snugly onto his head as he looked around. It had been a long time since he had seen so many armed men in one place, and it roused strange feelings in him.

"You alright?" asked Snorri, as if sensing his mood. "Well enough," came the reply. "This isn't exactly what we usually see, after all."

Snorri grunted. "I'd rather be hitting monks and villagers for profit, I'll grant you that."

"I can't help thinking that this king who's pushed his way into our business is not as glorious, or as good a guarantee, as we might want. He may even be venturing on the stupid – especially if he heads through this old settlement and goes chasing Njal all around the countryside. Why didn't he finish this last year? How come this Njal is still alive to cause this much trouble?" He growled in exasperation. "We could've been home by now, enjoying our fires and contemplating another winter of wealth and good eating, if it wasn't for an Irishman who won't die, and a king who can't kill him."

"Hush; for all that I agree with it, keep it quiet! He may or may not want to kill Njal, but that doesn't mean he won't finish us off if he feels he has reason. The best way to get through this is to keep cool heads, and try and outwit both Sihtric *and* Njal."

"Sound advice, as always, Snorri. Come on, we may as well fade back into the lines as stand out here where he can find us."

Einar's hunch about speech-making proved on the mark. With Svein on his right, and Dagfinn on his left, the king stepped up to a slightly raised bit of ground, and looked out over his forces. Hrolf had to admit, he looked the part: his war-gear was of good quality, and polished, whilst around his shoulders sat a cloak of red wool, edged in silk. A silver pin in the Gaelic style held it together, and more silver adorned the belt around his ample waist. His sword appeared to have a hilt of solid bronze, although Hrolf had not had the chance to examine it more closely; his spear bore coiled lines of bronze and silver inlay. As he stood, waiting, chatter ceased around him, and the silence of expectation took its place in the yard.

"We go to make our town safe again," began Sihtric, in a voice that carried well beyond his intended audience, into the streets and alleys beyond. "We have a wolf at the door, friends, that same wolf who escaped our spears last year, and now he takes the weaker-hearted from among us in the hope of weakening the rest.

"This time, I am determined, though; this time I will *not* be cheated! Spears I have given you, and shields, too, from my own hoard. There is food yet in the store-houses, for those who stay behind - but they, like I, are relying on you to stand with me and my bench-mates here. It is we, who are keeping their food safe; we, with our spears and our shields, who will go out, and dispose of this annoying little arse who thinks he can take *your* town, *your* livelihoods, and y*our* families, away from you!

"I know most of you are not fighting-men by choice; yet only last summer you fought beside me, and we drove this Njal away from here. Fight again; some did not survive, but then our enemy had to say the same to a lot more widows than did I!

"Trust in those I put to lead you; they will look to your safety, in my name, and make sure you do not fail either my pride, or your own. Proud is the man who can say that he stood firm when the spears met, and enemies glared over the shield's rim - and I take pride in each and every one of you. The men who lead you are seasoned at sword-play, skilled in spear and axe and bow. Listen to their words, do as they command, and all will be well.

"We go to the site of the original longphort, where the fences and ditches still stand. There we will camp, and there we will deal with this Njal, who thinks to be lord of Dubhllyn. Say your goodbyes, and welcome your new marching-mates; if the rain holds off, we will be there by nightfall!"

CHAPTER FORTY- EIGHT

Early the following morning, far too early for either one's liking, Brynjolf stood with Hrolf at the top of the bank that still stood around what were, clearly, the remains of the original
Dubhllyn town. Although the houses had fallen and sunk into the wet, muddy ground (they did not appear to have been any better built than the ones in the new settlement), here and there among the rotten posts and the windblown, mouldering piles of wattle, covered now in grass and with saplings pushing up through them, the lines of the streets could still be made out, and beyond, the small mounds that marked the graves of the more illustrious of its early inhabitants. Before them were the jagged, sodden splinters that remained of the palisade; the two ship-mates peered into the low mists beyond, and stared out to where Njal's army mustered between the two rivers that finally converged on the other side of the old town.

"Look a lot like us, don't they?" Brynjolf said at last. "It's only 'cos we're up here and they're down there, that we can tell who's fighting for who."

There was a lot of truth in his words. The makeup of the two armies was very similar, and it was only the marginal advantage of the bank's height (were they standing at its base, the top of the earthwork would have been about level with their heads) that allowed the watchers to distinguish between them. Native men from the surrounding farms and estates; townspeople, whether impressed or fugitive, a mix of Irish and Norse; and a small knot of armoured men, with longer spears of a distinctive shape, and round shields bearing conical bosses over the hand; these could have been men from Hrolf's own crew, except that he knew for a certainty where all of his were.

"Those men, the real militia with Njal: another ship, do you think? Or settled men, from out in the sticks somewhere?"

Brynjolf sniffed. "If it's another ship, they ain't in our haven, and according to both Sihtric and Kraki, no others have been for some time. Could be from somewhere else; nobody seems to know where Njal has been the past year, so he could've found 'em anywhere." He peered a little further, squinting his eyes to try and focus. "Ah, I can't tell from this distance. They could even be Englisc for all I can see, though I'd put more money on Dansk or Jutlandar."

"Hmm." Replied Hrolf. "This could get interesting, then. We might even know some of them."

"It's a chance you take coming into this bloody country; you never know who's coming after you next, or who'll be on the end of your spear. I just want to go home. I seem to have said that a lot lately."

"I won't argue that," said Hrolf warily, aware of a potential conflict looming, "but this time, we have to earn our passage." He shrugged, hearing the iron rings of his mailshirt jingle as they shifted over the leather jerkin beneath. "Not had to do that in a long time, eh?"

Brynjolf leaned more heavily on his spear, a frown etched deeply into his face. "Doesn't mean I have to like it, though, does it?"

He pulled his spear back out of the soft soil and, with a nod to his bench-mate, strode back to his own knot of men further along the bank. Hrolf watched him go, worried slightly; of the three who had sailed together before, Brynjolf was in many ways the most volatile, the least able to hold his tongue when angered or upset, and the hardest to predict as to what *might* anger or upset him. Snorri was hard to move from his placid, calculating view of the world, something Hrolf hoped to achieve in later years, when he had caught up with the events around him and didn't need to continually beat the people surrounding him into even vague acquiescence. His time always seemed to be too short to deal with everything that presented itself, and his temper always just that little bit too short to get the best out of either situations or people. It was a source of constant surprise to him that the people around him continued to trust in his leadership. At times like these, looking down at an army getting ready to try and main or kill him, he wished more than ever that it wasn't so, and that he could be back on his ship, doing things he understood, and taking risks that were stacked heavily in his favour. Like ball-games, fighting battles was not his idea of good entertainment, for all that he was confident enough of doing well in either.

Somewhere along the line of the slope, Njal and Sihtric had evidently caught sight of one another, for Hrolf began to hear shouted words in two different voices. The king's booming tones were easy to identify; the other voice was higher, coarser, and thick with accent. Hrolf couldn't hear the words, but he could guess them well enough. He turned to Jon.

"Get word to the lads, tell them to pass it down to their men. I can't get the words from here, but I reckon Sihtric and Njal are flinging no more than insults at each other so far. Soon it will be spears. I want our men with their shields up and ready. I *don't* want anyone throwing good spears down that hill; if they want to test their skill, let 'em chuck the Irishmen's spears back
at 'em. Oh, and watch out for arrows, though I can't see many bowmen out there as yet."

"We don't have many either," Jon reminded him. "Even you left your bow behind."

Hrolf patted his injured side. "That, in case you'd forgotten, is because I can't pull it again at the moment. And you left yours at home!"

"You done anything to protect that?" asked Jon, nodding at his lord's side.

"Wrapped a blanket round it – tightly - and now it's stopping me from breathing because it's pushed up tight to the mail! It looks to be healing alright, though; Einar did some good stitching, and it was a shallow, clean wound after all. He's been keeping an eye on it."

The two rivals for Dubhllyn's throne, as predicted, soon tired of each other's company, and the slanging match abruptly ceased. A tense, nervous silence descended, in which the wind in the trees, the songs of the birds, and the little noises of the land around them, all sounded impossibly loud and immediate. "Stand ready," Hrolf murmured, but whether anyone ever heard him, he did not know. He was too busy hoping that Sihtric had the sense and the power to hold his men up here, on the high ground, where the Irish could hardly reach them. Would Njal be so desperate, or so stupid (not to put too fine a point on it), as to try and assault them from below?

He was; at a sound from a horn, his men began to advance towards the ditch that sat wet, foetid and foul, uncleared for a generation now, below the men of Dubhllyn. Shouts floated up: insults, offers of terms, warcries, snatches of psalms and chants. As they came nearer, Hrolf put his own shield in front of his body, and hefted his spear to the horizontal in the other hand.

No spears came flying from below, nor arrows; Njal's men were better disciplined than that, although Hrolf noted with some detachment that it was the armoured men he had spotted earlier who appeared to be commanding. He was not unduly bothered; all his men had to do was stand fast and wait for them. By the time the Irishman's forces reached him, they would be exhausted from the climb, even up a bank this small, something that Hrolf found comforting and very welcome. He would not have wanted to be in their place; Sihtric had chosen well in coming here to fight.

Without any pause, from the bottom of the slope, the Irish were suddenly at the top. As they came up over the lip of the bank, through the broken bones of the old wall- timbers, Hrolf shouted the command and his men stepped forward, parting slightly to allow their lord back into the line. Spears jabbed over locked, overlapped shields: men fell away, over the backs and heads of their comrades, or crumpled forwards to make another wall for their mates to climb across. The dull thuds of iron on leather-clad wood, and the brighter ring of steel sword-blade on iron axe-edge reverberated over and over, without rhythm or pattern, just a constant, unending din around him. The pattern of the day was set, but it just went on and on. Behind him, Hrolf heard snatches of singing - he thought it might be Jon, or perhaps Frodi. He kept his shield tight against his chest, held firm by those on either side within the line; his spear was held high, one-handed, ready to stab down heron-like at any who came within reach. He was getting warm under his wool, leather and iron, but there was nothing to drink, nor time to drink it; his wound was hurting, a dull throb rather than any real pain, but there was nothing he could do about that either.

Spotting a useful vantage point, he stepped up onto the prone form of an opponent, and immediately caught another in the shoulder. His spear snagged on something; he had to lean backwards slightly to pull it free, and risked toppling over his own mates. At the same time, something banged into his shield, threatening to spin him sideways. He glanced across, and saw an axe being pulled from the leather facing of the board. He pulled his arm tighter to his chest, and the axe flew free, jerking its owner's arm away violently. More men were beginning to push around him on either side; he was suddenly, without realising how, too far forward to reach safety. Behind, further away now, he could still hear singing, and so assumed the rest of the line was still holding. They did not need him there, which was just as well, as he couldn't get to them anymore; he was nearly surrounded by foes, although thankfully most had not appeared to notice him, either.

He stuck his spear savagely into one last man - he must have burst his breastbone from the force of the blow - and as the dead man wrenched the shaft out of his hand in his fall, Hrolf took his axe from his shield - hand, sliding the loop over his wrist without even thinking about it. Now it was also necessary to push the shield a little further out, and use it more as a weapon than a defence. Axe swung; shield punched, a cone of iron pushing into faces, chests or other boards as the axe's thin, bright edge carved patterns of blood and hot air around him. His arms ached all too soon, but to drop either burden would be the end of him, and so he carried on just trying to clear the space around him as he stepped slowly, inch by inch, back towards his own men. Was it just his imagination, or were the men of Njal retreating back past him? Suddenly there was a hoarse, wild yell from behind, and familiar clothing began to appear on the men around him as his own line surged forward, pushing the enemy back, and parting just a little to let Hrolf back among them. He let them advance without him, catching his breath; then, spotting his spear jutting upright from a supine corpse, he lurched forward and retrieved it. He met Jon coming back from the edge of the rampart.

"How are they holding up?" Hrolf asked, with a flick of his head towards the townsmen they were leading.

"Well enough," replied the smith, "though I think the sight of so much blood has unsettled some of them a bit. What about you? I thought we'd lost you for a while there. And how's the side doing?"

"I don't know how that happened; I'll have to be more careful." He looked out at the retreating forces. "I reckon there's another rush in them yet, you know."

"More than likely," agreed Jon quietly, "more than likely."

"Regroup our lads; there's no ale to be had, so we just have to wait where we are."

"Somehow," answered Jon, "I don't think we'll be waiting all that long."

CHAPTER FORTY- NINE

Njal's men had barely got back down the slope - those of them that could still move - before the other ship-men (for Hrolf found he could not think of them as native men, so well were they handling themselves) were moving among them and marshalling them into fresh gangs, filling the gaps in their ranks and trying to present the best front possible before they came on again. Some of them had evidently spotted the Felag-men, for both Einar and Snorri sent runners asking if Hrolf had received any offers of terms yet. It was an interesting idea, but somehow Hrolf doubted his ability to scramble down the bank without catching an arrow in the spine from one of Sihtric's men. And quite rightly, he considered privately; once people started breaking deals, nobody knew where they stood anymore. He turned back and went over to his own men.

"Everyone alright?" he asked. "I'm not expecting you to be happy, and if anyone feels fit and relaxed, you need more help than I can give." He raised a gentle laugh, which was encouraging.

"Any wounds yet?" Around him, men shook their heads.

"None that are worth mentioning," answered Jon, "just cuts and bruises so far."

"That's because you held the line firmly," said Hrolf, "apart from me, that is, and I learned my lesson already. Do the same again, and we'll get through this yet." He risked a further look over the bank. "I reckon we might have broken them already, boys, for all that they're lining up for a second go. So when they do come up that hill again - their legs must be aching already, I reckon - we hold firm, we lock our shields again, and we stick our spears in their faces or their feet, where the shields don't reach. And remember, they can't keep together the way we can, 'cos they're on the move, uphill, and climbing over bodies already." He grinned savagely. "We can kill 'em all, if they keep on coming, and any wounds we get are going to be bloody unlucky ones, and no more. So hold firm, my boys, and keep your wits about you. Sihtric'll owe you dearly when you win this day for him, just as he does already for last year's work."

Jon, Hakon and Frodi sorted out their own little crews from the knot of townsmen gathered around the shipmaster, and once again the line began to string out along the top of the bank.

Hrolf detailed a couple of them to roll the injured and the dead back down the outer slope - just as an extra encumbrance to their attackers - and sent three others in various directions to try and find something to drink; although he doubted they would have much luck, the mere fact of sending them was good for the morale of the others, and he needed these men awake, alert, and willing to fight for him. He just hoped they had the stamina to withstand another bout of hard fighting; for his own part, he could feel his arms, legs and back already beginning to ache. His side was doing a little more, now, than just hurting.

Which reminded him: he pulled a whetstone from his bag (the only item he had spent silver on in Dubhllyn this summer) and carefully took out a couple of burrs on the edge of his axe. He was interrupted by a shout of surprise: one of his runners had returned with a bucket of brown, rather brackish-looking water. Ordinarily deemed fit only for animals – Hrolf would not have even considered washing with it, let alone drinking it, and as for Var and her dye-pot… now, however, the cup was passed around eagerly, and all too soon the bucket was empty. It had been well made, though, Hrolf noted absently: hardly any leaks at all.

Frodi rudely interrupted his reverie. "Lord: they're moving."

He looked in the direction of Njal's men, and sure enough, a multicoloured line of shields was moving unevenly forwards. "Look ready!" he shouted, seeing his men shuffle back into their own lines and awkwardly slide their battered, dented, dulled shields over their neighbour's in order to hold them together more effectively. "Remember my words: hold your places, put your shields together as before, and no throwing your spears! Let them come to us, and listen to your gang boss's voice - no others but mine and his!"

The force of the assault seemed a lot less this time: fewer men to come towards them, but just as much ground to cover. Instead of a hard line of men, they were separate people now, with worry and desperation in their eyes. Hrolf found himself suddenly hoping that none of his own locals would

recognise a friend, and waver before pushing a spear at them. Further along
the line, he thought he could hear Njal's voice again, and he wondered vaguely if the would-be usurper was now trading more than words with the king. If he was, then what went on around Hrolf was of no consequence: whichever warlord fell before the other was all that mattered, and word of *that* outcome would spread across the field faster than any fire. As these largely unconnected thoughts floated through the corners of his mind, he also called his own shield-wall forward to meet the oncomers, struck a foe in the cheek with his spear, and pushed forward just enough, just sharply enough, to send another overbalancing backwards, his arm numb from where Hrolf's shield-boss had rammed into the muscle.

"Steady!" called Jon from somewhere, but Hrolf was unsure whom he was shouting at. Then it became all too clear.

"Turn!" he shouted, "turn the line! Bear right!" Having the shields locked so tightly was suddenly useful, as Hrolf was able to bodily pull his neighbours round as he wanted them, and their momentum pulled the rest. Hakon was down; his part of the line was falling apart under a rapid onslaught by better-class men than they had seen so far. Hrolf cursed; the opposing ship-men were among them. He had to push them back, and soon, or they could be cut off, surrounded, picked off one by one as more came up and Hrolf's men would have nowhere to go.

"Hold fast!" he yelled, "step forth!" To their credit, his men were still listening to him, and they took the one step together, shields still together, spears still level and ready for blood. Hrolf had lost sight of Hakon, but he saw Jon, then Frodi, with their men still behind them, also wheeling round to meet the new threat. Hakon's contingent were standing steady, fighting hard with the spirit of men who know how dangerous their situation is; Hrolf frantically looked for a way to get over to them before they broke and ran.

"We need to go towards those men!" Hrolf called out, "and we need to spear these others and get them off our patch! Are you ready?"

"Ready!" came a voice he didn't know the name of.

"Step, then! Step! Step!" Three strides brought them to the flank of the incomers; rather than waste spears against what looked like good mail, Hrolf simply barged his men into their sides, sending them tumbling, before they could turn to face him. *Then* it was time for spears, and for axes, as the fighting grew close and sweaty; many on both sides dropped the long, unwieldy spears and grabbed for the shorter, sharp knives that hung from every freeman's belt. From that time on, it was just a haze of swinging arms and blood underfoot, of men shouting, screaming and cursing, of shields pulled high and then battered back down. At some point in the middle of the slaughtering, a shout went up from around the rampart, and men suddenly began to break and run if they could, or throw down their weapons if they could not. Their enemy began to fade away; the fight for Dubhllyn appeared to be over. As they stood together on the rampart, breath ragged, vision hazy, Hrolf refused to let his men relax or drop their guard until he was certain Njal's men were not among them any more. Even then, for long, long minutes, he found it hard to accept that there was nobody left to fight.

CHAPTER FIFTY

Everything hurt; from the top of Hrolf's head to the soles of his feet, there was an ache or a pain in every last part of his body, and one or two places inside the skin as well. The place in his side where the Welshman had shot him particularly hurt, with a lancing, stabbing pain that came on more strongly whenever he stretched or twisted - which, of course, he had spent most of the day doing. After that, he thought his back probably hurt the most, mainly from the weight of his mailshirt sitting on his shoulders with only his leather ship-gear between the iron rings and his overshirt - which was sodden with sweat, soil and blood for sure, and probably grease and oil from the armour as well. His head throbbed inside his helm, even after he had pulled it off: his brains felt as if they would boil in the heat, and the iron felt warm to his fingers. The padded cap inside it was only making things worse. Perspiration flooded down his face as soon as he took the helmet off, stinging his nose and his eyes, and blinding him to the activity around where he sat. The world seemed unnaturally quiet, or perhaps it was just the numbness in his ears.

He had found a place to sit, but even so he kept his feet planted firmly on the ground, for he knew that, were he to rest them now, they would only hurt even more as soon as he tried to stand again. But sitting was beginning to hurt his calves... there was no respite, and no rest. Somewhere in the back of his mind, he knew he had more to do today, before he could sleep, but for the moment his body just would not move. It was as much as he could do to get his helm off before his head melted inside it, and then get his hands out of his gloves and push his sleeves back up his arms in an effort to cool off. Somewhere, he heard a man calling that he had cool milk; Hrolf was so thirsty he would have drunk the curds without complaint. If that man had milk, he wondered if, somewhere, there might be beer heading towards them. Then he could have a *real* drink, and feel better. Finding clean water around here was unlikely in the least, to judge by the earlier bucketful.

Could he lift his spear? Arm-muscles protested at more work, but he gritted his teeth (even his jaw muscles complained) and tightened his grip on the slick, bloody shaft. It was a good weapon, Hrolf had to admit, and he was short on spears in the house; he wondered if Sihtric could be persuaded to make a gift of it. He got it upright, then had to bend and pull up a handful of grass in order to clean the worst of the mess from the wood before he tried putting his whole weight onto it. More aches, more pain, from his legs this time, as he pulled himself upright at last. It wasn't the wounds that hurt so much, he decided, absently noting a rip in the links of his iron shirt and beginning to feel the bruise beneath; it was the length of the fighting that gave out the real pain. To his blurred and somewhat unreliable vision, it looked as if the day was heading for sunset; they must have been at the spear-play all day, more or less.

He didn't think he would ever want to do this for a living.

As his eyes cleared of sweat and mud, he was able to look around. Taking in the field of slaughter, he began to remember some of his duties as a leader of men, and began to count heads and faces he knew.

He tried to call his men to him, but his voice was a dried-up, croaking thing that barely carried past his teeth. It was unlikely that anyone would recognise his spear, and lifting his shield was simply not an option. Half the leather was gone from it anyway, an annoying extra expense this coming winter. Did it still have a strap? It did; he spent a further agonising eternity wrestling it onto his back, which naturally protested at the burden. Hrolf was past caring; he grimly shut out as much of the pain as he could, and concentrated on finding his men.

The bank and ditches had served Sihtric well; most of the casualties on his side appeared to be from falling down it as the Irish had advanced. Of real wounds, he found very few as he walked the line of the palisade, and as he walked further, more of the men he had led looked up, and formed a ragged crowd behind him. Looking down the slope, he saw bodies everywhere; to the practised eye, most of them were clearly from Njal's forces. Not many appeared to be the better-equipped men he had seen at the start of the day, and in some strange way, that worried him. It might mean they were still out there somewhere, with a mind for vengeance. They should be found, and made safe somehow - and soon.

Further along was Arne, safe enough; Hrolf found this gave him an unexpected feeling of relief - until he saw Kol beside him, his hand bloody and his face white with pain. Jon had been beside him until the very last charge, when they had become separated; now he too looked up from under a tangled mass of sweat-filled hair and a stout leather cap, and grinned. Hakon sat nearby, nursing a bad gash in his thigh; Hrolf grabbed man after man as they passed, until he found one with a needle and linen thread, who he sent over to try and sew his men's wounds closed. Hakon was a hunter: he would need that leg as whole as it could be if he were ever to chase the deer and the birds again, and Hrolf knew he had an obligation to at least try and help. Thorhall had been left behind in the town, from his crew-share; so where was Frodi? Unable to see the man, Hrolf carried on walking, putting one leaden foot before the other, and struggling to stay upright beneath the weight of his armour. Absently, he felt for his sword, uncertain if he had ever even unsheathed it. As if to reassure him, it banged against his leg, and the pommel's three lobes nestled into the palm of his hand.

The other Felag-men were collecting their troops as well; gradually, without ever meeting or agreeing it, they began to converge upon Sihtric, pulling more and more of the army behind them. There were gaps in the lines; Einar in particular seemed to have very few with him so far, and Hrolf's spirit sank when he saw them. It fell lower still when he saw Snorri being helped along by Olaf and Ragnar, his face as pale as a corpse. If Hrolf had been capable of rushing to his old friend, he would have, but his legs just could not go any faster.

"How did this happen?" he croaked when he did finally reach them.

"Lucky spear," panted Snorri. "Olaf nearly caught it, but it just bounced and hit me in the shin. Can't stand on it yet…"

Hrolf looked at the leg. "That's because it's broken, old friend, though not, I think, as badly as Eyvind's was. We should be able to mend that; won't even need the onions in the stew."

"Don't mend it too soon; we should at least see what we can get out of Sihtric for it first."

Hrolf left them, and continued towards the king. Sihtric saw his approach, and stepped to shorten the distance, his hand out in welcome.

"Well fought, shipmaster! Well fought from all of you; I've sent runners with the news. Told 'em to bring the ale and the meat back with them, too; we'll stop here tonight. Nobody looks to be up for a walk just yet." He turned to observe Snorri's slow progress. "Especially not this bold wolf! You men, take your lord straight to my hird-fellows, and tell Arnolf to attend, on my orders. He has the skill with wounds, and knows the leechcraft to mend that leg properly. Lord," he continued, addressing Snorri directly, "when you are well enough, we will discuss a due geld for that wound."

"You chose your spot well, sir," answered Hrolf, unsure of what else to say, "and I could also use the rest tonight."

"For a lot of the time, your part of the line had the hardest knocks, my lord. You did well, your men also." He smiled and looked around, nodding to himself. "I said I'd like this place named as Njalshowe, did I not? And we certainly buried him this time." As if suddenly remembering, he turned to his nearest hird-man. "Take a few of the lads; find Njal. Bring him to me, whether alive or not. This time, I have to be sure."

CHAPTER FIFTY- ONE

"How goes it, old friend? Did this Arnolf do you any good?"

Snorri shrugged as best he could from his prone position on the ground. "We found him, and quicker than you found me this time. Glad I had Olaf and Ragnar carrying me, though: first thing he wanted was two strong men to pull the leg apart, so he could feel what was going on inside it. Then he bound it up, with wooden splints, and put various leaves and herbs under the wrappings. Bone-knit, he called one of 'em, but it looked like good old comfrey to me. I was more interested in the care he took in setting the bone - which took a while. My toes were turning blue at one stage, but last time I looked they were a better colour; Arnolf thought there was more smash and break than bleeding because of that. He also had a little bag of white poppy seeds, with which he was very generous. Sihtric kept trying to say how rare and valuable they were, but I've seen 'em before, both in Wessex and the Frankish kingdoms, and they're common enough there. It might be worth your while heading that way one summer, and bringing a load back."

Hrolf frowned. "You say that as if I'll be going without you."

"Well come on, be realistic, Hrolf! Gytha has made it plain enough that she'd rather I stayed home, my joints have been stiff and aching since we set off, and now this happens!" He shook his head slowly. "I think the message is plain enough: it's time to sell up my bench and live a few years longer while I can still get out of bed."

Hrolf rubbed his beard thoughtfully. "It's been a year for changes; I suppose this is just one more in the season. If we haven't missed it, come to the Winter Thing, and we'll do it properly, in front of Oslac and all the right witnesses. With luck, you'll have changed your mind by then."

"Don't forget I live outside his law- lands."

"You live outside *anyone's* authority! Oslac is the best – and the nearest - legality you're likely to get. It's what you get for taking lands nobody else wanted, without any near neighbours. But enough of this; we can sort business another day. I came to make sure you were still alive, and that your lads were all alright. Sihtric has decided to stop here for the night, and perhaps for tomorrow as well, but I'm trying to arrange a way of moving you sooner rather than later, so I've sent a runner of my own back to Kraki to try and find a cart for you. Otherwise, we'll have to carry you..."

*

"Can't we get the ship up to near here?" asked Ragnar from within shadows thrown in the evening by the remnants of a wooden wall. All around them, men were taking what little shelter there was from the ruins of the old buildings, making fires, trying to find comfortable lodgings in a town full of ghosts and bad memories. "If this really is the site of the old longphort, there must be riverfront somewhere, surely. The water's close enough, after all."

Hrolf raised his eyebrows. "Damn; I didn't think of that. Wonder if Kraki will?"

"Send another runner, if you can spare one," advised Snorri. "That way, we're rid of Sihtric sooner as well."

"If we can get him to agree to it. Also, I need to find out how many we lost from the crew first, to be sure we can row away again."

"I can help you there," put in Ragnar again. "We lost none; even the men from the town held up. Lord Snorri was our only casualty to my knowledge, but I think Olaf's gone to do a count as we speak."

"Fair enough; you must have had little to do if this was your only wounding."

"Ah," said Ragnar, raising a cautionary finger, "I said casualty. I've a gash in my arm here, and Olaf will have a limp for a day or so, but such things hardly count, do they? I think a couple of the town lads caught a busted rib or two when they held the Irish charge back - that was a fine thing to sing about! Ah, lord, you should've seen them, shields in front, shoulder to shoulder, with the rest piled up behind... Njal's boys came over the edge of the rampart and ran straight into us - and bounced!" He laughed, a high and rather nervy sound that Hrolf knew was normal for him. "A fine sight, especially their faces as they tumbled back down."

Hrolf grinned in appreciation. "Did you follow?"

"Down there? No way, not without the king's direct order - which he never gave, I'm happy to say. But by then, my lord here was down, and my duty was – is - to him. So Olaf and I stood over and marshalled the rest around us. I was glad of our bench-mates at that point, I can tell you."

Hrolf nodded. "Mine did me proud, too, but I've lost Frodi, and I'm bothered about Hakon's leg. I wonder if I could get Arnolf to look at him, too?"

Snorri grunted. "I wouldn't bet on it - Arnolf is one of Sihtric's hearth-men, and they're all gathered to await the ale wagon, toasting-horns at the ready."

"None around for us, I suppose?"

"I secreted a few poppy- seeds if you're desperate."

"Not very satisfying, I expect. I might go and see if I can find the supplies as well."

"Sure you'll stand that long? You're still very pale, and that spear looks more solid than you do."

"You could be right, at that. But I've got to either eat, drink or rest, and it all hangs on when the food gets here. When Olaf comes back, you might want to have yourself carried over to our fire, and hear the rest of the day's stories."

"Mm, more chance of getting food over to a big gang of us. I'm likely to be forgotten out here in a corner."

Hrolf looked down at his shipmate. "Not by us, old friend. We're not a full crew without you."

"Good of you to say; but we've replaced Eyvind - or he replaced himself, rather - so it's hardly the end of the worlds if I do sell up." Snorri looked up at his ship-master. "Think I could persuade you to lend credit to Kol and Arne for next season? I still like those two. How did they do today?"

"Snorri: I don't want discussions about retiring and selling up in this place, with these ears around us. We need to concentrate on getting out of Sihtric's reach - nothing else. Do I have your word?"

"You have it. I can see the sense in what you say."

"Then if Olaf isn't back in time, I'll send a couple of my lads over to carry you."

"If Kraki has his head together, you may yet be carrying me shipboard, eh?"

"We can hope, my old friend; we can certainly hope."

CHAPTER FIFTY- TWO

"We left Erlend in the Welsh lands," began Hrolf as he gazed through the firelight at his ship-mates, "and we left Thorhall, Otkel, Broddi and Hreidar with the boat in Dubhllyn. So we came to this place with, in total, twenty-seven of us." He took a deep drink of the ale that had finally arrived, and then took an equally deep breath. "Time for a reckoning, then."

Slowly, carefully, he counted around the edge of the fire. "Raise a hand if you bear a serious wound…" he counted again, and frowned.

"Bench-mates, we've not done too badly, but it's not good, either. We are ten men short, dead on the ramparts: Frodi, from my share of the crew, though he went down in a knot of men from the town; Snorri has lost Thorkel and Harek. Brynjolf is without Harald, Olvir and Thorolf, but Einar, you have lost the most of all. Eirik, Arnfinn, Steinar and Gisli, who sailed with you, are all dead." He paused. "Or did I get it wrong? Anyone I've just called out sitting here and having a laugh?"

"Sadly, no," muttered Brynjolf from beyond the flames. "Go on, count off the wounds as well and get it over with."

"Well, there's Snorri, obviously. Then Kol, who may lose his fingers, Hakon with a gash in the leg, Thorfinn from Snorri's hall - asleep still? Not good… Brynjolf's man Armod got a spear in the foot. Einar's men, if they got a wound, seem to have died from it already. Small comfort. It's an empty fire we sit around, friends, and fewer stools than we're used to."

Einar stared hard into the flames, his face thin and drawn. "Make it their pyre, then. Say their names, and send them to the hooded one, proud and upright, as they died,"

"Hael to that," replied Snorri. "None of 'em were churchmen, were they?"

"Not that I knew of. Brynjolf?"

"No idea, I never asked. Ah, if they were, I'm sure they'll find their way home just as easily."

And so the toasts were drunk, and poured into the fire; the names were spoken one last time, and a moody silence settled over the crew. The wood popped and cracked in the fire, sending little showers of sparks into the night; around them, at other fires, their comrades in arms celebrated their own survivals, their own victories within the day, and said their own farewells to other fallen comrades. Hrolf presumed that tomorrow they would be searching for bodies, specifically those who required burial within the grounds of the church in Dubhllyn, but for his own part he would rather see his ship heading upriver towards them, ready and able at last to take them homeward. Let the ground here have their dead, either within it or as ashes blown across it; those to whom it was done were beyond knowing, or indeed caring.

"I'll go to Sihtric in the morning," he said suddenly, coming out of his thoughts and back to the world around him. "Before I do, though, any of you wanting to ask for weregeld on your wounds or for those who died should come and talk with me. I think it best that only one of us go and deal with the king over this; he lost friends and bench-mates too, after all. Still no word from Kraki, either, so we might not be going back to the town for a while longer."

Snorri groaned. "That's something I could do without." There was a general murmur of assent from around the fire.

"What else could we do?" countered Hrolf. "Would you rather wait here, with living men as well as all the old ghosts, and the new? Or out there, where Njal could come again if he wanted to, and murder the lot of us?"

"Njal won't bother you, ship-master," answered a new voice, as Dagfinn stepped into the light of their fire. "We found his corpse; his surviving hearth-men came and asked for leave to burn him properly, and after he saw the body, made sure of who it was, the king agreed - so that's another problem solved."

He looked around at the remnants of the crew as they stared up at him out of tired, wide-stretched eyes. "Come to the king tomorrow; it looks as if we may be here for most of the day, if not the night as well. Come early; if you want, I'll take you in, and then you'll know he's awake and ready to listen.

"Gentlemen, you fought hard, and well, and the king should be properly grateful, whatever the cost to him. I've not forgotten he owes you for your cargo, either, and I can well believe you would want to be gone from here just as soon as can be. You have my word that I will assist you however I can. I don't think you deserve any less than that."

CHAPTER FIFTY-THREE

The mist of the following day gave the whole place a further air of unreality. Shadows moved around, slowly, methodically, painfully, as the grim task of searching through the dead began, stripping the fallen of anything valuable or useful, separating the friend from the foe, and finding someone who could decide what to do with either. Smoke from fires mingled imperceptibly with the surrounding fog, turning the world and the spirit fuzzy and grey.

It was not, Hrolf decided, the best of mornings to go asking favours of a king. Late in the previous evening, he had taken a quiet stroll away from his crew's campsite, heading imperceptibly towards the royal tent - the only one to be seen, but it did house both Sihtric and his entire hearth-troop, so it was worth the seeing. Like the Felag's benches, it too had space to spare after the fighting was done, and so it was with some trepidation that Hrolf, having taking casually careful note of Sihtric's losses, walked slowly - and alone - through the morning, on his way to the now undisputed king.

He had not found or seen Dagfinn yet, and, after hanging around his fire for a while, had concluded that his best course was to go and get the business over with. Thorfinn had not lasted the night, and that had only added to the growing gloom among his men. He realised bleakly that it was up to him to get things moving again, and the best way he could think of to do this was to free them all from the machinations of Sihtric. Which meant going to talk with the king, and asking - Hrolf would rather have demanded, but realised the prudence of caution - his permission to depart. Hopefully they would get paid before they went, but at the moment the general mood appeared to be swinging in favour of getting away from this place at whatever cost. It was hard to argue against it; they had not done well in Dubhllyn, and privately, Hrolf wondered how many of his regular crewmen would answer the call to oar next spring.

Mist swirled to his right, and Dagfinn stepped into view like some wraith of this place, walking suddenly and silently beside the ship-master. "My regrets at not coming to you sooner," the Reeve began, "but the day is already long and messy."

"You're busy with the dead, then? All part of your duty, I suppose. How is the king this morning?"

Dagfinn shrugged. "Well enough when I saw him; he had the tally of his losses even then, and he knew Njal was properly dead, so there's little to upset his mood, I should think. I saw you through the mist, and thought you'd be heading there without me - which is well enough, by the way - but since I was on my road back as well, I thought I could discharge my duty and my promise to you, too."

"That's well said, Dagfinn, and I thank you for it. Dealing with kings is, I suspect, always easier when there is another man to help you through it all."

Dagfinn smiled. "Sometimes; but people can get used to it. I had to, after all."

"I think my bench- mates and I will not be wanting to get *too* familiar with such high company, somehow."

Sihtric's abode loomed out of the murk: a tent made for a ship, Hrolf guessed from the faded paint on the elaborately carved wolves on the end- frames, but he was not aware of any vessel owned by the king. He'd not mentioned one, and surely if he had it, he would have sailed upriver to this place rather than slogging overland. Perhaps the tent was all that was left of it.

It wasn't important, Hrolf decided, but it could be interesting. A bargaining tool, perhaps? An indication of just how wealthy – or not - Sihtric really was?

Dagfinn led him to one end, where a man stood carrying both a spear and a fine set of bruises. He nodded as he recognised Dagfinn, and stepped aside. Something in his eyes, swollen though they were, suggested to Hrolf that he was recognised, too.

Inside, the fire-smoke more than made up for the absence of mist. Hrolf stood for a moment, his eyes stinging, before making a slow progress, relying more on his ears than his vision, deeper into the noisy and sweaty air.

"Ship-master!" boomed an all-too-familiar voice from somewhere to his left. His eyes had cleared somewhat, and now he could see Sihtric sitting on a chest to one side of the mess of bedding that littered the floor. "Come closer, the air is vile in here, but here is where my business is today. Hrafn, clear a bench there! Get beer, someone; and bring the war-chest, too. There are debts to pay, and gifts to give."

Hrolf bowed, and took the proffered seat. "You remind me, sir, I have a spear of yours, and no doubt there is other gear around our fire, too."

Sihtric's eyes sparkled. "The spear, did it do good work for you?"

"Admirable work, sir."

"Then keep it, my gift to you for your efforts yesterday. I will have to ask for helms and war-shirts back, though were I wealthier I'd say to keep those too." He took a drink, and tapped the smaller chest by his feet. "I said I would discuss a geld for the lord Snorri's wound, and there is the matter of payment for the cargo I bought from you - a mean trick for a king to play, but have it as a lesson I doubt you needed. Kings can be as tricky and treacherous as any other trader, and that, in a way, is all we are sometimes. How many others are you asking payment for, my lord?"

"We are eleven dead, now, sir, and three wounded besides the lord Snorri, who sends his greetings and so forth." Hrolf paused a moment. "It was a good fight, and a good victory, sir, but at quite a cost."

Sihtric nodded slowly. "You men bore the worst of it, along with my own, but you all showed that I was right to set you above the men of the town: you all held them together, and kept them safe, for the most part. It is no surprise to me that your losses are so high - but your deeds were noble, and worthy of remembering."

He bent to pick up the chest, and slowly opened it. Then, balancing it on one thigh, he turned it to show Hrolf the contents. Silver gleamed: a few coins, but mostly the reassuring bulk of rings and bracelets in there as well. Hrolf twitched a slight, fleeting frown, and raised an eyebrow. He could feel his heartbeat quicken, and began to feel warmer than before. He reminded himself sternly that this was just business – nothing more. He needed his wits about him.

"I take it Snorri is not yet well enough to move?" continued the king. "I'm not surprised, but Arnolf assures me that his leg is well set, and he should have the use of it yet. I would rather have him here to discuss his price, but I am sure he would trust your judgement. Have you scales?"

Hrolf smiled. "Always, sir." He pulled a smaller bag from under the folds of his shirt, and unpacked a folding balance, complete with a set of weights. Sihtric inspected the latter, and presently nodded his satisfaction with them.

"So: what worth has the leg of a lord and a leader of men?"

Hrolf carefully placed three of the weights in one pan, and looked to Sihtric to fill the other. The king considered for a moment or two, slowly stroking his beard; then, with a glance at
Hrolf, he removed the smallest weight, and began placing chunks of cut silver into the balance. Eventually, the scales swung, and balanced, then tipped slightly over as Sihtric added a further half-coin. "How would that be to you, ship-master?"

"Reasonable, sir. Have you anyone who can write? I could take this figure back to Snorri and see if he'll take it..."

"Put the other weight back, and take him that figure instead."

Hrolf allowed a fleeting smile to reach his lips. "You are generous, lord. I thank you for this."

Sihtric grunted amiably. "He earned it, ship-master; I would not wish to argue that point." He scratched his cheek absently. "Think he'd take a sword as a gift as well?"

Hrolf inhaled sharply: here were gifts indeed! Now, though, the game became trickier, for if he got the balance wrong they would be back to owing Sihtric something again, and that was the last thing he wanted. Should it happen, he was not at all sure his crew would not hang him from the nearest oak in consequence.

"I could ask him, sir; I would be glad to."
Sihtric chuckled. "But your admiration is set against your desire to be free of me? Don't worry, I won't be offended; you wouldn't be the first, and I doubt you'll be the last. I am impressed by your caution, though, and your canny handling of all this. There are no hidden ties to the sword, my lord. I would give him a spear, only I suspect he'd view it as a

walking-stick, and then he *might* take offence, hmm?

"So here is my offer, then: what sits in the scales for the lord Snorri's wounding. I will give a silver *ore* for each of your other wounded men. I will give you your spear of yesterday, a sword of good lineage to Snorri, and a weapon of choice to the lords Einar and Brynjolf. You may all keep spears and shields, should you wish, as part of this offer, too. On top of all this, I will pay, oh, say three more *ore*, in silver, to each of you lords for your work here yesterday, and I will deliver the full price of the cargo I had bought in the town before you sail. Furthermore, I thank you and your ship-men for your fine, fine services to me this summer, and give you leave to depart whenever you see fit - but you are to guest with me at least once before then. And on our parting, I will send you off with gifts more fitting to your enterprises than weapons and shields." He held out his hand to Hrolf. "How say you now, shipmaster?"

It was a magnificent payment; Hrolf could not find any fault with it. Lest the proffered hand be withdrawn, he spat on his own palm and grasped the kings firmly.

"You are generous and open-handed, sir, and news of that will travel wherever else we may sail. I take the offer, and pledge our friendship in return."

"That's good, shipmaster," smiled the king. "Those are indeed welcome things to hear."

And Hrolf came out of the meeting convinced that Sihtric meant every single word of it.

CHAPTER FIFTY- FOUR

Ragnar had been right: the place of Sihtric's victory did indeed have a waterfront, and although access to it was none too easy now, what with the collapse of the timber revetment holding up the rampart and the young shrubs and trees that obscured the road down to the river, Hrolf had chosen to post a watch there every day since the battle. He had finally got an answer from Kraki, who had sent any members of his family that could be spared down to the ship in order to assist in rowing it upstream. Now that they had the king's permission to go, the crew were eager enough to take their turns in watching for a sign of the vessel, and it became usual to find up to half-a-dozen of them sitting around on the shore. However often Hrolf reminded them of the obligation to see Sihtric one more time, nobody seemed to be taking any notice.

It was only towards the dusk of the following day, quite a rapid trip by Hrolf's estimate, that their ship slid into view. The faint rhythm of distant oars was the first sign, and those on watch sent word back to the fireside. Even as Ljotolf was scrambling back towards his bench-mates, the sounds became louder, and the grey-brown bulk of the vessel became clear to everyone's eyes. By the time those aboard had noticed the wild shouts of those watching and altered course to beach, all of the Felag able to walk were already heading down as well.

Brynjolf smiled - the first time in many nights, Hrolf thought - and clapped his hands as they strode onwards. "This, my friends... this is a day I've been looking forward to!"

"I'd never have guessed," muttered Einar with a grin. "Feels good, though, I'll agree. Homeward bound at last, eh?"

They half-ran, half-slid down the mud slope to the shore, just in time to see the ship pushing up out of the river to meet them. In the prow, Thorhall and Hriedar stood up to wave a greeting, whilst others pulled the oars inboard and Broddi threw down a line.

"Is Kraki with you?" called Hrolf.

"No, lord," answered Otkel from the steer-board, "he was attending to matters in town. He says to bring his people back downstream with him and let them off within the new ramparts, if we would."

"Easily done, and the least we could do. We have other payments to leave with him, too, and the latest news about Sihtric's plans."

"Shall we stay the night? It's getting a bit dark to go a-rowing in this current."

"Make fast these lines, then - there's plenty of trees to tie them round - and come up to the fire. We'll sort it all out come morning."

Unable to welcome the ship, Snorri had set his energies to foraging. So far, his scavengers had procured another cask of ale, a basket of edible bread, and enough meat to put in a kettle over the flames. All in all, it promised to be a better night than the previous one, when the ghosts had crowded round the fire as if seeking warmth, and nobody had found much to say that was cheerful. They were tired, both in mind and in body; the reserves they had drawn upon to stay alive in the thick of the fight were spent, and there had been nothing to renew them. Tonight would be different: they had food, they had beer, and – most importantly - they had their passage home again. The mood felt definitely brighter.

CHAPTER FIFTY- FIVE

"I would have been a poor host, and probably a worse king," said Sihtric to the assembled Felag-men, "had I not roused myself early enough to come and say my farewells." He sniffed the cold of the morning air. "This mud stinks a bit, though; I'll be glad of my bath-house when we get back. No wonder my forebears moved downriver, and left this place to moulder."

"Well sir," replied Hrolf, "we are happy to have had a part in securing that place with you. But we have homes of our own to reach, though I don't think any of us yet own a bath house! It might be a useful thing to do; less messy than washing at the hearth."

Sihtric shrugged. "Don't make it too far from that hearth, shipmaster, or you'll only regret the walk to and fro. That could be a kenning for kingly policy, I suppose. I for one have no intention of walking out into the wilds beyond my walls; I reckon that's where my predecessors got it wrong."

"I'd not argue that one," said Brynjolf. "It strikes me as just asking for more trouble than anyone could handle. Let the natives be, happy in their own little squabbles."

The king stroked his long beard thoughtfully. "Could be a useful source of silver, though, should times ever get hard… they like paying for good men like us. You saw it yourselves, in Njal's army. Plenty of work in that direction, should you want it…"

"Not for us!" laughed Hrolf. "I think once is enough. Did you catch any of those men alive? They might have a ship somewhere, and it would be worth the finding, perhaps."

Sihtric shook his head. "All dead, or run for home before we could get to them. Pity; they fought well, and I have gaps in my shield-wall, just as you have empty benches. We could both
have offered them a better ending than they've had."

"We are heading east, but if we veer off-course and meet them, we'll pass that offer on."

Sihtric nodded, and beckoned one of his men to step forward. A small box was handed over-not the same one as before, Hrolf noted - and the king drew out a small bag.

"It would not become me to see you off without a further token of my thanks for your time and your work in my town, my lords. Your men fought valiantly, and bravely, and well, and there is an ale-cask aboard for their enjoyment, and fresh bread, too. They have their share of the silver, now they have food and drink as well, so by the time you reach home, they'll be happy again. And I will have the memory and the song of how the men of Wirhalh turned the might of a usurper, and my heart will be the gladder for it.

"And you, my lords: men who are higher in the world, with finer tastes, would, I think, appreciate something rather more permanent to show for your hard knocks. You led both your own men and mine, and brought most of them through the fight to hear the songs of it, and for that, once more, I thank you. I have gifted you weapons, I have given silver both as geld and as gift; now, finally, I give these with my promise of friendship, and a warm welcome whenever you should return." He tipped open the bag, and held out four golden rings of twisted wire.

Einar slowly, hesitantly, reached out and took one. "I will return my friendship, sir, and a promise of help and support should our roads cross again. More than that, I will carry this and be proud to tell the tale of how I came by it." The shining metal slid onto his finger, catching the faint shine of the sun behind the clouds. Hrolf took two, and passed one up to the rail of the ship, where Snorri was already safely aboard. Brynjolf waited a little longer, seemingly caught in some unfathomable internal dilemma, but in the end, he too slipped his gift onto a finger. Hrolf watched his friend carefully, and realised suddenly that he had been doing that for almost the entire trip. Perhaps, he thought with a twinge of guilt for the idea, perhaps it *was* time for Brynjolf to sell up and attend to his farm. Not perhaps for his own sake, but for everyone else's...

"You have kept us... *entertained?*... for the summer, sir," Hrolf said finally, with a smile, "and we thought ourselves well rewarded with our spears and our share of the loot. We would have offered you our friendship and support without these final gifts, but they are handsome, and we will remember our words and pledges here. It is unlikely that you would ever have reason to travel into our lands, but if it should happen, you can be assured of our welcome and hospitality."

He held out his hand; the king grasped it firmly, a smile in his eyes. "You should go," Sihtric finally said, "you've come higher up this river than the tide does, and you'll be wanting high water beneath you before you get back downstream, in case it's on the ebb. Oh, and I'll not insist on your coming to wait on me within the longphort. You've been doing that for long enough, I think." Once again, there was a warmth in his smile as he spoke, and Hrolf found himself almost able to like the man within the kingship.

Sihtric stepped back among his men as Hrolf, Einar and Brynjolf climbed up the ladder-pole onto their familiar deck. Arne and Asbjorn untied the ropes before following them up; the king's men put their shoulders to the strakes and, feet digging deep into the soft shore, they pushed the ship off the mud and into open water. Already settled in their places, the surviving crewmen had the oars out in moments, and a few strong strokes were all that was needed to set the vessel straight in the river, and moving away downstream from the watchers on the shore.

CHAPTER FIFTY-SIX

"So," murmured Kraki, sitting by the light of his own fire within the mad, rambling warren of streets and alleys that made up the new longphort of Dubhllyn, "I see you are still somewhat entangled in the plots and doings of kings." He nodded towards the golden rings that sat on his guest's fingers.

"Well, at least you still have the fingers to put them on - or most of you do," he added, remembering Kol's injuries. "It's no bad thing, and good stories are already coming out of it."

Hrolf shrugged. "I'd have rather stayed here selling our cargo honestly, there's no secret to that, but when wyrd sends you down another road, then there's little else to do but follow it in the best way."

"Ah, that's the difference, you see," smiled their host. "I set my feet on my road, and no man or wyrd is going to make me turn off it. But then I don't have land, and tenants, and obligations like you do, cousin, so perhaps it's easier for men like me to say that. After all, Sihtric is less likely to knock on my door than he is on yours."

"True enough," nodded Brynjolf, whose mood had been improving with almost every oarstroke away from the king. "But I think we acquitted ourselves well enough, for all that we have dead to mourn, and wounds to nurse. Not an easy road, I grant you, and like Hrolf, I would rather have stayed where we were. But it's not been as good a trip all round, I think. Been a lot of bad happenings, and odd little incidents."

"And yet," added Einar, "things *have* tended to our favour in the long term. I know I hesitated about throwing those bloody monks away as we did - but we couldn't have sold them here even if we had kept them, could we? For one thing, there's no markets open; for another, they'd only have made more trouble the longer we kept hold of them; and finally, I doubt the kirkmen would have allowed such a sale anyway! And how much trouble would that man of yours been, Hrolf, when he heard of Njal's approach, I wonder? Could we have trusted him to stay with us, and not run off to try his luck elsewhere?"

"I wouldn't have put him anywhere near the king's ear, that's for sure," agreed Hrolf. "All in all, as you both say, a very strange trip indeed. I too will be glad to be home again - not that I expect to get much peace or stability there, either."

Kraki smiled. "You're starting to sound like I do, going on about the joys of home and a good family, rather than the fame-ridden shipmaster I know you to be!"

"Time enough for all that tomorrow. Tonight we will take your offer of hospitality while the lads clear out our houses; we will tell you the tales of what really happened in the place of the old town - because we've not had much time to tell each other our stories yet, either - and we will pay you for our time here, and for your help and support, too. And certainly, I for one will pledge my friendship anew." Hrolf was both happy and relieved to hear his fellow-owners echo his words; he considered that Kraki deserved no less from them.

The talk lessened as Kraki and his sons set up the tables in the little house, and his wife attended to the contents of the pots wedged in the edges of the fire. Hrolf leaned back and closed his eyes against the smoke that somehow, as in their own rented day-house, seemed unable to find its way out. For the first time in days, if not weeks, he felt able to just sit, without wondering what was happening around him, or what was about to come along. He would have been very surprised if any of his shipmates felt any different, and he was sure in his bones that they would all be glad of the first sight of home. Tonight, also, he did not have to delegate someone to cook, he did not have to be certain of the ale supply, he did not have to have sent someone for firewood, he did not have to intervene in any of the little disagreements and disputes that inevitably occurred when close to thirty men were cooped up in the same house for more than a day. Tonight, all he had to do was eat someone else's food, drink someone else's beer, talk if he wanted to, or sit and be entertained if he so wished. He suddenly realised that this was a rare and unaccustomed thing: he was a guest in someone else's house, with no cares or responsibilities beyond those of any other guest. At some point in the night, he had to speak thanks to Kraki for his help while they had been in Dubhllyn, and with those thanks went silver rings and coins; but that was hardly a chore. All in all, he considered, it was a good end to their time in this place. Tomorrow, their prow turned for home, bringing a welcome end to a long, difficult summer that had been full of unexpected turns and surprises. Truly, Hrolf reflected quietly, they had been deep in the serpent's coils this voyage. Now came the time to start cutting their way loose.

CHAPTER FIFTY- SEVEN

Their serpent had one more twist for them, and it came as no surprise to anyone, looking back, that it was the barb in the tail. No sooner were they away from the jetties and walls of the longphort of the Black Pool, and heading out into open ocean instead of tidal river, than the skies began to darken and boil. Rain fell, gentle at first, but swiftly chilling and getting harder, a fierce westerly wind pushing every last drop at a slant, to sting the face and blind the eyes. Hrolf rapidly sent Thorhall to get his satchel from its snug little hole in the hold, but by the time it got to him, he was already soaked and chilled. Around him, the crew gritted their teeth and made ready to try and run the storm. At least, Hrolf realised, even while the rain was battering into them, the wind that drove it was still filling their sail. He simply hoped that it didn't veer round, and begin to push them off course. The waves were growing, too, from little white-flecked seahorses playing around the bow, to bulking, oily-black monsters, full of fluid, rolling power and strength that ran alongside them, spitting foam, and sometimes threw themselves sideways into the flanks of their own ocean-steed. The ship rolled and lurched, snaking its way through the swirls and eddies of the sea; the strakes twisted and curved, the withies that held them to the ribs stretched and slackened as the sea played around the hull. But the sail stayed taut and bellied out, pulling at the lines that held it. Drops of spray bounced off the stretched leather and linen, making patterns in the air that none of the crew could see, or would care about. The men huddled into the curving walls of the hull as best they could, something made easier by the absence of the cargo, and kept the baling-buckets close to hand.

Olaf and Ragnar made their way back to the aft platform. "We'll take our lord into the hold!" shouted Ragnar over the wind, as Olaf began to untie Snorri from his safe holding by Hrolf's feet.

"About time!" replied the old man, "I was beginning to soak here!"

"Mind that leg," cautioned Hrolf. "Slide him along, don't try and lift him by it!"

By setting a couple of the deck-planks back into place, the two men were able to make a gangway towards the middle of the ship, close enough to other pairs of hands to allow Snorri's being lifted to a safer spot among the crew. Brynjolf, already in his weather-gear, relieved Hrolf at the steer-board long enough for the ship-master to don his own leathers. "Want me here, or can you manage alone?" he asked.

"I can steer on my own, but the company would be good."

Brynjolf nodded, though most of the motion was lost in the folds of his hood. "Fair enough. I think they can do without me further forward, and we don't need a lookout this far from shore."

Hrolf grinned into the spray. "Only idiots would be sailing in weather like this!"

"Or men so desperate for home…"

And so they ran before the wind, the waves and the rain, wishing for a lull in the storm, if only to try and see where they were, yet at the same time happy for the speed away from Dubhllyn and the doings of its king. If he squinted and peered hard into the spray that lashed over the length of the boat, Hrolf could see Einar crouched in the prow, apparently searching for something. Quite what that might be, Hrolf had no idea, but he found himself hoping that his bench-mate had tied himself to some part of the vessel. For his own part, two lines held him at his oar, stretched as tight as the lines to the sail, and Brynjolf had already secured his own ropes to the stern-post.

"Going with the wind?" he shouted into Hrolf's ear.

"Nothing else we can do," replied the ship-master, "we can't see where we're heading, beyond broadly homewards, and the wind and waves are too strong to fight: they'd smash us apart, for all the old ship's bending and snaking like a new one. No bearings to steer by, no sun, no stars… look on the bright side, we're still heading in the right direction."

Brynjolf nodded, but said no more. Hrolf peered down the length of the ship again; he could see nothing amiss, and his ears told much the same story. The lines were all holding up to the strain, even the walrus-hide ones; the sail was full and taut, with no evidence of rips or thinned patches in its weave. If he looked hard, he could still see members of his crew ranged around the ribs of the ship, checking the nails, testing the withies between ribs and strakes, looking for leaks or signs of stress in the timbers. The water was nearly up to their ankles, but Hrolf was not unduly worried, since most of it was coming in from overhead - and people were already baling.

He looked up into the sky, and saw nothing but layer upon layer of dark, brooding clouds, that seemed to tear along their lower edges and drift in strands down to the sea. This showed every sign of being a long storm, and a hard trip over the ocean to their homes. The men were fine for now, but if this carried on, it would wear them down still further, and when they raised sight of land they would have to be awake and alert. There seemed to be no obvious way out of this particular problem, but then it was largely out of their hands. The storm would do what it would; if it stayed with the ship all the way across to Wirhalh, well, they would have had a faster passage, and if need be there were coves and bays to north or south that might give them haven for a day or two before the final run for home. If it blew itself out before then, so much the better to Hrolf's mind, both for ship and crew. The only thing he was really worried about at this stage was if it turned around and blew them back towards the Irish lands again. If that happened, and they made landfall anywhere else than one of the longphorts, they would be in the hands of the natives, and their lives would be measured in hours.

CHAPTER FIFTY-EIGHT

Night fell, although it was only a subliminal awareness of time's passage in the broadest sense that let any of the shipmen know it had come, since in weather like this, the day was as dark as the evening. The firebox was flooded; the water in the bottom of the ship was lapping higher than the ballast-stones, and certainly higher than anyone's shoes. Most of the crew had discarded them, preferring the ability to feel and grip the timbers with their toes over the minimal comfort of sodden, cold leather around their feet. Snorri was snug in the hold - providing somebody kept watch over him and prevented him slipping under the bilge water. Olaf and Ragnar had appropriated the spare sail to wrap him in, and Hrolf had not felt the need to argue over it.

At some point in the blackness of the night the wind began to lessen, and the rain began to ease. Exhausted though he was, Hrolf could not bring himself to relinquish the steer-board;
he was ship-master, so it was his place and duty to bring the vessel home. Memories of his father floated up into his mind's eye at times like this, and now, he found, Eyvind was at his father's side. He

wasn't entirely sure what it meant, to share the aft-deck with two such wraiths; nor was he certain whether he was comforted or disquieted by them being so close in his head. But he knew with a certainty that he could not leave the oar to another; and so he called for drink and food whenever he needed them, safe in the knowledge that none of the crew would be sleeping much through this night either. For one thing, he kept on reminding them to bale.

Dawn showed faintly, eventually, a thin line of slightly less-dark than the rest of the skies around them. There was more colour in the clouds, and Hrolf, conferring with Einar, considered that they were not moving so quickly across the sky.

"Wind's not as strong," commented the new Felag-man, handing Hrolf another cup of ale, "I can see some sag and give in the sail, and the wind-lines aren't standing straight out any more. From what I could see in the prow, the waves aren't as big either, and they're moving more slowly than before." He looked around, at the ship, the men, and the open ocean around them. "I'm beginning to think we might just be through the worst of it."

Hrolf nodded slowly. "I reckon you might be right, friend, but I'm staying at this oar for now. Until we spot land, at least, or until I see clear skies and a bit of sun."

Einar looked closely at him. "Those of us who could sleep are still tired and weary; you must be even worse by now. Whatever happens, don't leave it so late to hand over that you get it wrong, and send us off-course."

Hrolf smiled thinly. "That won't happen, I promise you. How is Snorri?"

"Sleeping, I think. He's warm, and he's about as dry as any of us, and he has his lads watching over him."

"If the rain continues to ease, it might be worth trying to get the fire lit again."

"I'll see to it, or I'll get Brynjolf to when we swap watches. How long on a straight run from Dubhllyn to home, usually?"

"No idea, we've never had to do it before. Always gone by way of Mann, or the Western Isles, or

Ongle-sey." One gloved hand rubbed the other absently. "Got sidetracked towards the lands of Pawl the Welshman last year, and what a mistake that turned out to be! I wonder, now, if that was the start of our ill-luck, though it didn't feel like it at the time."

"Could we have turned it back by now, do you think? What with our doings for Sihtric?"

Hrolf shrugged. "If this storm hadn't brewed up on our tail, I might have thought so. Now I'm not so sure."

Einar was right about the storm, though: as the day progressed, the wind blew less and less fiercely, and by what Hrolf thought would normally be day-meal-time, the rain had gone and the sun was beginning to shine through gaps in the ever-lightening clouds. Somebody got a spark into the firebox, and with carefully-stored dry kindling, the fire slowly came to life, greeted with a muted, ragged cheer. By the time Brynjolf came aft with his man Asbjorn, bringing warm beer and heated strips of mutton, Hrolf was ready to let go of the steer-board and stumble into an empty spot between the benches. He was asleep before he even got to eat a mouthful, and his ale spilled, unnoticed, to mingle with the water in the bilge.

CHAPTER FIFTY- NINE

"Never," said Snorri towards the end of that day, his voice full of exhausted emotion, "never, I say, has even the sniff of a coastline been so inviting…"

"Steady on," smiled Brynjolf, "this one isn't even yours! But I know what you mean. I'd say this was a trip to bury in a verse or two, and start looking forward to better next year."

"There's still time to take you back to your own hall," Hrolf reminded them from the stern, his hand once more on the steer-board. "All you have to do is say the word - but say it soon, before we hit that cross-current at the rivermouth."

"No, I'm happy to come home to our Felag's haven, as we always do. I'll not tempt wyrd further by doing things that differently." He rubbed his broken leg, feeling the splints beneath his trews, an innovation inspired by the men of Sihtric, some of whom had taken to the long, loose garments in preference to the more usual high-breeks and hose. "I think we've broken enough new ground for one year."

"Look on the bright side," chuckled Hrolf, "at least I made that spot you lay in, warm and comfortable long before you needed it."

"True enough, and it's a lot better than sitting on those ballast stones, I can tell you! I don't know if my arse will ever stop aching."

And so they headed steadily, if slowly, homeward. The waves were still large enough to roll the ship from side to side a bit, but now, with clearing skies and a manageable wind, it was no more than they were used to. Damp they could live with: it was all part of spending time in an open boat, after all. But storms and gales, the weariness of constant vigilance against leaks and cross-winds, the repeated snatching away of sleep and the cold that seeped into the bones, were all things they could well have done without. But the storm had passed, or they had somehow managed to outrun it; now, Hrolf was grateful for light breezes and only mild currents at last, as with their depleted numbers, and after that harsh a crossing, rowing against any serious tide would tire them far too soon. The homeward approach was always harder than the outward journey, as the motion of water and wind were, for the most part, trying to send them away from the wide mouth of the northerly river, into which they had to head. This time would be even harder, with so few able to row for any length of time.

His thoughts must have been loud, for Brynjolf was joined by Kol and Arne, who all looked just as worried as their ship-master. It was the lord of the burgh who broached the subject first.

"Do you think we're strong enough to row home as we usually do? I can't remember ever coming home this badly mauled before, in body or in mind. And you've had far too little sleep for tricky thinking."

"My brother and I are still new in this size of ship," put in Arne, "but might we not be better to beach where we put our boat? The shore is shallow, and soft..."

Hrolf raised an eyebrow. "It's an idea; I hadn't thought of it. Must be tired... as for being battered and short on men, I would agree it's not happened since the trip when Dubhnjal died - which is before most of us began to sail. You're the last of the old crew, Snorri, unless I'm mistaken. Maybe not, though; what about Otkel?

"Arne, your idea has some merit; it's not so far from the beach to the noust, and after a night or two of resting, we should be able to muster enough extra hands to portage the ship over.
What do you say, my fellow ship-men? The keel is sound, it stood up well enough to the Dubhllyn mud, and I'm not inclined to put the lads to rowing more than we have to."

"Beach it," answered Einar wearily. "Anything to just get ashore and lick some wounds. I'll send word homewards for extra men, should we need them." Beside him, Snorri nodded.

"Sound advice to me," agreed Brynjolf. Hrolf accordingly went to the prow, and sighted his target, before taking the steer-board again and pulling the ship slightly to the south. Brynjolf and Einar went forward to get men onto the sail ropes as the breeze began to fill it once more, leaving Snorri laid by Hrolf's feet, out of the worst of the spray and wind.

"How's the leg?" asked the ship-master. "Still there," answered Snorri. "I dread to think what Gytha's going to say when she sees this."

"Oh, I can imagine there will be quite a while of harsh rebuke, and a strong lack of sympathy; on the other hand, there will probably also be a lot of worry and concern, and an even stronger argument against you sailing next year - as if you needed one. You'll have a serious headache from it all long before spring, I should imagine."

"Encouraging words!" Snorri sighed as he looked into his own future. "As I said after the fight, I can't see me resisting the urge to stay behind next year, somehow; this leg will barely be healed - if it heals properly at all - by then. Olaf and Ragnar wedged me into the base of the boat as best they could, but I think it still took quite a battering at odd moments. Well, we'll see, I suppose; to be honest, I'm just happy to have lived through it all. I reckon we're late home as it is; you three may even have missed your Thing by now."

"Oslac won't be happy if that's happened; come to that, nor will Var, or Thordis, or Asa. Well, we made a profit, we have silver coming home with us, we can pay the lads and keep the surplus, even after the weregelds; but this time, there's little joy in it somehow."

Snorri nodded. "We got hit, and no mistake, and in places where we weren't expecting it, and so weren't equipped." He looked down the length of the ship, seeing the aches and pain in the faces of the crew - and the empty benches here and there. "I reckon it's that part of it that is bothering us all."

"Aye. It's a good lesson in staying well away from the doings of kings."

"Mmm. I said we should have run when we had the chance."
"Do me a favour and don't rub it in too much…"

"Sorry; I meant nothing by it, I got sucked in as much as the rest of us." He tried to stretch up in the hope of peering over the rail, but sank back from the effort. "Are we nearly there yet?"

"Soon enough; the coast comes ever closer. We'll have to find some way of softening the blow as we beach, or we'll smash that leg back open again for sure." Hrolf retreated into thought for a few moments, then called out for every cloak and blanket they had aboard. Olaf and Ragnar were given the task of wrapping their lord as securely as possible, and then roping the consequent cocoon tightly into the side of the ship. Once this was achieved, Hrolf left the steerboard to Ragnar and went forward.

"Listen: we aren't going to make you row into the river…" a ragged cheer greeted these words. Hrolf grinned briefly before continuing. "We're beaching the boat on the open strand instead. It still means work at the oars, but it's only a swift sprint instead of the usual hard slog. It's the last stretch of the journey, lads, short of portaging back to the noust in a day or two - but we'll have extra help for that.

"We'll be taking the sail down very soon - stand ready for the oars if you're not on the ropes. Brynjolf, Einar: with me at the benches, if you please, we need every fit arm we can find. Otkel: take the steer- board."

Brynjolf grimaced as he clambered onto an empty bench. "We've not done this in far too long; my hands have gone soft!" He chuckled. "My, what an education this trip has been!"

"Otkel," called Hrolf, "we need you to call when we are… oh, about a furlong or two from the beach. Further out is good, closer is bad - we won't have time to get the sail down and the oars out. Come to that - oars out, now! Keep 'em up, lads, lean on 'em if you have to, but don't let them dip in the waves! Otkel, watch the shore and sing out when the time comes!"

Otkel waved absently, his eyes fixed over their heads on the approaching beach. All other eyes were set on him, tense at their benches, awaiting the sign. It came soon enough. Tired, protesting arms hauled on ropes to lower the sail into its rests; ordinarily they would have rolled it around the yard and roped it, but there was neither the time nor the energy now. They just wrestled and kicked it out of the way of the rowing-crew.

Exhausted, aching backs pushed oars into the foaming waves, pulled them through the harsh, resisting ocean, then lifted them out to repeat the stroke: again and again, over and over, seemingly without end. Gradually, the ship gained some speed, the timbers creaking as much as the men's muscles as it twisted through and around the waves. The one thought in all their minds, the urge that kept them pulling on their oars, was the thought of home coming ever closer.

Hrolf thought his arms would explode from the pain within them, his back break clean in two with every stretch and bend as he pushed his oar up, out of the foaming, hissing water beneath him, and back for the next stroke. He could not recall who had the foremost bench up in the prow, but their voice sounded loud and clear as they called the stroke again and again, over and over. From the way his seat moved imperceptibly beneath him, he could tell that they were winning, that they were gaining speed in water deep enough still to take the keel. But that would change soon enough...

He needed suddenly to talk to Kol and Arne. Just how steeply did this beach slope? He had seen for himself the difference between his ship and their little boat, and they had put this suggestion forward based, surely, only on what they knew. A slope that was too shallow might let their skiff all the way to the dry shoreline, but leave the bigger vessel stranded in the surf; and then they would have no choice but to wait and see what the tide did, and pray they could float the ship off again. Moreover, if that happened, they might never get Snorri ashore in his current state.

More strokes, and the overpowering need to heed the stroke-man, listen to his rhythm, keep his own oar in time with those around him - or risk smashing them up against each other and, more desperately, losing their momentum in the confusion that would follow. They only had one chance at this; they only had the strength for one go, even if time, tide and the ocean-gods would allow them another chance. It was too late for worries: he had to trust his choices, and the men who had helped him make them. He had the power to refuse to beach, and he had jumped at the chance as eagerly as the rest. So, one way or another, beach they would.

Almost as the thoughts crossed his mind, tumbling like a rockfall, the ship gave an almighty lurch. A shudder ran from prow to stern, straight along the keel, accompanied by a long, scratchy, hissing growl. Their progress stopped abruptly; Hrolf leaned on his oar, catching his breath, waiting for his head to stop swimming. Around him, the men looked at one another uncertainly, then to their leader.

"Well," came Brynjolf's voice from somewhere towards the stern, "I reckon that means we've arrived."

Hrolf stood up slowly, and, grabbing the rail, leaned over the side to look. Below him was water - but only the faintest, shallowest remnant of the sea. He could see kelp waving in the cloudy murk as it swirled around the keel; they had driven up a lot of sand, but sand it was - they were home. The ship was beached - and within easy reach of the shore.

"In oars!" he shouted, his voice rasping and ragged. "Someone find the lines, and run them out from the prow. Lads, we made it!"

Around him, his battered, wounded and exhausted crew struggled to their feet, some to look overboard, some to just stretch the aches out of their bodies. But all of them bore smiles on their faces, and the trials of the past months began to fade away into saga.

CHAPTER SIXTY

Hrolf had no way of knowing how long there had been a lookout kept from the rock on which his own hall stood, but he suspected the job had been going on for long enough to become onerous. At any rate, hands were running towards the beach as they rowed into the sand, ready to catch lines and push timbers carried over a mile from the boatshed under each side once the vessel had finally stopped moving. Thanks to Sihtric, there was little to unload; the hardest part was Snorri, who had difficulty in trusting the people who lifted him over the rail and into waiting arms below. Happy though Hrolf was with the way the bones had been set by Sihtric's own men, he still sent a runner back to the homestead to find Halldora, his family's own cunning-woman. The other wounded men did better, for all that it looked probable that Armod would end up losing his damaged foot, so blackened and devoid of feeling had it become. Snorri claimed he had heard of a man who had survived having a foot cut clean off, but Hrolf thought it unlikely to be true. Hakon limped, but at least the limb was still whole, and would even bear his weight a little. Thorhall had already promised to make his neighbour a crutch before winter.

From his place on the sand, Hrolf could see the smoke rising from his home-fire, and guessed that Var and her ladies would have the welcome-feast deep in the flames already. He wasn't sure he could face it; it meant being lively, telling the tale of the voyage, laughing and joking and acting the Lord of the Rock, when all he really wanted was more ale than was good for him, and a long, long sleep. As so often, however, he knew it wasn't an option, and further, he knew that he had to pull the rest of the crew up with him.

"Form up!" he yelled, turning to face them all. "Make a line there! It's been a bad time in Dubhllyn, aye, but until that time we were doing well, and had the better of monks and Welshmen! Remember those bits, those fine deeds; remember, also, that we fought for a king, and won his crown back for him! So when you speak the names of those who sit in halls beyond us now, forget not how they got there, and how we *all* won fame and glory on the fringes of Dubhllyn, and how Sihtric paid us handsomely for our efforts.

"Tomorrow, we share out the silver; the day after, we come back and drag the boat over to the noust.

But tonight, we must feast, and drink, and make our oaths and our boasts, and live and act as the heroes we are. We got through this trip, and a hard one it turned into, the further on it went. And I give you my promise now, that next time, we'll go northwards, to the western islands, maybe even to Hrossey, anywhere where there are no kings to embroil us in their plots, and where all the ancient natives have been either married or killed! I think we've earned the rest."

Laughter: a good sound, and not too forced or false. Satisfied, Hrolf walked to the head of his weary band, and they headed for the cliff that loomed barely an hour's slow walk away. Much to his surprise, Hrolf found his spirits lifting with every step. But he was glad he had someone else to carry the mailshirt this time.

GLOSSARY

Anglian: originally one of the Germanic tribes believed to have settled in Britain following the withdrawal of Rome. By the time of this novel, a cultural "label" applied to certain facets of Northumbrian society.

Berserkir: a specific style of fighting- man, reputed to have gone into a wild rage during combat, in which state he was believed to be impervious to wounds or hurt.

Boarsnout: a military tactic in which a triangular wedge of men pushed forwards to break an enemy line. The man at the apex, or tip, bore the brunt of the assault.

Bondsman/ Bondar: freemen attached to a social superior, usually in return for support or wages.

Boss: the iron cone or dome at the centre of a shield that protects the hand holding it.

Breeks/ Breeches: knee-length male legwear, often but not always tight-fitting.

Brortches: long wooden pegs used to secure thatch or turf onto roofs.

Burgh: an Anglo-Saxon term originating in Wessex (see below), denoting a walled or fortified settlement.

Curds: a sour by-product of cheese-making. Often offered in Sagas as insults to unwelcome guests.

Day-Meal: the Norse generally ate only two meals in a day. Day-Meal was taken around mid-morning, whereas Night-Meal was eaten at or just after sunset.

Dubhllyn: modern Dublin, Ireland.

Felag: a term meaning "fellowship" or "brotherhood", in the sense of a collection of individuals bound together by a common factor or purpose.

Frankland/ Frankia: modern France.

Fyrd: a term denoting a non- professional, seasonal, or conscripted body of fighting-men.

Hauldr/ Hauldar: a position within Norse society. Lower to middle aristocracy: literally, a holder of land.

Hazel Rods: the traditional boundary set out to demarcate a duelling-field.

Herred: the Norse equivalent of the English Hundred (see Wapentak).
Hersir: a position within Norse society. Usually a fighting-man of independent means, and often, therefore, also a Hauldr (see above).

Hird: a term denoting a professional or semi-professional body of fighting men (see Fyrd above).

Holmgang: a formal duel, to strict protocols, usually fought on an island. Literally, "island going"; in the absence of convenient islands, the duelling field would be marked out with hazel rods (see above).

Hooded God: Odin, who reputedly travelled the world with his features concealed.

Howe: a burial mound.

Hrossey: the modern Orkney Islands, specifically Mainland.

Jarl: a position within Norse society, equivalent to an English Eorl or Earl.

Jorvik: modern York.

Kenning: a device in Norse poetry, whereby an object or idea is expressed in terms of another object or idea. "Whale's Road", for example, is a kenning for "ocean". Many kennings were taken from mythology, as well as from everyday life.

Lawman/ Lawspeaker: an official whose function was to memorise, recite and enforce the local law codes.

Longphort: a term denoting fortified ship- bases, specifically in Ireland. Many modern Irish cities began as longphorts of Norse incomers, especially on the eastern coast.

Mann: the modern Isle of Man.

Mast-Fish: a central timber in ship construction. Sited amidships at the level of the deck or upper ties, this timber supported the mast and prevented its shifting. Masts were not stepped into the keel in this method of shipbuilding, and the timber often assumed a vaguely fish-like shape, hence its name.

Meols: a site on Wirral, thought to possibly have been a beach market. Finds from the nineteenth century are currently (2006) undergoing re-evaluation, and it may be that Meols was actually a burial site.

Mercia: one of the English kingdoms, covering the modern Midlands and North-West England.

Mere: a lake or pool.

Northumbria: a kingdom of the English, covering modern North East England, the East Midlands, and South East Scotland.

North-Way: modern Norway.

Noust: a boat shed.

Ore: a monetary unit; due to the non-money nature of the Norse economies of the time, an Ore was also a specific weight of silver, usually around 25 grams.

Ormsness: modern Llandudno in North Wales.

Oslofjord: southern Norway, at this time still a separate kingdom. Site of the Tune, Oseberg and Gokstad shipburials.

Portage: the practice of hauling a ship overland between waterways.

Pottage: a barley-based stew with herbs.

Raven-God: Odin, who relied on two ravens for information storage and retrieval.

Reeve: the origin of the modern "sherrif". Administrator of a town or settlement.

Rime-thursar: the ice giants of Norse mythology.

Roves: metal backing plates used in conjunction with iron nails, to hold the strakes of a ship to each other.

Saga: a traditional form of Norse story-telling, analagous to a modern historical novel.

Scarf: a method of jointing wood longitudinally, involving a diagonal cut between two lengths of timber and securing with pegs.

Se' en-night: literally seven nights, ie, a week.

Shambles: term denoting a street or area used for slaughtering and butchery.

Skald: a poet; often also genealogist, propagandist and keeper of other useful information.

Snickleway: a narrow alley off a wider street.

Stallar: term denoting a professional fighting-man, equivalent to a modern junior officer.

Steer-board: the side-mounted oar by which Viking-Age ships were steered; the origin of modern "starboard".

Stone setting: boulders placed around a grave in lieu of a ship or boat.

Strakes: the longitudinal timbers comprising the sides of a ship.

Strandhogg: literally "beach clearing": coastal raiding, usually for food rather than profit.

Strathclyde: modern South West Scotland.

Straw-death: a term denoting a quiet, peaceful death, usually from old age, in one's own bed. Anathema to many in Norse society.

Tafl: a generic term for a number of similar board-games. Also known as Hnaefatafl, or King's Table.

Thing: a meeting of free-born men, of all social strata, for the purposes of law-making and legal disputation. Roughly analagous to a combined District Council and Magistrate's Court, and often including trade fairs and social gatherings.

Thrall: a slave, although this was not necessarily a life-long or immutable state.

Tripod: an iron stand set over a fire, for hanging cauldrons from.

Tun: in English, a village, but in Norse, a farmstead. One of a number of interchangeable terms.

Twenty-bencher: above a certain size, possibly eight or ten oars, ships were referred to by the number of oar-benches, with one man per oar. Smaller boats were named for the number of oars, but one man rowed with each pair of oars.

Vestfold: modern South West Norway.

Walea: modern Wallasey, on Wirral, Merseyside.

Wall- plates: long horizontal beams placed along the tops of wooden or wattle walls; part of the house-frame which took the weight of the roof down to the ground.

Wapentak Court: the Norse equivalent of the English Hundred: an administrative unit of land, roughtly analagous to a modern county. Each Wapentak had its own court which settled internal disputes.

Weregeld: a payment, usually compensation for blood-letting or killings, made by the perpetrator of the crime in order to avoid either outlawry or revenge-killings.

Wessex: one of the English Kingdoms, covering South West England.

Westmorland: modern Cumbria and Strathclyde.

Withies: pliable willow strips used to tie the strakes of a vessel to its internal frame, imparting great flexibility to the whole ship.

World- Serpent: in Norse mythology a great serpent sits at the bottom of the ocean, encircling the whole world. On one occasion, the god Thor hauls him to the surface whilst fishing.

Wyrd: usually interpreted as "fate", but in its original context, wyrd is more flexible and subject to change at every moment.

Printed in Great Britain
by Amazon